Emigree

Jane Ireland

THE CRYING TREE SERIES BOOK 1

Emigree © 2020 Jane Ireland.
All Rights Reserved.

No part of this book may be reproduced in any form or by any electronic or mechanical means including information storage and retrieval systems, without permission in writing from the author. The only exception is by a reviewer, who may quote short excerpts in a review.

This book is a work of fiction. Names, characters, places, and incidents either are products of the author's imagination or are used fictitiously. Any resemblance to actual persons, living or dead, events, or locales is entirely coincidental.

Cover by Melinda Childs @studioorchard

Internal design by Book Burrow www.bookburrow.com.au

Printed in Australia

First Printing: March 2020

Second Edition: January 2025

Published by Wild Magenta Books

Paperback ISBN 978-1-7637599-0-9

eBook ISBN 978-1-7637599-1-6

Hrdback ISBN 978-1-7637599-4-7

 A catalogue record for this work is available from the National Library of Australia

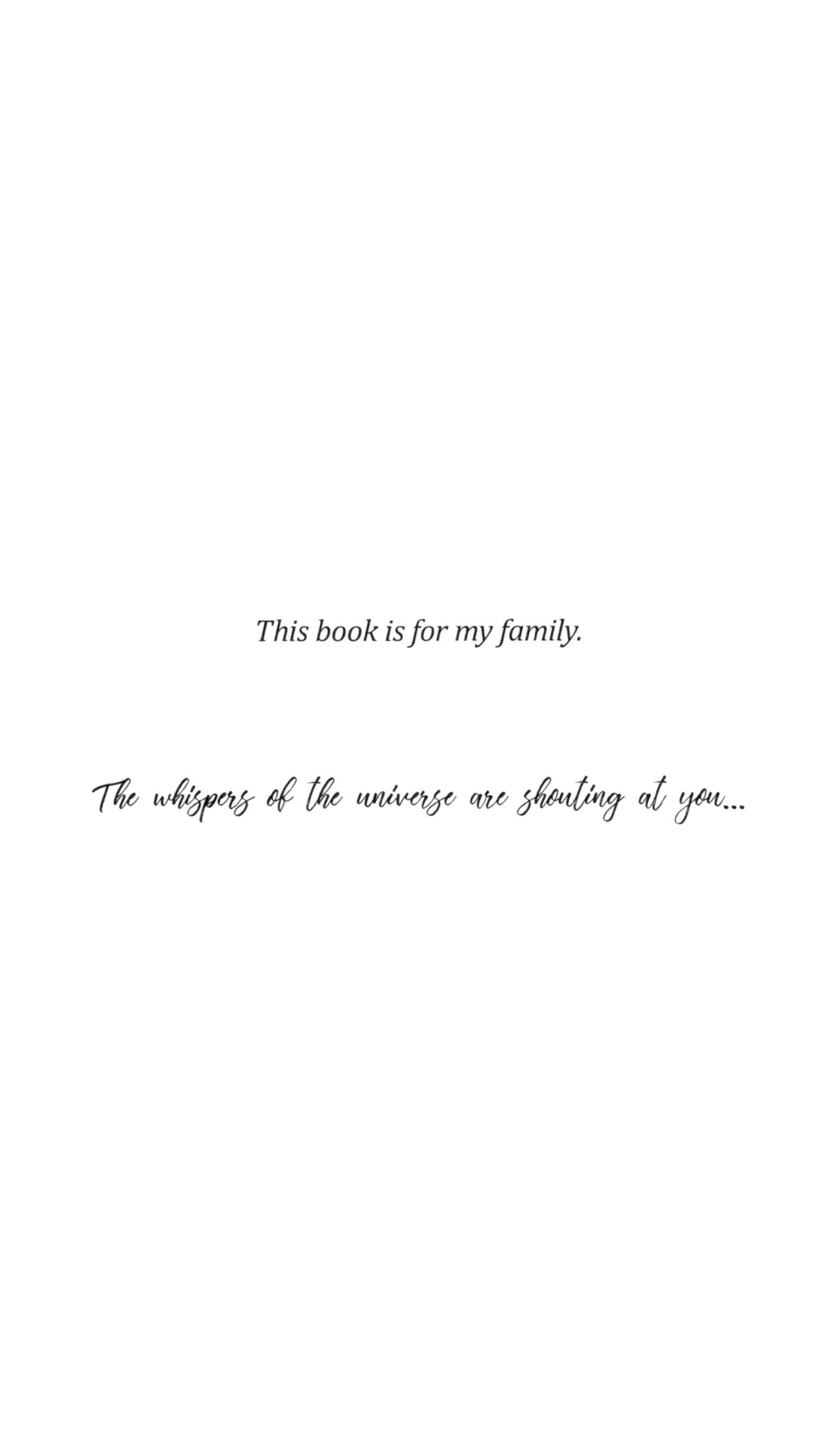

This book is for my family.

The whispers of the universe are shouting at you...

The Crying Tree Series

Book 1: *Emigree*
Book 2: *Niche*

"The smallest thing may speak to a man of the whole round world..."

WALTER DE LA MARE

1942 – One Year After

The trigger for the flashbacks was a spider—fittingly, a creature with a trap. They overwhelmed Grace with their perfection, their breathtaking power, the sharp bursts of detail almost more vivid than reality. They were also harsh and cruel, akin to the actual event. There, then not there—like transient summer storms they struck her with the force of lightning.

Grace wished they would bring her welcome surprises, like those from when she was an adored baby perhaps, or ones that brought whiffs of her favourite flower—freesia. Audacious: she liked the way the plant sometimes refused to be coaxed from underground. And fleeting: The Spring appearance or non-appearance of its flowers made her crave them all the more. The waiting felt to Grace like waiting for God.

But the niggling new memories of old—the unwelcome visitors— once reacquainted with their teenage host, flooded through her like warm waves of blood. Once they took hold, Grace couldn't push them back.

The school day having dragged to its dull conclusion—and late enough for all teachers to have gone home—three fourteen-year-old girls make their escape to a creek behind the running track. Still in their uniforms hitched high with low belts, they sit in a clearing near the bank, leaning back on their arms with heads tilted skywards in reckless abandon to catch the remaining sun. The ground is rough. When Grace looks at her palms, she discovers little temporary indentations caused by sharp twigs and stones. She can feel things digging into her thighs too. The other two girls smoke Grace's father's tobacco while Grace just coughs occasionally. Having made the tobacco heist in a hurry, she didn't bring with her the little rolling papers to wrap with, so they are improvising using newspaper.

Having just returned from another visit to the headmistress's office, Marjorie holds the title: 'The Day's Most Fed Up'.

'What was it this time, Marjorie? Talking back again?' asks Julia.

'Not back, just talking. Miss Prentice makes me want to scream, so if I can't scream in class I'll talk instead.'

'Why not just scream? I thought she was deaf anyway, but I must have that wrong if she heard you and sent you to Miss Titless, oh sorry, *Miss Titmus*.'

'She is as deaf as a post. Only reason she heard me this time was because Erna whispered that she liked Tom Ford and I yelled back: No! He thinks he's the ant's pants and he has the brain of a frog. Which is quite true, and I couldn't possibly have waited until the bell to tell her that important piece of information. I swear Titless hates me with a passion. She always finds something to pester me about, the bloody bitch, bloody bitch,' says Marjorie, squinting her eyes, pursing her lips, making a fist with her empty hand—looking to Grace like a constipated Buddha.

'Hating your fobbles would be the only passion that old dragon ever gets. She should be thankful,' says Julia.

'I think you mean foibles,' interjects Grace.

'Foibles? I tell the truth!' whines Marjorie.

'Yes, perhaps, but you don't always have to let everyone everywhere know about everything,' says Julia.

'Whose side are you on?' says Marjorie airily.

'Your side, my sweet chum.' Julia puts her arm around her best friend.

'And you, Graceless, whose side are you on?' says Marjorie, glaring at her.

Grace has no answer, so she simply stares into the water, its rhythmic flashes and bubbly flow starting to take hold of her. She wills it to do its work.

Marjorie stubs the butt of her durry into the ground and she, then Julia pulls another bundle of earthy-smelling tobacco strand from the pouch. In tandem each girl rips small squares from a newspaper sheet, stretches out some stringy plant bits, places them onto her paper and licks along one side. They hold their partially made cigarettes towards Grace.

'Here. Be a honey and roll this for me, Grace. My fingers are sore from writing,' says Marjorie.

'Do mine too, will you?' adds Julia. 'Mine are sore from wrapping care packages for the war effort.'

'But I was in your class too, and I wrapped more,' says Grace.

'Yes, but I had knitting class before that and what's more, I've caught Mum's arthritis.'

Begrudgingly, Grace forms two neat cylinders, tapers one end of each, then hands them to the girls. They snatch their fags from her and light them, taking long drags before releasing sideways streams of smoke. Marjorie's eyes widen. 'Erk, look over there, a spider! Get rid of it! Do it Grace!' With a wriggling finger Marjorie points to the offender housed in its web on a nearby bush, then jumps up and backs away, swiftly followed by Julia who runs to cower behind her.

Grace wonders why she hasn't noticed the St Andrews Cross spider before with its distinctive yellow stripes—female, she understands. Zigzag configurations of white silk traverse a quarter of the web to form the shape of a cross. Is it for stability or as a display to ward off predators?

Suddenly Grace is looking down upon herself sitting with the bad girls, somehow appearing different. She is the one out of place, doesn't belong here. Is she who she's always been? Why be with girls she has no affection for, let alone respect?

'But it's not hurting us. Just leave it be,' says Grace, trying to act natural despite the shock caused by her interesting new perspective—floating in the air.

'If you won't do it, I will,' says Marjorie. With that, she rises to her feet, walks over to the spiderweb and pokes the fine silk with the furnace-red tip of her cigarette. The home of the arachnid shrivels as it melts, leaving a widening then gaping hole as the terrified spider retreats to its web's extremity, shaking furiously on what remains of its shelter. Marjorie and Julia roar, doubling over with laughter before they fade from Grace's sight.

She closes her eyes and drifts back to her bedroom, to one stifling day in 1941.

When Grace returns to the scene, the spider is scuttling over her hair. Dispassionately, she reaches up and flicks it away. A stick flies out of Marjorie's hand. Yelping, she shakes herself to exorcise what the creature may have left on her body, then both she and Julia once again cackle like chooks. Grace notices filaments of web tacky on her hair and fingers, almost as real as what she's just remembered.

Chapter Two

Norman Park, Brisbane, Australia

1941 - The Day Of

Grace peels a damp sheet from her legs and fans herself with Hemingway; a hot, humid Sunday afternoon. Her parents, Connie and George, have driven to the nearby bayside suburb of Manly, its gravelly beach reminiscent of Blackpool in Old Blighty—England—according to Connie's mother. She's lukewarm about the sentiment and the drive, but Grace looks forward to fish and chips for dinner tonight. For now, alone in the house, she's enjoying the seclusion of her bedroom; *For Whom the Bell Tolls* has her hooked.

Yet a noise niggles her. Under the eaves just outside her window, a spiderweb has become a battleground; a fly screams and whirs its tiny wings as a huge Golden Orb slowly mummifies the small insect in its tight silk. Earlier Grace had tried unsuccessfully to reach up and release it. So, she closed the window but it did nothing to dim the racket. Now as the screams intensify, the fight more frantic, she wonders why it's taking so long for something so small to die.

Three measured knocks on her bedroom door, each an exact second apart. Demanding, different to the polite hesitance of family tapping. Grace hears them as three gunshots smashing the tranquillity of a remote valley, its echoes ricocheting off surrounding hills, terrifying all life forms, doing some damage there. In her mind she can see the place quite clearly: beautiful but struck with the sound of death.

Whatever it was she just heard, she is certain of one thing: she must help. But how, from here in Brisbane? Was this another premonition? Having experienced several recently her skin prickles.

She jumps from the bed, having startled at both noisy intrusions, sending book pages flipping through the air. Hemingway hits the floor like an inflated piano accordion. Must get her bearings. She hadn't heard her parents come home. An intruder? Please ... no.

Her fingers tremble as she automatically skims them through her hair and down her sides, to make herself presentable. Another knock causes her to jerk, move to the door and lean against it.

'Who is it?' Her small voice shakes.

'It's Archie.'

Archie. Friend of her father. A veteran of The Great War. Her godfather.

'Can I come in? I've got something for you,' he sings.

'Archie? I wasn't expecting anyone. Lots and lots of schoolwork to do. Mum and Dad have gone out.' Grace speaks to the door.

'I know they have, the car's not there. Let me in! I've got a present for you and it's *really heavy*.' His words ring of pain.

She eases the door open. He rushes in, kicking it shut. Her eyes dart towards the door he's closed, the line he's crossed. A sudden chill makes her fold her arms in a protective hug. Her bottom lip wobbles, she tries to settle it with her fingers.

Archie balances in his arms a large wooden box, about three feet in length.

'Just let me put this down somewhere. Good Lord, those front steps and this blooming heat ... and my poor arthritis!' Even when complaining, he sounds like a jolly, pompous Englishman. He dumps the box onto her bed; the mattress sinks in response.

'How did you ... get through ... the front door?' Grace's hushed voice comes in a pant.

Archie is much taller than she is, but she can still count five bundles of wispy white hairs sprouting from his pate, glowing in the window light like tiny winter poplars. She remembers those spindly trees from books, leafless and sort of desperate.

'I let myself in, Grace m'girl. Your dad has a habit of not locking it and he didn't today. Lucky for me, eh?' He winks. 'You mustn't have heard me knocking. Where've they gone?' he asks vaguely.

'They've gone to Manly, but they'll be back any minute. Any minute. Minute …' she trails off.

He comes to life, straightening his back. 'That right?' Frowns. 'I'm sure we'll hear them, won't we?' He flicks his head around until he finds his focus—the closed bedroom door. 'You should be more careful about locking the front door while they're out though. I might have been a burglar. But it's only your poor old godfather.'

Archie turns his attention to the box. 'I made this just for you. I think you'll like it. Go on, have a good look.'

Easing herself down onto the bed, Grace looks at the wooden box. She opens its hinged lid to reveal six internal compartments of differing size, little rooms separated by walls of faultlessly sanded and polished timber.

Archie beams. 'It's a toolbox, you see, your very own.'

How many times has Grace asked her father for a toolbox? On how many occasions has he denied her? She's always wanted to help him around the house with painting, grinding, winching, sawing—a multitude of boyish pursuits. Harping to be included until George acquiesces. Her work inevitably eclipsing her father's low expectations. And then, the accolades! Always the same, round and round in slap-stick pantomime, with an unwelcome edge of gravity.

She wishes her father had given her this present.

Archie plonks onto her bed, the box a barrier between them.

'I made it myself. Mahogany—the finest timber, finest grain. It's all been finished off, see. Bit too good for holding tools really, but I had to make it perfect for you, Grace. Think about what you'll put where.'

Grace nods mutely, horrified about him sitting with her on her bed.

'Do you see?' He points to each compartment. 'You can put your hammer here, your saw here, spanner, wrench, pliers … every tool has its place in this unit. See, I've put a screwdriver in here for you. To start you off. You'll just have to get your dad to buy you some more tools. I can put a word in to him for you if you want.' He studies her.

'Well, do you like it?'

'Very much. Thanks, Archie,' she mutters, chewing her bottom lip, looking towards the door, willing it to open to the sight of her parents' smiling faces.

'Go on, feel the workmanship. I'm proud of it. It took many hours,' Archie's voice is husky as though he's been doing physical work.

She tries to concentrate on the wooden box. Reminds her of a maze for mice.

Placing a trembling finger on one corner of the maze, she runs it along its smooth rim. He runs his finger from the opposite corner, meeting hers in the middle. 'Hello, sweetheart' his fingertip 'says' to hers. He sounds like Jimmy Cagney. A child's game. Hastily, she retracts her finger. Jumps up from the bed, glaring at Archie.

The man's beady eyes dart around her things, her precious, personal possessions. 'You've a fine room here. Nice bric-a-brac. It's sort of girly, isn't it? Not at all like you! Well, what I mean is, you are a bit of a tomboy, aren't you?'

She feels herself blush, shot to the heart. 'We can fix that.'

What does that mean? She doesn't care about the present. *Get out of my room!*

Looking down at him sitting there, the poplars sprouting from his bald head amongst beads of sweat, she also notices brown patches staining its taut, shiny skin. A map of somewhere? She's drawn to the bridge of his Plasticine-like nose below, smeared sideways and covered in large pores that look like orange peel. A Plasticine man. He's been sniffing loudly through that nose since he entered her room. Still exhausted from climbing the stairs? Why doesn't he use his mouth? When he does open it, she wishes he hadn't. His breath smells of chemicals—something mechanical, to do with a car anyway. Perhaps he's swallowed a car. Perhaps he is a car. Wishes he'd drive off.

Alone with Archie. Grace reads her dictionary every day and when she read the meaning of the words *sleazy* and *repugnant*, she thought of him. The toucher. She couldn't count the number of occasions over the years when he's stood too close, rubbed against her, beckoned her onto his lap. She hasn't told her parents but thinks they're aware of him being an embarrassment. Just an embarrassment; she tries to convince herself.

'Tell me now, Grace, what are your dreams?' He looks up at her.

'What do you know about my dreams?' Her premonitions.

'That's a peculiar thing to say. Do you have something to hide?'

Winks, simultaneously clicking his tongue. 'Your plans for the future, I mean, of course. As your godfather, I should know these sorts of things. I do care deeply about you, you know.' Such a natural request sounds all wrong on Archie's lips.

Grace secures a lock of her golden hair behind an ear, tries to stand tall. 'I want to be a nurse, I think.' She peers out the window, searching for an escape.

'You *think?* Now, that doesn't sound very enthusiastic!' He taps the bedspread beside him, gesturing for her to once again join him. 'Sit with your old godfather. Please? How often do we get to spend time together, just the two of us?'

She sits on the far end of the mattress near the wall, her hands in her lap. Her heart is pumping so fast that her blouse is moving.

'Now, that's better.' Archie stares at her. 'Such a pretty thing you are really. Do you have a boyfriend, Grace? Bet you have lots of boys after you. Is that why you want to be a nurse? So you can marry a handsome doctor? Yes? Come on, tell me.' He licks his lips.

Why is he being so stupid? It's as if his entire life is a bad comedy and she could almost raise a laugh if she were viewing him from anywhere other than from within herself. She closes her eyes, but his rhythmic sniffing keeps her in the room. She sneaks a look at his face. His eyes don't match the wide-eyed smile he attempts—dead down the bottom of two holes gouged below his large forehead. It couldn't have been God who put those eyes in there. But God made Grace. 'He poked a hole in your tummy to make your belly button, announcing, "You'll do".' Her mother once told her this. She clings to such things.

'What are you now, a teenager?'

'Thirteen, young … little,' she rambles, each word more hushed than the last. She feels like a ten-year-old in his overbearing presence.

Archie emits a vile, sour laugh she can almost taste. 'Young? I thought you'd be bragging about being thirteen. Quite an age. You're almost a young woman now.'

He pushes the toolbox aside and inches towards her until he has her pinned against the wall, blocking her escape. He places his firm hand on her knee. That sniffing. That stench. She clasps her hands between her legs and winces, trembling. Her parched tongue tries but refuses to wet her parched lips. The fingers of his gnarled hand crawl up her leg. Another game. She wants to tug her skirt back down but her body won't work, as the determined spider scurries beneath, searching for prey.

'What do we have here? A toy for *me* to …' his words fade away as he lifts her skirt, peers under there. As she closes her eyes, she can feel his smile. She's been trapped, become limp and helpless.

Grace feels as though she's looking at a scene that has gone before, that dull thud of knowing what is about to unfold.

Of course…

1942 - Eighteen Months After

At almost fifteen years of age—Grace by this time having discovered Daphne du Maurier—when the movie *Rebecca* comes to the Regent Theatre in Brisbane city, she naturally makes plans to see it.

It's a strange early Saturday afternoon. In an unusual occurrence, a heavy veil of morning fog still hovers, leaving the familiar theatre venue as Grace imagines 'Manderley'—the grand de Winter estate from du Maurier's novel—to be: imposing, shrouded in mist.

Her mother is ill. Grace has few real friends and the only person she knows who would have come with her is Marcie her neighbour, who she doesn't really like. Which is why she has braved town and the cinema alone, but she's edgy about it.

Also nervous about the movie's content—she worries it could be too creepy—she buys a small packet of jellybeans from the theatre shop for something else to focus on. She ascends the magnificent staircase and takes her seat at the front of the cinema near the screen.

Waiting there, she realises that even the beginning of the book had unsettled her. She'd related intimately to the unnamed female protagonist. Shy, socially awkward, eager to please—she could have been reading about herself. Grace doesn't think she's always been this way, but she has become so. She needs a boost and hopes to experience the protagonist's journey of becoming braver, more confident over time. Perhaps Grace can do that, too.

The lights dim to a barrage of war-time patriotism as the Movie tone News rolls out. She's yawning by the time the film begins. Pops a couple of jellybeans into her mouth.

Speaking of clouds, moons and dark hands, the narrator's voice sounds mellow but foreboding in the blackness. Grace shudders, arms folded as she sucks on the sweet's sugar coating.

Oh, there she is! Joan Fontaine looks even more like Grace than in the magazine photographs she had seen of her. The sinister music and dialogue continue their assault. Engulfed in cigarette fug, it could almost be the fog from outside but the smell gives it away. Perhaps she isn't the only audience member feeling nervous? She turns around to discover a sea of intermittently glowing red dots coming from the tips of lit embers, like little lighthouse beacons confusing her as to which direction would be safest.

The hushed, scurrilous voice of that evil housekeeper, Mrs Danvers—exactly as Grace had imagined. Both she and Joan wring their trembling hands, Grace's tacky from the lollies. Certain words start to come through as distorted muffles, some dialogue amplifies as if meant just for Grace. She watches wide-eyed as the poor young woman stands beside the old witch, trembling precariously at full-length French doors Danvers terms a window. High above the mist, the cruel woman is coaxing the poor thing to jump, to kill herself, telling her not to be afraid, that she has nothing to live for, baiting her … Grace wipes away a tear then pulls her feet up on the seat, rocking back and forth, terrified of falling.

The screen splinters in a black and white explosion as Grace's lollies jump from their paper packet. Gunshots, then silence. The commotion of the scene over, her heart pounds on. She is barely aware of the remainder of the film. The movie reel of Rebecca coughs, splutters and abruptly stops. The end. She sits in darkness as people mumble and shuffle all around her, leaving one fog for another outside. Alone, she takes some huge smoky breaths, coughs, then closes her eyes.

A cacophony of piercing sounds shoots from the speakers then whooshes around her to create a buzzing breeze, assaulting her senses. She pops open her eyelids, darting her head and eyes around like a deranged doll. 'What's going on?' she whimpers into the darkness in her little girl voice; it wasn't meant to be a double feature. The hisses and blurts piece themselves together to form words.

And suddenly she is watching another film. Every detail blazes in full-colour cinematic perfection, as clear as cut glass. Grace is the main character. The veil has lifted.

It is the performance she had never asked for …

1941 - The Day Of

Tick tock, clock on her bedroom wall. 5pm. Grace watches its slow hands edge towards her death.

Must focus.

Archie is a car and if he touches her further, he will stain her, and she'll never be able to rid the marks. He has to stop; she can't let him do this.

Sudden rage courses through her body, enabling it to work again. With a sharp intake of breath, she reaches behind him and grabs the lone screwdriver from the box. Forcing her eyelids shut she jabs at the air in front of his face, then hits something.

'Ahh,' Archie yelps.

When Grace manages to open her eyes properly, his hands are cradling his left eye. Between pats Grace notices the damage: bloodshot and watery eye, a bleeding scratch to the cheek. It's the red that surprises her; she's surprised to see he bleeds. She pants, wild-eyed, shaking, still clutching the screwdriver in her shaky fist.

'How could you? You, you …' Her words jolt as she jumps from the bed.

Archie gets to his feet. With gritted teeth, he takes a handkerchief from his shirt pocket and gently dabs his face, grimacing as he discovers specks of blood and watery discharge on the fabric, checking it in the mirror. He stares at her. 'Here, look at what you've done, you could have blinded me,' he snarls, dropping the hankie on the floor, pointing to his face. 'What the hell kind of nurse would you make? Why did you do this to me? To me?'

'What were you doing to me?' Not quite sure if her words came out, she backs away.

'To you? I think you've got me all wrong, my girl. I have standards. Who would want you anyway—an insipid, gawky imbecile like you?'

She realises he must have heard her.

Archie paces—back, forward, back, forward. 'Don't go whining to your parents. They asked me to educate you in the facts of life. Obviously, you still have some lessons to learn. But, dear child, we'll leave that for another day, if you ever show promise of becoming a real woman that is. At this point, it looks doubtful. But keep the faith!' Spitting on his palm, Archie damps down his poplars and moves towards the door.

Grace throws the screwdriver at him. 'Get out!' Her tone low, guttural, which surprises her as she's trying not to cry.

Archie turns to her as though second guessing. His face devoid of emotion, he picks up the screwdriver and places it back in the toolbox. Closes the lid then gathers the box into his arms like a rescued child. As he approaches the door, he nods down to the heavy load he carries and smiles at her.

'You won't be needing this, ever.' A look of puzzlement. 'Not a boy, not really a girl, never a woman. How very confusing. How very sad it must be to be you.' Archie departs Grace's room with the sensitivity of someone having visited the toilet.

When she hears him waddling down the front stairs, she shouts to his back in a wobbly voice, 'Mum says you're uncoot.' Grace knows that's not quite the word she's looking for but it's similar.

She slams the front door then locks it—all thumbs. Runs along the gloomy cedar hallway to the bathroom. Showers hot, scrubs herself hard.

Returning to her room, Grace notices the spider has moved down on its web closer to the window, away from its victim which now hangs immobilised and silent in its tight sheath. She pushes open the window, severing the web which causes the large leggy creature to reel, release its hold and land onto her bedroom floor. The fly is left dangling dead in silk, waving defeatedly on the slight breeze.

Using the sole of one of her shoes she uncharacteristically squashes the spider dead. Thump! She bangs her shoe on the window ledge to dislodge the mashed spider, banishing it to the garden outside. Shuts window and curtains. Puts herself to bed, hoping to test her wings, striving to experience some dire premonition about Archie.

It's all about focus and sentience.

Two Days After

She hears her mother's voice as a frantic muffle through her bedroom door. 'You must come out now. Please darling.'

Grace has been considering what happened, what to do about it. She almost gags when she thinks about Plasticine man insinuating her parents approved of what he was doing to her. She'll not let herself believe his words or even remember them. She'll try so hard ... Girls she knows never share anything personal with their parents, let alone something so horrible. But Grace trusts her mother; she's always felt safe confiding in her and that trust is reciprocated. Perhaps it's because Grace is an only child. But this is big and scary and she has no idea how her mother will process it. Grace will take her deep breath and spill just enough to help herself, and punish the man who dares call himself her godfather.

'Come in.' Her tiny voice surprises her. She sits up in bed and tries to prepare herself.

Connie enters and marches straight to the window, opening the curtains, saying, 'It's so stuffy in here.' She returns to sit beside her daughter, whose eyes squint against the dense afternoon sunlight.

'You're looking awfully pale, dear. No wonder, after so long without sun.' Her eyes move to the tray of half-eaten lunch withering on the side table. 'And you've barely touched your food. What's this all been about? All this ... hibernation. Please tell me. Dad and I have been worried sick.'

'I didn't know how to tell you. I don't know how I can, even now after all my hibernation, as you call it.' Grace swipes her hand across her forehead, looking towards the ceiling. She takes a deep breath.

'Something has happened,' states Connie.

'Something could have happened, yes. Something really bad.'

'Goodness Grace, what is it?'

'You've always spoken highly about men who served for our country, haven't you? You've always carried on about how good and proper they are.' The look Grace shoots her mother is near accusatory and she can't help it.

'I don't know about *carrying* on, but indeed, if not for them, we would be overrun with enemies by now. Why?'

'But what if the enemy is right here at home? At our home. My home?' Grace searches her mother's face for some kind of recognition or understanding.

Connie places a trembling hand over her décolletage. 'Whatever are you saying, child?'

'It's Archie. He's my godfather, isn't he? Isn't he, Mummy?' Tears well in Grace's eyes.

'Heavens above, what's he done this time?'

The tut-tut of dismissal in her mother's voice makes Grace want to hit her.

'*This time* you weren't here. You and Dad weren't here, were you? What do you think he did? *My godfather.*'

'What do you mean we weren't here? Listen, Grace, I don't want to play games. I know sometimes Archie can be a bit silly with you. Did you see him recently?'

'He came over when you and Dad went to Manly.'

'Why on earth would he do that?'

'He offered me a toolbox, said he made it for me.'

'Well, that's very nice of him.' Twitchy smile of mouth, not eyes. Grace is seething.

'There's nothing very nice about him. Nothing!' she cries. 'His words ... He touched me,' covers the area between her legs with her hands, 'there.' She looks down. 'That's what he did. My godfather betrayed me. And if you betray me too, if you don't believe me, I think I'll just die.' Grace rubs her hand under her wet nose.

Connie stands slowly and walks to the window where she peers outside. Grace sees her breathe in and exhale through pursed lips. Her mother's mouth looks ugly.

'Look at me, Mummy! Tell me you believe me. Please tell me you believe I'm not lying.'

Connie turns to Grace. 'Why would you lie about a thing like this?'

Lying? 'Tell Me. You. Believe me.'

'You've never lied to me before. Why would you start now? I do believe you. I'm just *sorry*. Just so sorry.'

Connie sits and embraces her relieved daughter. 'Did he say anything to you?' says Connie.

Grace pulls away. 'I just … Mum, I just can't say. Too hurtful.' She wipes away a tear, reaches into her bedside drawer then hands her mother the blood-splattered handkerchief. 'I hurt his eye, stupid old fool.'

'That's my girl. That's my girl.' Connie pats Grace gently on her back with one hand, taking the soiled fabric from her sobbing daughter with the other.

'Now, let's get rid of this disgusting thing.' Connie walks to the door to leave. She turns back to Grace. 'Dad will have to know. He'll have to talk to your … to Archie about what you've told me. You know that has to happen, don't you?'

'Yes.'

'And Grace?'

'Yes?'

'Come out soon.'

When George summons Archie to the house, and he swaggers in as though he'd done nothing wrong, Connie ushers her daughter away. Grace races from kitchen to bedroom. Slams her door. Begins moving her silky oak dresser to block it—marvelling at how light-weight the furniture feels—then realising she'd hear better without the barrier; she drags it back. Hears her mother's high-pitched shouting. A slap— skin against skin.

Her father yells, 'Never set foot in this house again!'

Archie grumbles what sounds like a protest. Her father's growl stifles Archie's voice.

A heavy object crashes to the floor.

1942

Grace eventually floats out of the cinema; she thinks it strange to be floating while carrying heavy thoughts. She is going home. Home: something is no longer right about that word. Home means refuge, doesn't it?

On the bus, she sits trying to look prim with gloved hands clasped politely over her female parts so no-one can look at her. The Story Bridge takes the bus over it while Grace turns her head to the right and takes in shattered glimpses of city interspersed with hard, dark stripes of the bridge's steel pylons. Another movie reel. Why is life so topsy-turvy? She wants something more stable than flickering images. But why are her thoughts so seamless? Resting her head against the windowpane, she closes her eyes. Not even the mechanical jolts can stop the tirade.

All that remains of the rot descends upon Grace on her ride home to Norman Park. When she arrives back to the house at sunset, she notices that the fog around Brisbane has lifted. She can't lift hers.

Archie doesn't come to the house anymore; his name is not mentioned again. But Grace never feels totally secure. And even though her mother believed her, and Grace knows she didn't really do anything wrong, she decides to keep quiet about anything bad that may happen to her in the future. Easier for all that way. No more friendships broken, like the rift she inadvertently caused between her father and Archie. She tries to imagine the episode was just a nightmare. Never really happened.

One thing has come of it: Grace has vowed to never let herself, or anyone she loves, be hurt again. She's always known there's something special about her—the ability to see, hear and feel things that have later come true. But since the day Plasticine Man tried to take from her what wasn't offered, she's been learning how to hone her true abilities, to ignite them. If she just keeps quiet about her gift, *beyond* will retain its powers, it will transfer them to her, and she and her loved ones will be protected; that's the promise.

Focus and sentience. Prescience that is incomprehensible, yet so very real.

Chapter Four

Indian Ocean, 1948

Izabella's face is stinging. She feels it's become a magnet for iron filings, instead it collects piercing shards of ice as they spear through the roar of gale-force winds. Standing on the ship's open top deck, her long dark curls are getting soaked. She should really have worn the grey scarf from her meagre collection of possessions she brought with her. Grey, like all her clothing; she resolves she will only wear bright colours in Australia. Somehow, she's not really bothered about the elements tonight; the bracing shock makes her feel alive, diminishes the pervading stench of smoke, disease, death and takes her mind off the long voyage. She vows to try to overcome the ghosts of war and experience something new: freedom, which she can barely remember. She will banish to the sea all the horrors, subversion and heartache—too much baggage for nineteen years of life.

But the memories still linger. The Siege of Budapest from late 1944 was when her 'strategically significant' city was encircled, coming under fire from a battle between Soviet troops and allied Hungarian and German troops. The city was almost obliterated, the population decimated. Izabella and her parents somehow rode it out, having retreated to the Buda's hinterland, the hills west of the Danube River.

They huddled in the underground cellar of an abandoned home, cold and without power, managing to stay invisible. As waves of ammunition fired from tanks rained down from the hills into the city below, the soldiers were seemingly oblivious to the clandestine presence of the little family. The godsend of cheese and wine kept them fed and drunk during the cold winter. She knows they were lucky: her father has told her of people resorting to eating horses and bugs to keep them alive during that time, drinking water from the increasingly polluted, frozen Danube.

She and her parents escaped Budapest in a van driven by a man dressed, possibly disguised, as a soldier who bartered bundles of cigars for their freedom—why, she'll never know. They were driven to Austria where they stayed in a refugee holding camp before being transported to Italy. From there they were given safe passage, as displaced persons, to travel by ship to Melbourne, Australia.

The sky is clear tonight, igniting the visibility of a multitude of stars. Through her large, dark eyes, Izabella thinks she recognises a stellar constellation she's learnt about from her on-board English lessons—the Southern Cross—its points reminding her of an arrow piercing through the sky, a device to safely navigate the ship and its passengers to the land down under. She thinks of the Star of Bethlehem leading the wise men to Jesus. She and her parents are Christians, but Christian or Jewish, no-one was safe during the siege. The yellow Star of David leading the Nazis to the Jews, herding them onto trains to concentration camps, to death ... The Red Army raping women and girls, plucking civilians—even non-Jews— from the streets to perform *malenky robot*—a 'little work' which meant three to five years of hard labour in camps in the Soviet Union ... The Arrow Cross of the 'Hungarist' fascist party guiding Jews to the ghetto, to the gun, to the Danube, to lie with the corpses of men, women, children and horses, in a river of ice and the rubble from the German-bombed bridges ... She recalls the horrifying sight of the iconic Chain Bridge; still attached to the towers, its cables draped into the river. Izzie remembers being struck by an image of her mother's fallen bra straps, the bridge ironically appearing so delicate and nonchalant in its destruction.

She shuts her eyes and inhales deeply. Teetering from the ship's relentless pitch and roll, she opens her eyes and grabs hold of a railing for balance. There are many women up here Izzie has had to dodge, sprawled like corpses on the deck. But they are alive and their eyes remain open. They've chosen the glittering galactic star show, or at least the fresh air, over trying to sleep on triple-tiered bunks in tiny cabins way down on the decks below, segregated from their partners. Izzie likes the segregation, hopes she's far away from her father. He'll be drunk on the vodka he smuggled from their departure port, and no doubt attempting to flirt with the women passengers. She couldn't bear to witness it.

Feels bad for her poor *anya*—her mother. Lying in her bunk in a dolls' house of a cabin, hit with violent seasickness. Izzie has been caring for her as best she can, but after four weeks of hearing her mother moaning and having to clean up her vomit, she sometimes must get away.

Only one week to go until they reach Australia, the free country that will lift them from their pains, their woes. She can hardly wait.

Chapter Five

Norman Park, 1949

Let me tell you about when I was small. I have a secret I want you to know because there is no one else here who really understands me and I'm supposing you may. I feel if anyone will inherit my gift, it will be you, dear Treasure, because you will be kind of the same as me—in your head, the way you think, see and feel. Strange and wonderful things may happen to you too, and I never want you to be afraid of any journey life may reveal to you.

For the longest time, I flew inside this house, the house I, your mummy, grew up in. It was nothing frenetic, just floats, indolent leaps and landings, my limbs synchronised in precise tandem. A bit like air breaststroke. Graceful almost, which is unusual for me. Like Esther Williams—the actress in 'Bathing Beauty'.

I don't know why I don't fly anymore, it's not that I wanted to stop. I told my Mum, your grandma, about it and she just smiled at me, but nicely, not like I was an idiot. I want you to tell me if it happens to you—I'll give you my widest smile. I'd like to talk to Mum more about flying—style, aerodynamics, trajectory etc., but I'm afraid I might jinx things, or word will get out and I'll get thrown in the loony bin. So, I've shut up about it now to preserve my dignity and freedom. In this world, I've shut up about lots of stuff now ...

The bloody phone is ringing. 'Mum? MUM!' No response.

Grace drops her notepad and pen, races downstairs to the lounge room, picks up the telephone receiver.

'Hello?'

'You are coming tonight, aren't you,' Marcie declares as Grace spreads herself over the green velvet and mahogany armrests of the loveseat. It's an automatic search for escape from the loquacious Marcie; every part of Grace recoils from the assault of the girl's tinny voice. She will only reel herself in to alternate receiver between shoulders and ever- reddening ears.

'My day was simply divine, thanks for asking, Marcie.'

'Didn't think it necessary to make small talk. Figured you'd be more worried about what to wear tonight for Frank.'

'I'm not wearing anything tonight *for Frank*.'

'Ha ha. He'll love that.'

Grace moans. 'Listen. Stop being silly. And stop being so upbeat about tonight.'

Marcie drones on. During long conversations with the girl, Grace's manicure kit, which she keeps on the side table nearby, keeps her productive. Soon she's achieved the required contortions to paint the nails of all fingers and toes, but she'll ruin her work if she squeezes the small, ripened blackhead on the top of her left arm. This inconvenience starts to irritate her.

'I'd better go, Marcie. I've just done a nail,' she lies.

'Oh, you're doing your *nails*? Tres chic! I'm shocked and almost impressed. So, you'll come? Please poppet!' pleads Marcie, having made her predictable slur.

'I'm not sure. I don't want him getting the wrong idea.'

'He won't. It's just going to be a fun night out with your three best buddies. We all care about you and you've been studying too much lately. Frank knows you're not looking for anything serious, for now.'

'I'm not looking for anything serious with Frank—period. Sorry Marcie,' she mumbles, cranky at herself for apologising.

Slight pause. 'Sure thing, poppet. Don't worry about it. Frank's happy to take things easy too, for now. I'm sure of it.'

Grace rolls her eyes, blows her fingernails. 'Well, alright then, but on the condition that you don't leave me alone with him, not for one second.' She smacks her forehead, carefully—so she won't muck up her nails—with her palm, in a swat at her indiscretion. 'He's nice really, but we're just friends, okay?'

'That's wonderful! Yes, he is a lovely chap. Frank will be thrilled. If you didn't come, he'd be beside himself! We'll pick you up at six tonight, okay? We'll have such fun!'

Grace hangs up. Long ago, she decided if Marcie's brother Frank was beside himself, she wouldn't choose either of them.

Connie has appeared at the telephone, releasing the smell of grilled lamb chops as she wipes greasy hands on her apron. She's been preparing dinner while Grace's father is, as usual for four-thirty in the afternoon, at the bowls club for his daily injection of mates and beer. Almost every day the same routine. Grace gives an exaggerated sigh.

'What's wrong, love?'

'It's Marcie. She's stupid.' Noticing her mother's frown, she adds, 'Sorry, but she is. She craves self-gratification. Takes everything at face value. I want to yell: Use your senses purposefully! She has no intuition whatsoever, well, unless she's on a scent. She never considers *consequences*. She never listens to me. Constantly puts words into my mouth. She pretends I've said what I haven't. And she is gullible, too. If it's something she wants to hear, she believes it. Anything! Like, I could tell her that Clark Gable had been staying at our house and she'd believe it.' Grace almost flaps her hands off.

'Well, if she is so gullible, I hope you haven't taken advantage of her.'

'No, I said it was Bing Crosby.' A harsh laugh escapes her. 'Honestly, if anything, *she* takes advantage of *me*.'

'I really have no idea what you're talking about, Grace.'

'Oh, don't worry, Mum. I just don't want to go out with her tonight, that's all.'

'Perhaps it will do you good. You've been moping round home a bit aimlessly, to be honest, darling.' Grace can't believe her mother is encouraging her to go out with Marcie, a girl they can barely tolerate.

'Hmm.' Grace chews on her bottom lip.

Grace knows that her mother is always sensitive to Grace's needs, especially during 'post-exam malaise', which also means giving her daughter some much appreciated space to recover. But she obviously thinks it's time to move on.

Two weeks ago, Grace arrived back to her parents' house from the hospital, having endured what she hopes were her final nursing exams. It's been a protracted, frequently road-blocked journey to attain the status of Nursing Sister and arrived at more from obligation than passion. Grace remembers trying to explain her displeasure to her mother.

'You look happy to be home, love,' said Connie.

'Relieved, more like it. And I always like seeing you and Dad.'

How could she tell her mother that she dreads returning to this house, especially to her now tainted room? She wants to escape—everything.

'I don't know how I'm going to keep going, Mum, with my nursing I mean. Please try to understand. The nuns and matrons are so prim and proper. I honestly tremble every time they come near. I keep praying they won't appear beside me to check that I won't slip up when I'm giving an injection. Don't they know that their very presence always makes me slip up? They sure don't bring out the best in me.'

'I can't really imagine they've ever been any different, Grace.' 'It's not only the penguins.' Grace gave a coy smile. 'It's the claustrophobic, mildewy nurses' quarters; the sloshing of ungodly contents of people's stomachs and bowels presented to me in shiny silver pots; the heavy fall of stained calico curtains; the toxic smells of ammonia, ether, chloroform, urine, faeces, disinfectant. It's hell, Mum!'

Grace despairs these nasty assaults on her senses—evoking memories of sickness and death—may haunt her forever. What scares her most is that this is meant to be the beginning of her career.

The telephone call has left her exhausted, as have recent night shifts. She heel-walks outside to the dunny—the toilet—at the back of the house, silently thanking her father for the flat concrete path, because any bumps could ruin her toenail polish. George has planted what is sometimes a rainbow of spring flowers along the path, as though leading somewhere nice. But it's winter when neither wisteria nor freesia bloom, so nothing masks the stench wafting from the outhouse.

With care she climbs the stairs and goes to her room. When her nails are completely dry, she squeezes that beastly little blackhead. Deciding to grab a nap before going out tonight, she folds the pink chenille bedspread halfway down her single bed and creeps under it, enjoying the security of just enough swaddle. Puffing up her pillow, she cocoons her head to block extraneous noises.

Brooding about the night ahead, Grace attempts some magic instead. She stares, as always, at the porcelain figurines on her dressing table: tiger, bear, dog—knowing exactly the strange things that are about to happen.

Chapter Six

Concentrate. Look. Listen. At last, the near meditative state overtakes her. Fixating on each object, one at a time, she catches the animals' little painted eyes and mouths moving. Some are animated— widening to convey amazing secrets from exotic lands. Some are more introverted— revealing barely a snippet of a secret. What are they telling her? She knows it's important, wants them to know she cares as she strives for the thrill of an audible whisper.

As her hooded eyes move to the rabbit, the weight of her eyelids becomes too much, and they close. She lets her arms relax and fall to her sides, lets her breathing regulate. Crazy, random thoughts sneak into her head, evoking a little smile with the realisation that sleep is descending. She's dully aware of the familiar, gentle coo of a pigeon outside. Her mouth lolls. The little Cupid's bow pouts above the exposed gap in her front teeth, through which she whistles.

Grace finds herself perched atop a huge blue Ulysses butterfly. Little terracotta-tiled rooftops below expand as the land rises to meet her too quickly. She's going to crash! She jolts awake as the front door slams, wondering how dreams can synchronise so well with real life. Is it real life? Her heart pounds. Tries to settle, slow its rate.

'Konnichiwa? *Konnichiwa!*' Affable mood. George has almost forgiven the Japs since his Kokoda stint. Or perhaps, thinks Grace, he can afford to now the war is over. He has a series of funny nicknames for Connie. One day he'll be calling her Constantinople, when everyone knows the song.

'Shush! Grace's sleeping, silly moo.' A playful mother.

Her clumsy father has fallen into the house in his predictable alcoholic haze. The comradery of the diggers at the club always emboldens him. If George is recognised by Grace and her mother as a little too reliant on the bottle, the issue is rarely discussed, and they accept the pattern as 'just the way it is'. It could be worse. Grace knows that some men who'd seen action took their own lives. Some became blithering idiots or recluses—hollow shells of the men they once were. Some became a little too indecent—failing to decipher right from wrong, like her godfather— the word and its meaning forever defiled for her now.

Grace knows her father fancies a woman down the road, Peggy McBride. Her mother knows it, too. How could she not? George becomes visibly stupid in her presence, talking too loudly, fussing over her. Grace has seen her mother trying to keep the two of them apart. Whether her father was a flirt before the war she doesn't know, she doesn't think he would have been; Grace cannot imagine her mother being attracted to that. She thinks he's never acted on it, prays to God he won't.

She can hear him talking loudly but can't make out the conversation. George hasn't taken Connie's advice; Grace hears crockery and cutlery banging, little ting-tings of the cruet—never one for subtlety at this time of day. He's having a late lunch or early dinner.

Standing too long in the shower, she lets the heat of the hard water do its soothing work on her body. She shudders when the bracing cold water contracts the pores of her skin. Dries herself off with a fresh towel, shakes on a puff of floral talcum powder and shoots a long astringent spray of 4711 cologne over her body. Dresses.

The late afternoon sun shoots an ethereal glow through her open bedroom window, casting leaf-shaped dappled light and shadows through the diaphanous white muslin curtains. The light is fading but holds enough to finish getting ready without Grace having to resort to her lamp. She sits at her dressing table, applies rouge, powder, fuchsia lipstick and critically assesses her look in the mirror.

She removes a large roller from her fringe to reveal a neatly tamed roll. Gives her hair a quick brush. 'Hmm,' she annunciates while nodding, 'almost suitably preened. God help me. Sorry God, for swearing.' The nod has dislodged a few stray gold hairs, so she sprays a strong waft of hairspray to tame it, set it back down on her forehead.

As she raises a hairbrush to perfect her fringe, she catches her sapphire gem-like eyes reflected in the mirror. She's struck by a phenomenon lasting an indeterminate amount of time, as time and place blur confusingly.

A strand of bright, almost neon light inches along the outline of her body. The strange light trail has originated from her hip and is picking up momentum to wind its way around her entire reflection. As it traces around her arms, she sees little fair hairs she hadn't really noticed before standing erect and glowing—all downy like a baby's. Frozen, she stares in wonder as her torso illuminates the mirror in traces of spangled gold. What springs to mind is a sight she saw as a child, while she and her family holidayed in North Queensland. They were driving past a line of fire as it forged its destructive path across a sugar cane field at night. The before, the recognisable, and the after, unrecognisable; at least for a while to come, until nature laid down a flurry of even more prolific growth.

How will tonight's vision change her? What is it showing her?

As the light encapsulates her body, she stretches her right arm up high, appearing as some unwitting idol. Lady Liberty. She tries to smile, but she's suddenly been struck dumb and paralysed, so she carefully regards her reflection which has morphed into a strangely beautiful apparition. Daring what she sees to stay, she diverts her attention to the trees outside which are starting to move haphazardly in the building-to- blustery westerly Brisbane winds.

Taking a deep breath and returning her gaze to the mirror, it's with a mix of bewilderment, sadness and relief that she notices the spell has broken. And back is the familiar, now not so vivid, palette. Her regal aura faded, all that's left in its wake is a steamy blur, like a used branding iron plunged into the shock of cold water. Her rouged cheeks look clown- like against her pallor, a ghastly glow in the hastening darkness. The brand has claimed its property and Grace knows she won't be the same now—at least for a while to come.

Gasps. Something inexplicable has occurred. She gives a quick glance down her body which appears unaffected. Giggling, she says, 'Sometimes I kinda feel like I'm the centre of the universe.' With renewed vigour, she tests her reclaimed mobility, searching for clues to the source of the apparition. The only discernible change to the room is the appearance of stirred-up dust motes hovering around the mess of windblown curtains. Outside, the light fades as nature whips up her fury. She closes the window on the encroachment of night.

A sign—that's what it is. This familiar, yet seemingly innocuous whisper upon her body could signal changes as awakening as a new love or as darkly perilous as a visit from Beelzebub himself. These phenomena have only ever signalled good, but she never knows. Grace has become in tune with a force she calls *beyond*. So much so, she's enticed it to show her a mutual respect she trusts is afforded only few. Her preposterous childish wish on a falling star that was realised; the fox with pup in mouth inexplicably sauntering right up to her toddler body, dropping it at her feet as she sat playing with her doll in a field of dandelions; the huge heart-shaped hail stone she found—to her knowledge, the only piece of hail produced by that storm. These encounters, as startling and exciting as they were to her individually, trail blazed significant, and positive moments in her life. She touches wood every time something like this happens.

Like what has just transpired, some of her encounters she can only call supernatural. One imprinted memory involves when Grace was about eight years old: the ghost of her recently buried grandfather lounging in his chair, smiling up at her with a flash of gold tooth, slippers donned, the smell of Scooters cigars rendering the air thick and oppressive. She now keeps such experiences to herself, afraid of the disruption. Despite the dismissals, Grace can't help but wonder how many others secretly harbour similar experiences. Or if she's just plain weird.

Strange things have happened to her, and seem to be occurring more frequently, since Plasticine Man, at least since her recall of the incident, as if some kind of bond, a secret pact has formed and is being cemented. Grace thinks it's almost as if *beyond* now feels comfortable to present its powers to her without ridicule, as each new episode seems to further push the boundaries of daring. Grace's mysterious vault of secrecy, a silent provocation to the unknown to come clean. As a keeper of secrets, she's unwittingly become *beyond*'s trusted confidant. She tries to keep her crazy side from her parents, fearful of disclosing anything much anymore.

Grace hopes this afternoon's mirror incident with *beyond* is a precursor to some magical event about to happen to her, perhaps even tonight, although she's at pains to see how the upcoming occasion could spell anything but disaster. Grace squirms, telling herself that she's being rendered silly and dreamy, yet she cannot shake her conviction that the strange omen was lighting a pathway to tonight's outing.

Chapter Seven

Cloudland, Brisbane, 1949

Four young adults enter a taxi and are whisked away to the Bowen Hills tram stop, from where they'll make the ascent to Cloudland Ballroom. Grace plonks herself inside the funicular carriage. As the climb progresses, so does the wind and the rattling. She's squashed next to Marcie, opposite James and worst of all the unfortunate Frank, who stares leering at her.

'Wow!' he finally blurts. Grace fears the leering would turn to dribbling if he'd let his body do what it wants. All but Grace stare at him. 'What I mean is, what a pretty dress you're wearing, Grace,' he announces, looking chuffed about his restrained words. Grace is close to telling him he'd look just right in it, cursing herself for its low, low neckline. She crushes the stole across her cleavage.

'Grace does look pretty, doesn't she?' continues Marcie. 'It's a miracle.'

Instead of killing her friend, Grace grinds her teeth.

'I'll bet she even looks good in her nurse's uniform. The lovely Nurse Love,' says Frank.

Marcie nods at her with wide eyes as if to say, *be grateful Frank doesn't think you're ugly.*

'Good God! Can't you people find anything remotely meaningful to talk about?' Should Grace be flattered? Not when it's coming from Frank, she decides.

Ignoring Grace's request, James reaches over and tickles Marcie's ribs a little. She responds with the first of many giggles. When she's spent, James looks lovingly at his date.

'You look fine tonight too, Marcie.'

Free of the cyclonic capsule, the group disembarks atop of the hill, each one gazing up towards the familiar, bright lights of the Cloudland Ballroom archway. They move through the impressively domed entrance. According to Grace's father, during the recent war American soldiers invaded Cloudland in big numbers, playing mental, sometimes physical fisticuffs with our troops. Invaded the whole town, he said. 'The Yanks came and went, in and out of Brissie like Errol Flynn, bearing nylon stockings like the proverbial bloody wise men.' Grace wishes they were here now; they'd surely save her.

Grace finds herself in a similarly precarious predicament to being squashed in the rickety tram: sitting on a crescent moon prop with Frank, for the inevitable photo. He's leaned his head against hers, limpet-like, a thick layer of Brylcreem smearing one side of her shoulder length hair. He is not THE ONE. In the photograph they are given as a souvenir, Grace has her head turned away from him. Like Frank, this photo won't be kept. It's a shame really, because apart from the low neckline, she'd felt quite fetching in her blue dress.

They perform a strange mix of foxtrot and jitterbug to Johnny Pace and his big band playing 'I'm Looking Over a Four-leafed Clover' as Grace artfully overlooks Frank. Marcie's smile flips as she notices Grace's distaste. The ballroom floor sways with each rug they cut, and, after four dances, 'Now is the Hour' signals her cue to escape. The others may have planned a big night in town, but Grace knows she won't be part of it.

'I'm afraid the funicular and all these lights and frightful noise have wreaked havoc with my vertigo.' Grace knows Frank is dumb so plays to it.

'Huh?' grunts Frank predictably.

'I have to get away from you. No, not you really. It's this place. I'm not well. I have to leave. Sorry,' she adds, 'I know the music is fabulous, but I honestly feel I'm not up to it anymore.'

'Let me take you home, gorgeous,' chimes in Frank too quickly.

Grace gags, suspecting he's hoping for some action.

'No, no, I won't hear of it. Dad's given me money for a taxi. I just want you all to go on enjoying yourselves. Please don't worry about me.' She backs up. 'We must do this again soon. I've had such a pleasant time!' Grace feels her face flush.

Marcie and James stay for the final slow dances while Frank follows Grace, attempting to lead her to the station.

'I'll be fine to walk myself, thanks,' she says in staccato.

Frank moves towards her for a kiss as she sighs dramatically, turning her head away at just the right moment.

'I'll be alright when I freshen up and get out of here,' Grace splutters.

She almost trips in her haste to be rid of him. First, she dashes to the cloak room to collect her stole, then attempts to duck unseen into the ladies' toilets. Grace glances over her shoulder and sees the abandoned Frank standing miserably under a chandelier, his rheumy eyes illuminated by the twinkling lights. She knows she'll never go out with him again, whether he likes it or not.

Boys huddle around the bar. She can feel their stares as she passes. Two of them make lewd remarks. She knows they're lewd because the word that rises high above the rabble is tits.

'Cut it out, stop being a drongo,' Grace sneaks a peek at the tall blonde doing the accusing. She slows her pace.

'Who's gunna stop me?' torments the drongo.

'Come on, mate. Take it easy.'

'You threatening me?'

'Take it how you will. I've met the guys working here tonight, every single one of them. They told me they'd look after me, told me if I encountered any trouble, they'd be right onto it.'

He watches as the group scans the room.

'They can hear what you're saying and don't take blokes insulting girls lightly,' he says. 'So, watch out! All of you. I know what they're capable of when it comes to keeping things nice and straight around here. I think it's about time I took my cue. Good night, chaps.' He claps his hand on his companion's shoulder. 'I'll see you back at the house, Jimbo. You might want to get moving soon,' he adds cheerily.

The nice boy beams at the boys, turns and walks to the cloakroom, leaving the group nervously scanning the room for someone who might want to fight them; there look to be several contenders. Jimbo disappears in a gallop towards the entrance.

Grace hides for a while in the security of the ladies', shaken by the night's events, hoping Frank has gone. She splashes water on her face, pats it dry with a hand towel. With head bowed, she hurries her thin, vertiginous body to the station, where she flops onto a bench, huddling her stole tightly around her cold shoulders. She watches the rear of the funny little funicular disappearing down the 330-foot hillside. It's a westerly windy August night, even more ferocious than when Grace arrived. But she's pleased to get some air into her lungs and won't mind the wait or the solitude.

She did try to stay, didn't she? What will be her penance for leaving?

Chapter Eight

Grace sights who she thinks is her nice boy from the bar, standing tall and windblown under a lamppost near the bench upon which she's sitting. Hand to head, he's determined to keep his hat plastered down. She envisions her family at the beach huddled under their trusty beach umbrella, the wind failing to hoist it from the soft white sand. His hat offers security for him, she supposes.

Through gritty eyes, her gaze lingers longer than intended. When he lifts his head, as she notices he is the nice boy, the light's shadow catches a small cleft in his chin—a peculiar charm. He glances at her. She smiles too widely at him. Horrified, she looks down to her hands fiddling with her hankie.

Moving to sit beside her, he removes his hat and runs his fingers through a flash of blonde hair.

'Hi, I'm Grace Love!' The middle syllables got caught on the wind, and she fears he may think she's called him love. Their eyes meet. His chiselled face. Dark amber eyes—sly cat in the lamp light. She looks down to forage about in her handbag for the gloves she can't find.

'Do you need some money?' inquires the familiar stranger. Grace cowers, fearing he's intimated that she's a prostitute. Surely not.

'For the trip home, I mean. I'd be happy to pay for your fare.' His voice comes as a squeak.

'No, no, I'll be fine thank-you.' White knuckled, she shuts her bag and wraps the stole tightly over her breasts.

'Anyhow, let's start again. That kinda came out wrong. Hi! I'm Charles Alton. I'm here to show my sheep,' the cracks sounding more pronounced than before.

And there they were: the almost first romantic words uttered by her soon-to-be husband.

'Sorry, that sounded stupid. What I mean is my so-called mate Jim and I have driven up here to Brissie from New South Wales for the Ekka. Strange name, Ekka.'

'It is I guess but it's so familiar to me, to all of Brisbane, you know? We love our Queensland show. It's great fun, especially the rides and the showbags.'

'We don't get to do much of that, I'm afraid.'

'Well if it helps, I won't be having any fun there this year. Last year I got the flu from all the germs. You two had best be careful.'

'Put it this way, if sheep can spread colds, we're in trouble. We're sheep farmers. Jimbo is a jackaroo on his family's neighbouring farm. We've organised to show two of our best merino sheep. We're in the category of 'Best pair of Ewes'. The sheep, not us!' he chortles, loosening up.

'I thought as much. It sounds interesting.'

'That's the first time I've heard a girl say that showing sheep was *interesting*. Tell me about yourself.'

I have china animals on my dressing table that talk. Oh, and I used to fly.

Despite herself, Grace's words emerge with a touch more eloquence than she predicts.

'Country life is in my blood, I suppose. I grew up on a farm too—a wheat farm in western New South Wales. Dad completed his internship in Sydney, and when he became a doctor, we moved to Brisbane. He set up practice on The Terrace, Wickham Terrace in town where all the doctors are, but he's now retired. Says he relishes the leisurely lifestyle here, compared to a big city's hustle and bustle. I wasn't quite five when we moved, but I can still remember lots of little snippets about the farm.'

'That's pretty grouse—seeing you were so young.'

'Mum tells me I'm kinda clever, or I could be if I'd only put my mind to it,' she mumbles, aware she may sound like a bragger.

'Nothing wrong with a decent dose of grey matter. So, what do you remember about the farm?'

'Let me see ... the dust, flies that landed on your tongue if you had your mouth open, the shed with its rusty tools, two scruffy dogs, the decrepit old windmill, the horse and cart.' She stares at the sky, worried about not remembering crucial details; worried about remembering ...

'We had a maid ...' Grace murmurs, unnerved by the fervour of her sudden thoughts. Memories of Frannie: kind and caring in her quietude. Grace as a toddler, careful to keep her dirty feet outside the kitchen while cleaning was in progress. From the doorway, watching Frannie down on her knees—knobbly when they poked out from under her skirt—furiously rubbing beeswax into the timber floorboards until it had disappeared then reappeared like magic in a mirror shine, her whole body shaking with the effort. Was Frannie trying to make herself fade away too? Grace hoped not because she loved her in her little girl way, and loved the way the waxy scent lingered on Frannie as though announcing she, like the floor, had been polished.

' ... Frannie has a white heart.' Remembering those words, spouted to all, even Frannie, often and with immense pride by Grace's parents. Did their words help them justify the woman's harmless presence in the house? Did her status as another 'good' member of the household make it easier for them to leave undiscovered what truly hid inside the little lady with the white heart? Frannie: always dressed in white to reflect her true self. Grace suspects her parents' misguided attempts at praise would have felt like a knife attack to the woman they—hopefully inadvertently—tried to dumb down just enough to be of use to the household without being a bother.

Grace glances at Charlie who has been waiting patiently for her to snap out of the memory. 'What else? The miles of flaxen wheat. It was hot, yet the heat here in Brissie is so humid, stifling in summer. Oh, there's so much more. I *hate* having forgotten so much. But I guess what I can't remember I can still live through Dad, or I used to. His stories always sounded so alive and honest.'

'Why doesn't he talk about the farm anymore?'

'Oh, I don't know. It's almost as though he wants to start again with a clean slate.'

'Was it the war?'

'Yes, I think so. No-one seems to look after returned soldiers, do they? Their emotional state, I mean. All those prisoners of war. Shell shock is a terrible burden for so many families. My dad worked as a doctor in New Guinea in the second world war. He saw some action at times, and he sure saw the results of it in his patients. He's not shell-shocked as such. He bungs on as if nothing ever happened to him in the war. But I see it in him, the pain.' She feels the lump in her throat and tries to swallow it away. 'Anyhow, where are *you* from, Charles?'

'Geez, I called myself Charles, didn't I? Sounds a bit toffee, eh? Call me Charlie, okay?'

'Okay, Charlie then.' She quietly practises it. Either version feels just fine. She likes the way it plays on her mouth and tongue.

'We run sheep for wool. The irony is the part of New South Wales we live in is called Pig Peak, where there are neither pigs nor peaks.'

'That's kind of hilarious. Why is it called that?'

'Well now, Sheep-pastures would be too obvious, wouldn't it? Why did they name it that? I dunno. Stupid if you ask me. Someone's idea of a joke perhaps. I'll tell you about one place name that works well: Cowpastures. You heard about the time, soon after settlement, when the colony's small herd of cattle went missing near Sydney Cove and then turned up years later at the place they now call Cowpastures—hundreds of them, having multiplied? When they found them, they were as rough as blazers, so they shot 'em, or they may have been thriving. Same story, different interpretations. In any case, there was lots of shooting going on in those days.'

'I'll bet we don't know half of it. I hate guns. I've never actually seen one, you know? But I can imagine exactly how they would sound.' She knows *exactly* how guns sound. Disguised as a blast in *Rebecca*; the jolting door knocks from a Plasticine man, telling Grace of something sinister happening far away, warning her about a place she knows she'll see one day. More visits from *beyond*, no doubt.

'So, Pig Peak eh?' She forces a smile. Her voice sounds frantic in her attempt to talk about something silly, cleanse her mind of toxic memories.

'Sure, pigs were introduced there but the only ones we get nowadays are feral. Lots of animals introduced from England probably shouldn't have ever been put here in the first place ...' He trails off. 'By the way, I'm not a fan of guns either.'

'Pleased to hear. So, tell me, do you like being a farmer?'

'It's a good industry to be in, but crikey, we've faced some setbacks.' He shakes his head dispiritedly.

'Keep going. Please.'

'Promise I'll tell you all about them one day soon. I'll tell you one thing though. During the shearing season, I keep a close eye on the shearers, making sure it's done properly, you know? Carefully. I'm like my dad in that respect. To be honest, some of the shearers have copped it from me, especially the casual ring-ins Dad has had to get when we've been pressured by the wool stores.'

'You don't seem so scary to me, Charlie Alton.' She's a bold girl tonight.

'No need with you—so far anyway.' A melting wink.

'They have this stupid contest—the quest to be the day's ringer with the highest tally of sheep shorn, so they can get shouted drinks at the local pub. They get all inflamed and rush the process. I mean sure, a little blood's unavoidable, but you should see some of the poor blighters afterwards—look like they've been ten rounds in a boxing ring. Dead set. The sheep, I mean. Well, they soon learn the deal—my expectations.'

'The sheep?' she laughs.

'The shearers!' Nice boy, nice smile. 'I'm a hard taskmaster, Grace.'

'So, I'd better watch myself?'

'Well now, I just can't *quite* see you in a shearing contest, dear Grace.'

Don't underestimate my capabilities, dear Charlie.

Grace folds her arms, sticking her bottom lip out in a fake sulk, subsequently wrestling with admiration for this ethical farmer, and hurt, as she is once again labelled incompetent for being female.

'Hmm, what else can I tell you? I'm twenty-three,' says Charlie.

'Twenty-two,' says Grace.

'Back home on the farm I work as a general hand, learning the ropes 'cos one day I'll take over running it from Dad. At night, I've been going to college, studying animal husbandry. Just graduated.'

'Congratulations. I'm pleased you're celebrating in Brisbane, if that's what you've been doing. I've been studying nursing, but I'm afraid for me it's all been a bit of a drag. I would much rather it had been veterinary.'

'Nice. Hey Grace, by the way, I'm sorry about those loudmouths in there. I hardly know them, well, I'm afraid I do know one who just happens to be travelling with me.'

'Jimbo?'

'Afraid so,' says Charlie, smiling.

'It's okay, really. I know how boys can get with a few beers in them.' She doesn't really know much about boys at all.

'Those other turkeys at the bar with the bad manners? Turns out they're here for the show too. They're woodchoppers, so that's what we were talking about, their sport. Being new to Brisbane was all we had in common really. Jimbo and I somehow managed to land ourselves at the bar with that lot. Not saying Jimbo is a saint—he doesn't hold his alcohol well.'

'But he's your friend and you left him.'

'Jimbo? He's alright. He needs a bit of a wake-up now and then. He was being a drongo, so I called him one. Needed to hear it. He caught the last ride down the hill, the one we missed. Ran out of there like a shot out of a gun! You can bet he would sure've been alright to leave his mate to cop the heat if the pack decided to attack. By the way, did you have friends back there, or do you always hang around funicular stations alone on cold, windy August nights?' asks Charlie.

'Only when I think I might meet someone interesting.'

'So, you think I'm interesting?'

'Not sure yet. Keep working at it.' What is this spell?

'Seriously Grace, why did you come out here on your own?'

'Let's just say I was trying to get away from someone.'

'Aha—can I assume you mean a boy someone?' Charlie ventures.

'Perhaps.'

The funicular carriage looks as though it's imbibed a few too many cocktails at the bar as it nears the top of the hill. In their seats they lean back and close their eyes, smiling as the wind whips things up around them.

'Funny, isn't it? That we're the only ones on here,' says Grace.

'Yes well, it took a fair bit of organising you know. I slipped the driver a few quid and he seemed surprisingly up to the idea of leaving the hundreds of other potential passengers waiting up top. Did you notice them all trying to claw into our carriage? Did you notice his total disregard for their welfare? All for you, of course. I did think about getting him to add some music, perhaps a half-decent string quartet or something more to your taste. A little Gershwin maybe, to go with your blue dress? On second thoughts, that'd be going a bit too far, first meeting and all.'

She wonders if he always talks this much. She basks in his words: first meeting.

'No really, perhaps it was meant to be,' offers Charlie.

'We must look funny from above, like we're riding on some kind of amusement—all illuminated like at the real Luna Park in Sydney,' says Grace, trying to lighten the mood, conscious of Charlie's warm hand on hers. 'Have you ever been there?'

'No, but I want to. Maybe we'll go there together one day.' Charlie turns away. Embarrassed? She can't tell.

'I'll hold you to it,' she whispers.

In a move so out of character Grace swears she's someone else, her head drops onto his shoulder. She wonders if and how far that tan runs under his flannelette shirt. A little electric current makes her wriggle and smile. They stay like that, contented and still despite the occasional jolt from the machinery.

It's been a long time coming—Grace's hormonal cusp. An aging ingenue—she's innocent when it comes to love.

On arrival back at Bowen Hills, Charlie makes sure Grace is safely in a taxi before he sets off, but not before they share addresses and telephone numbers. Something about this boy makes her trust him.

The bright full moon floods its protective light, the man tipping his hat to the couple below, approving wholeheartedly of this new, still fragile, beginning.

Chapter Nine

New South Wales, Australia, 1949

The large man she first thought was a thief, the man she finds at once repellent and appealing, is outside her shack again—Izabella can only call the house in the middle of nowhere her father half built then left for her and her mother to live in a shack. The man with the big jacket and the pack over one arm and the fishing rod in the other is grinning at her with crooked teeth. Should she laugh or cry? She hasn't seen him for weeks and can't decide how she feels about seeing him again. She knows nothing about him.

He strides boldly over to Izabella, who stands with her body bent over an iron pot which balances on a small fire. She uses a stick to agitate the sodden washing, submerged in the water she collected earlier from Lantern's Creek. He dumps his pack down beside her.

'Where you been this time?' she asks curtly, stirring with gusto.

'Hello, beautiful.' He bends down, kisses her cheek. 'Where do ya think I bin? Away fishing, of course. Don't get all upset on me. I've found that as much as I try, as sweet as I am, and you of all people know how sweet I am, the bloody fish just won't come to me and I haveta hunt 'em down, even if it means travelling miles away from you. You and your gorgeous ...' He looks her up and down, smirking, 'washing.'

He stares at her, as though mesmerised, as she stirs the steaming pot. Back forth, round and round. His hot breath on her neck, his eyes drilling ... She's getting cranky and is just about to tell him so.

'Better be careful you don't burn yourself on that. Here, let me.' He deliberately immerses both arms in the near-boiling water, up to his elbows. 'Shit!' Retracting them, he flicks a fine shower of boiling water over Izzie, then raises his hands, now bright red, in surrender.

'Hulye, stupid.' Unhurt herself, she can't manage to stifle a burst of laughter. 'Here, I'll get you some cold.' Shaking her head, she dawdles over to the shack and comes out with a bucket of water. 'Put in,' she instructs.

He thrusts his arms into the cold water up to his elbows. 'Thanks, but I gotta say, you ain't real sympathetic, are ya?'

'What you say? What?' She wishes this man would stop using words she doesn't understand. She learned to say 'pardon me' on the ship, but somehow those words don't fit with this man.

'Nothin'. By the way, where's yer mother?'

'Anya at little shop.' The only shop for miles. Why does he always show up when she's away?

'Ah, so we're all alone. You know, beautiful princess, I never did ask you your name.'

'No,' she smiles. At last he asks this, but he will have to work hard to get to know her.

'Well? Tell me.'

'Izabella.' She notices his reddening arms.

'Izabella ringing?' The large man's belly jiggles as he gives a hearty chuckle, obviously impressed with his remark.

'No, Izabella.' His belly rolls remind her of waves on the ocean.

She could get seasick if she looked too closely.

He gives his head a shake. 'Why do you wogs have such funny names?'

'And your name? Something like tiger I think you would like.'

'It's Joe.'

'Ha! That not even name.'

'It's enough for me, and I could even get used to having a girlfriend with a name that sounds like a church bell if you play your cards right.' He shakes his arms and hands as if trying to ease the sting.

'I not play cards.' Why is this man so confusing?

'Silly duffer. Look, I brung youse more fish.' Grimacing, he bends to his pack where he retrieves and opens a brown paper package to show her two large flathead and six whiting.

'So, I see. *Kosz*. Thank you. Put them there.' She waves an arm as though shooing away a fly.

Joe places the fish on the tree stump she has indicated. 'That should keep you going for a couple of days. I have something else for you.' He opens his jacket and reaches inside another large pocket.

How many pockets does this man have? How many secrets are hiding inside there?

He removes a picture book about Australia, presents it to her.

Forgetting the washing she drops the stick, wipes her hands on her apron, snatches the book and opens its glossy cover. Examines each page of beautifully coloured photographs of waterfalls and beaches and cliffs and cute animals and ... 'Oh Joe, thank you!' She smiles widely at him, her dark eyes bright.

He studies her. 'See, just saying my name makes you smile. Where did you come from, little gypsy girl from far away?'

'We come from Budapest, in Hungary.' She wishes he wouldn't interrupt her concentration.

'That on the continent somewhere?'

'In Europe.'

'What brings you to Australia—this big land of sun and ocean and bad guys like me?'

'What?' Narked about being dragged from the book she wants to devour; she stares blankly at his face.

'Why are you here?' His words are flat.

'We escape war.' Can't bring herself to go into this. 'First in Australia we stay weeks in migrant centre.' She pronounces each syllable of the place names she has learnt, slowly and with care like a school teacher. 'The place was Wagtail, but we not wag our tails there.'

There is a bitterness in her voice. In Wagtail she remembers feeling like a downtrodden, runty dog in a cage. No-where to go and nothing to do. There was one upside: she and her mother were segregated from Izzie's father. Unlike some residents who fretted for their loved ones, they weren't upset about the separation.

'You know that a wagtail is an Australian bird, don't you? A willy wagtail,' says Joe.

'Are they trapped too?' Izzie's mouth wobbles with the start of a sob, causing Joe to produce an almost embarrassed offhand huff.

'Then my father, he get work away from this place building big bridges and roads. He not want anya and me there so we here in house not built yet.'

'Why doesn't your old man, your father, want you with him?'

'He say we to guard this land, this bit house.' Her voice is becoming cold and clipped. She was thankful to have had the chance to leave Budapest in the wretched state it was. She knows Australia is full of possibilities, but she feels trapped here in the ragged bush, with no toilet—let alone any luxuries—in the half house where her father abandoned them so readily.

'He come here sometimes. You not be here when he here.'

'Why not?'

'He get angry.' *You have not seen wild anger like my father's in your life, Joe.*

'So, we'll just have to keep it our secret. I've always liked secrets. Our secret romance.'

'What romance?'

'I'll show you, gypsy.' He grabs her in his red arms without flinching, as if feeling no pain, then leads her inside.

Chapter Ten

Norman Park, 1949

Here's something else for you, Treasure. Sometimes things happen which are beyond our realm of understanding or mastery. You see, I'm certain a higher power controls us all. People struggle against it, lamely fighting something far greater than humanity.

Life tricks us into thinking we have full control, daring us to make choices. Despots head gung-ho into battle, forever legitimising their inevitable, dogmatically recurring divide and conquer. Just because they can. Hindsight no match for precedence! So fervently, but with a twitch of unspoken uncertainty, on we go with the game. A choice, a reaction, the resulting balance at play or out of sync. A bad deed punished? Not always, but conscience always leaves its calling card, even if some of us claim to be illiterate. A good deed rewarded? Sometimes, when it's ripe for it.

I guess what I'm trying to tell you in what you may call my ramblings is that you will always have choices in life. People have been granted free will. So, choose wisely and do good deeds, learn from the ramifications of your choices. I'm sure you certainly will, but don't always expect a reward for every good deed you do. Life is like that—uncertain. Sometimes bad things happen.

But sometimes, just when you think the bottom has fallen out, good things can be found in the most unexpected places.

Grace slips the notepad into her gold painted box and wonders: What was my deed tonight? Good or bad? Have I been rewarded for tonight's good deed of going out with Frank? Rewarded with Charlie? But I wasn't nice to Frank, not at all. She reopens her note pad and reads what she just wrote: *A bad deed punished? Not always, but conscience always leaves its calling card.* Doesn't want to think about it.

She lies wide awake for two hours, then falls into a dreamless sleep.

Sunday morning, George finds Grace sitting bleary-eyed in the kitchen in front of a bowl of steaming rolled oats. Elbows propped on the table, she frames her chilly face in chilly hands, closes her eyes. The steam warms her, making her want to go back to bed, except the familiar aroma is rich and enticing, so she'll eat for now.

She wonders about the apparition yesterday afternoon in her bedroom. What was its meaning? There must be one. Grace looked like the Statue of Liberty in the mirror. Perhaps Charlie will marry her, and they'll go to live in New York! She luxuriates in the warm feelings swimming around her body.

'Sweet dreams?' Grace starts at her father's deep voice. 'Judging by that smile on your face they are. Good to see you're up to getting your breakfast this morning. Surprising though. Heard you come in late last night. Big night with a boy, was it, love?' he teases loudly.

'Sounds like *you're* dreaming, Dad. I was with the effervescent Marcie most of the night.' A sarcastic 'effervescent'. She soon realises that George is more likely to find innuendo in the word 'most', and that would be too much to bear this morning.

'Well—all night really,' she adds.

'That confounded girl *is* effervescent, about as effervescent as Epsom salts. She produces the same results, too.'

'Dad! If you can't love thy neighbour, at least tolerate her—I do. I snuck in around midnight. Didn't want to wake you and Mum, well that was the plan anyway.'

'Very thoughtful of you. You should know by now that your mother still waits up for you. Heavens above, I think she'd still do it if you were forty! Keeps me awake with all her bloody huffing and puffing.'

'I promise one day I'll be out of your hair, Dad.'

'Can't come flamin' well soon enough if you ask me.'

'I didn't know I had,' laughs Grace. 'What are you up to today?'

'The car could use some new spark plugs.'

'Need any help?'

'Sorry possum, I know you're my little bright spark, but when it comes to spark *plugs,* well let's just say it's best to leave that to the expert.'

'Oh, so you must know of a mechanic,' teases Grace.

'Smart arse,' says George, loving this banter.

'And who made *you* the expert?'

'God's way, I guess'

'Ha! You know I could easily learn something as easy as changing a light bulb,' says Grace, serious now. Enough play.

'It's more complicated than that. Look poss, I know what you're trying to do. Just help your mum today, will you? She will need help, seeing she's been up *all night!* She's only just nodded off now. Best leave her for a bit of a kip.'

And with that settled, George picks up a bowl from the cupboard, scrapes into it a few spoonfuls of congealed oats from the saucepan, covers it with the remaining creamy top of the milk, pours honey on top and takes his cold porridge back to bed.

He always wins.

Grace concedes that she may never amount to anything. 'Just tell them what they want to hear,' pleaded her mother ineffectively throughout Grace's school years as she read her less than glowing report cards, having boldly questioned the logic of her teachers, something most school girls would never dare do.

Grace sometimes wishes she were a boy. An only child, she feels the pressure of trying to embrace both feminine and masculine pastimes, to prove to her parents they don't need a son to realise their dreams in this man's world. Her choices are both magnanimous and self-centred. She plays piano, originally at her mother's instigation and now for her own pleasure. She used to go to church to keep her mother happy. She joined the Girl Guides so she could erect a tent as well as any boy. But they hardly ever went out bush, the main reason she joined, so she left. At least her father could boast of spawning a wreath knot-tying-savvy offspring.

Not a boy. Not really a girl. Never a woman.

I hope I have a boy one day, so he won't have to feel the pressure only girls feel.

Grace shakes her head to flush out her fears.

Obviously too impatient to wait for the 'respectable' hour of nine o'clock to arrive, at eight Grace can see Marcie outside from the kitchen window. Her long mouse-grey hair is down, bouncing like it belongs to a feral animal as she runs her dumpy legs in clumsy lurches past the two houses that separate hers from the Love's.

Grace watches the girl notice a flying fox fried fast to overhead power lines. Today Grace wonders if Marcie will even mention it. Opening the front door too soon after her obligatory four loud woodpecker knocks, she barges inside. She'll be pleased Grace is the only one up, having no doubt calculated her parents to be in bed with breakfast and newspaper at this hour.

'Hi Grace.' Flat. Grace? Not poppet? Things must be bad.

'Hi Marcie.' She takes another spoonful, slowly, licks a stray oat from her bottom lip, biding time.

'We missed you last night.' That hateful, accusatory look. No mention of the fruit bat. Grace sees that without last night's ponytail, Marcie's eyelids have plummeted to where they belong.

'Give me a break, Marcie! I really wasn't feeling the best. Anyhow, where did you end up going?'

'Troccie. I thought I *told* you we were going to the Trocadero. Anyhow, Frank was a bit low. He ended up with an allergy attack when we got home. Blamed it on all that rotten wind. It seemed to go on all night.'

'Sorry to hear that.' Grace tries not to laugh, picturing Frank affected by another type of wind, sitting on the loo with a bad dose of the farts. She bites her top lip, hard.

'Anyhow, I assume you got home safely?' Marcie looks Grace up and down disapprovingly. 'Obviously, you did.' She rolls her eyes then takes a good look at her friend.

'What's with you anyway? You look like you did when we used to get the giggles in school assembly,' says Marcie, 'I hope you're not laughing at Frank. The poor thing. Grace?'

'No, of course not. It must have been terrible for him.' Grace can't help but smile.

'What is it?'

Grace looks up at the ceiling, trying to take herself out of the situation, away from the vacuous Marcie.

'Grace. Grace! You're not going all weird on me again, are you?'

'What do you mean, Marcie? Stop saying that!' Feels her face heat in anger.

'You know, loopy.'

'I'm not loopy! I'm tired, that's all.'

'I don't think so. You're planning some kind of escape.' From you, yes, Grace wants to say.

'Or do you want to escape?' Marcie fixes her with an intense stare.

'Stop analysing me!'

'You're too happy.'

'Oh alright! I have a secret,' says Grace, wanting to shout it to the world now.

'What is it? That you suddenly got ill when YOU got home? That would be nothing to be happy about. Oh … poor Frank.'

'I met someone.' Loving this now.

'You MET someone? When? Where?'

'He was waiting for the funicular. We were all alone there and we just started talking.'

'JUST STARTED TALKING?' Marcie squawks.

'Yes—he's a farmer, in Brisbane for the Ekka.'

'Or so he says! Grace, he could have been Jack the Ripper! What were we told about never talking to strangers?' Jealous for sure, Grace knows it.

'I'm not a child, Marcie. I know what I'm doing. And he is NOT a stranger. He's wonderful. Just wait and see!'

'A farmer, eh? Being a farmer's wife would suit you. You'd never have to try looking pretty again.'

Marcie's face is smug. Grace's is blank with shock.

Just as expected, because it happens whenever Grace is happy, another cutting remark from Marcie. Grace knows she'll do anything to keep those two apart. Guilt through association. She can't stand snobs or sycophants, and Marcie fits into both these categories. She wonders why she puts up with her. Thinks it's because she knows Marcie doesn't have any other friends. And Grace realises why: it's because she's too 'much'. Grace feels increasingly stifled in the girl's presence.

Unwilling to play the thinly veiled games of jealousy and spite she's seen acted out by her peers, Grace knows this is why she herself doesn't have many friends. But she's proud to be selective, so she tells herself, but swallows hard. More and more frequently Grace is thinking she's too needy, somehow not trustworthy. How on earth is she going to get rid of her?

Chapter Eleven

Charlie and Jimbo are staying with Charlie's cousins, John and Honey, in Bulimba. Grace lives with her parents at Norman Park. Only a couple of miles apart, two perfectly placed locations for ease of courting in Brisbane.

The couple rendezvous each night after the showground gates have closed, and this involves Charlie collecting his new girl in the truck from her home. He'd like to appear street-savvy to Grace, rather than like some ignorant country bumpkin, but he's hardly heard of any nightspots in Brisbane. Cloudland was recommended by a bunch of acerbic bushies the boys met the first day of the show.

During one of the weekends Charlie is in Brisbane, on a Saturday, Grace navigates as Charlie drives them south to the Gold Coast, having talked Jimbo into taking over show duties. Jimbo insisted that Charlie pay him a few bob, but Charlie didn't mind—he'd do almost anything to spend time with this girl.

On the advice of the fishmonger as to what seduces whiting on a line, they purchase live worms—wrapped in newspaper, muscular and wriggling in a large pat of sand, and hire boats and rods. They navigate the Tweed River, fishing from sandbars. The hauls are bountiful—big, fat silver and yellow whiting which they take back to share with Grace's appreciative parents for dinner. Grace can't easily stomach the kill, grimacing as Charlie knocks the doomed fish senseless and then decapitates them. Even the act of beheading the worms and skewering them, still wriggling, leaves her cold. She fakes it for the sake of heroics.

On the Sunday night dinner at the Surfers Paradise Hotel, Charlie woos Grace with prawn cocktails, lobster mornay and Bombe Alaska. The ambrosia is kind to Charlie and works its magic, resulting in a long kissing session on the beach.

Jimbo is miffed at Charlie's perpetual absences in the Chev truck, sans stock crate which Charlie has unceremoniously dumped in the front yard. But ebullient Jimbo thinks he's sweetened the deal for himself by rigging a couple of dates with Charlie's delicious cousin Honey. John has agreed to lend Jimbo his car in exchange for a little cash, so he'll have wheels for the dates. Money talks and John is happy. Honey has gladly taken the pound Charlie offered her for the dubious privilege of a date with Jimbo. Charlie has rigged this deal in case he gets the chance to bring Grace back to the house. It doesn't eventuate. The deal involving Honey has been arranged, naturally, without Jimbo being privy to it. In his blissful ignorance, Jimbo has lined up not one but two dates with Honey: the first to a restaurant and the second to a picture show. One pound for Honey turns to two—Charlie hopes it's worth it. The dating schedule and venues have been carefully configured by Jimbo: loosen her up with food and wine with lashings of compliments at the dinner, then make the kill at the pictures. Charlie still reckons he's secured the best deal as he has the best girl as well as the Chev, a much newer and more reliable vehicle than John's bomb of a Holden. Although Charlie's not usually prone to bribes, Jimbo's been acting almost jealous lately, plus Charlie is really doing him a favour—dates with Honey.

But later Jimbo confessed to Charlie that picture show night didn't go to plan—surprise! Starting out with nerves and gauche, the darkness soon emboldened his libidinous cravings.

'Pleeease Honey. You look so gorgeous tonight and I just want to show my appreciation. Just one little peck, that's all I ask. Don't make me wait any longer. I'm dyyying here!'

'Oh alright, but nothing more. I'm not that sort of girl.'

Charlie can imagine Honey looking bored and tired of the harassment. She reneged, probably hoping to shut him up and leave her alone, once and for all. Jimbo took more advantage than was on offer, turning Honey's offer of a cheek peck into a full-blown kiss. Charlie cringes about the details Jimbo is so readily supplying.

'Eerk!' Charlie imagines the shout of the flustered girl, rummaging in her purse for a tissue to spit into, then quickly popping an all-day sucker into her mouth. *Ha,* Charlie imagines Honey thinking, *let's see him get through this.*

'What do you think you're doing, ya cow cockie?' She muffled through the lolly ball that was so large it almost blocked her vocal cords, according to Jimbo.

'I thought you liked me,' Jimbo pleaded as he rapidly deflated.

'I only went out with you for the money, ya dipstick!' Honey jumbled.

Charlie imagines that she disclosed this because she figured she had well and truly earned it. He blushed when Jimbo said this, knowing he had initiated the bribe, but his mate either seemed not to know or not to care. Pride?

They sat silently for the remainder of *It's a Wonderful Life,* said Jimbo, Charlie conscious of the cruel irony of the film's title. Perhaps Honey would have stormed out of there but was enjoying the movie too much. Did Jimbo wonder fleetingly who had paid Honey to go out with him? Was his concern short-lived because he soon realised, he'd French kissed a girl? Oh, the people he could tell!

The late nights are obviously of the boys' choosing, but ten early mornings in a row are getting more taxing with each dawn. They've been topping each night off with a couple of nightcaps before crashing into bed, exhausted. Grabbing coffees, pouring on clothes, they head out before dawn, always in a mad last-minute rush, with pounding heads so thick that no amount of aspirin counters the damage. They drive straight to the livestock pavilion at the Ekka—Brisbane's Royal Queensland Show. Splashing on Old Spice aftershave in the car doesn't cover their body odour caused by only sporadic showers. Nor the bottom-of-birdcage breath, so they chew mints before facing the public. Truth is, the minute they're within cooee of the animal pavilion, their breath problem fades to insignificance.

The boys clean up the previous nights' faecal offerings in the stalls. They ensure all equipment is in order: food and containers, blankets for night-time, wool trimmers, foot clippers, harnesses. They've organised a daily schedule whereby one of them is always with the sheep. The other usually hangs around the show, sometimes seeking out an adrenaline rush in the amusement area with a sneaky ride, but always keeping a close eye on the animal pavilion.

The pace could easily get to them, particularly to Charlie who's often out when Jimbo is home at night hanging around the house, hoping to spend another evening with Honey, but dubious about the realisation of such a prospect.

Charlie hasn't yet broached the subject of Grace during his daily phone calls to his parents. He tries to focus on the ewes' welfare, but when his mum Edith is on the line, the talk inevitably turns to Charlie's welfare. So, he tries to keep the conversations chirpy and matter-of-fact. He fears he sounds manic.

Charlie has been collecting Grace regularly in the Chev truck from the Love's house. Before leaving for their first date, he felt compelled to stay for a while. The meeting went considerably well despite George stumbling into the sitting room complaining of some shouse truck some drongo had parked in their driveway. But by the time the young ones left, in a cloud of blessed relief, they were all getting on sweetly.

Chapter Twelve

When the inevitable judging arrives, on the last show day, Charlie and Jimbo are flustered. At least they look sharp; both have bathed, preened and dressed themselves suitably in clean, smart long trousers, matching shirts and Akubra's, their appearances defying mood. They're self-conscious, knowing the spotlight is on them as much as the sheep. They worry the animals are picking up on their tension, and feeling stressed from the crowds and cramped conditions. Nelly looks wayward and Elsie slippery, skittish.

The final clipping was done yesterday. Today, the ewes have been fed and watered and physically are ready to go. The men have agreed to use halters to lead the ewes around the ring, rather than relying on holding their lower jaws; they don't want to take any chances. Each man sits with his ewe, gently stroking and talking softly in hypnotic fashion, as the tension wanes in both the animals and themselves.

Ready to perform, the crescendo of months of practice, they lead the surprisingly cooperative ewes around, with hands gently but firmly on their docks to show who is boss and encourage movement. They shoot each other slim grins. When called, they stand their girls square as the scrutinising judges glare piercingly over bottle-rimmed glasses, occasionally turning and muttering to one another. Knowing they are up against some prized stock, including best in show from the previous year, Charlie and Jimbo hold a collective breath.

'We've got some big celebrating to do, my man!' Jimbo is cocky and hankering for some matey good times, which inevitably involve large quantities of alcohol.

Exhausted, they locate the nearest watering hole—the Cattleman's Bar at the show. As the night wears on, Jimbo becomes increasingly rumbustious, bragging of their winnings—a cup and two ribbons—meagre in material worth but priceless in terms of potential contacts and sheer bloody pride. The alcohol takes its toll.

Charlie keeps a close eye on his mate, having limited himself to one beer. Noticing the crowd dispersing and Jimbo fading, he studies him: piercing eyes which are now watery and red, pimply face, a mop of hair to put his to shame. He's not too bad looking but his ostentation lets him down. Charlie is suddenly hit with a surprising pang of sympathy. Barely able to muster his strength for another toast, it doesn't take much for Charlie to convince him that they should leave. In the car, Jimbo still holds his right hand up, clasping an invisible schooner in a mock toast, forgetting the fans have long gone, not realising they were never even there.

Charlie finds a phone booth on the way back to his cousins' house where he makes the necessary phone calls, the last one being to Grace. Waiting for her to pick up, his mind drifts. He decides he likes the gap between her teeth and the little 'm' shape of her cupid's bow, a permanent stamp of agreement, saying yes to him over and over. Her gentle voice. Her ease: confident, not cocky. Charlie is chuffed with the win but has other things on his mind. Only one more night in Brisbane. There is a relationship with Grace, he has no doubt about that, but will it last the distance? He must find a way.

He cringes as he thinks of the prospect of Grace returning to the farm with them now. He can just see it: his darling squashed between himself and Jimbo; his mate a bundle of perspiration and nerves and talk; his body touching hers—in his wayward mind having the perfect excuse to unleash his uncontrollably dirty mouth upon the poor girl. Shuddering, Charlie realises he wouldn't dare ask Grace to accompany them on their return journey.

Charlie takes an audible breath as Grace picks up; he suspects she can hear it through the receiver.

'Hi Grace. We won!'

'Well done! I knew you would. You've certainly put the work in.' Her voice is loud.

'True. You know I have to leave tomorrow night.' Straight to the point. The words sound thin and brittle, not like him at all.

'Yes.' Quietly now, Grace suddenly sounds just as fragile.

'Listen Gracie, let's make the most of it tomorrow. Whatever you want to do.'

'I don't want to spend the whole day driving. Let's just have a picnic down by the river, okay? It'll be fun. It's your last day and the next will be a tiring one for you. Let me organise the food, okay?'

Charlie is only too happy to agree. 'Okay.'

Jimbo wakes with a sore head. When told of his mate's plans for the day, he's not pleased. Since Honey has decided to totally avoid him, and John has repossessed his car, he's been moping around, sulking.

'And what if I want the truck today?' moans Jimbo to Charlie over breakfast.

'Sure, the truck belongs to you, well, your dad really. But I've paid my way in petrol, and besides, we've hardly spent any time together here.'

'Come on, mate! It's my last day with Grace. Look, promise I'll give it to you for a couple of days when we get back, okay?' says Charlie.

'Yes, you will,' says Jimbo, turning and stomping away.

Uncomfortable about hauling the metal stock crate, especially as it will signal to Grace and her parents the finality of his stay, Charlie rolls the Chev truck and its freight into the Love's driveway. He notices George hovering around downstairs in the front yard. As Charlie considers the unlikelihood of a quick getaway, he grinds the gears, slowing the truck to stationary as George strolls over. Charlie gets out of the truck for the inevitable chat.

'Morning, Mr Love, sorry, Doctor Love.'

'Morning, Charlie. I hear you're shooting off tomorrow. I'd imagine you're keen to get back to the farm then?' Hedging.

'Well, I don't really have a choice now, do I?' He bites back, can't help it, anticipating Grace's mood. The unwelcome game with the father in rehearsal for the showdown with the daughter. The shock on George's face reiterates Charlie's shame, leading to a mumbled 'sorry' as he acknowledges his overstep. Doesn't want to be this way this morning; he wants to make the day rosy and bright and full of promise for Grace. He must get himself in order, quickly.

'Wish you'd take old Gracie with you. She's like a bear with a sore head this morning. Don't you have room in that cage thing for one more little lamb? Come to think of it, she's more like a hairy goat, that's how she's been running around the kitchen,' says George, studying Charlie before disappearing under the house.

Take her with you? Perhaps he is reading more into the statement than he should, but he draws comfort from the old man's words. Were they subconsciously deliberate, a Freudian slip?

Standing alone, as the Love's house magnetises his gaze, he lets loose his imagination. Sitting across the tram track stamped road, one block from the Brisbane river, it's a proverbial Queenslander, he knows. Quintessential stilts stand it high and proud, the breezes throwing parties underneath its floorboards. Or it may be on guard, ready to be deployed into battle at a moment's notice, yes Siree! Its neighbours appear stalled on their platforms. The rumours reverberating about the treacheries of the river, sung loud and clear on a putrid pong of a breeze, causes them to have second thoughts about any movement towards it. They know of a Japanese submarine sighted in the river, too! Never know when the armada will arrive!

Jolting at the slam of the front door, Charlie watches Grace gliding down the rickety verandah stairs, a red cardigan thrown carelessly over her dress, the pleated material of her red and white spotted skirt swaying with the descent, looking almost part of her. The wind is causing her skirt to misbehave as much as the stairs are doing, and she releases her hold on the rail and grabs a fistful of material for the negotiation of the last steps. In her other hand she holds a picnic basket. He reckons she looks like a blonde Little Red Riding Hood, except she's tall and she doesn't have a hood.

Having alighted the stairs as gracefully as possible in high heels, difficult for Grace in *any* heels, so she's told him, she gives him a comforting smile as she overbalances onto the grass. Charlie gasps, but she quickly recovers to get up. They walk to the truck, Grace a bit giddy, where Charlie dusts her off, checks for injuries and grass stains, and opens the passenger side door for her. She sits clasping the basket. Charlie remembers Grace previously saying to him, 'I wish I could just feign frippery for a perfect fit'—at which he laughed. He now understands what she meant.

As they drive away, Grace catches her mother waving frantically from the verandah. Grace winds down her window.

'Have fun, you two!' Connie yells, blowing them a kiss, then holds her hand fast to her heart, looking as though she's worried it will either fail, or fall out.

Chapter Thirteen

Deciding on Hardcastle Park in Hawthorne, they find a grassy spot adjacent to the ferry wharf. Grace wishes the amethyst jacaranda flowers were in bloom, even though their association with exam time always causes a nasty pang of panic. Today however, a new kind of stress grips her.

Charlie spreads the tartan picnic rug Grace has borrowed from her parents. They sit in silence nibbling the little crustless ham, cheese and lettuce sandwiches Grace has prepared. They take in the uninspiring sights of the wool stores across the river at Newstead, and nearby, the dull tinman-silver smoke-billowing chimneys of the powerhouse at New Farm. Grace is secretly waiting for the one o'clock whistle to blow, signalling the workers' lunch break. Sounding more like a foghorn, it's known by all living near the river as simply 'the whistle'. It also signals the moment her mother sits down to listen to 'Blue Hills', her new favourite radio show.

The rank smell of mud hangs thick in the air. The river is its usual khaki sludge; a colour reminiscent of Grace's father's army uniform. Appearing even murkier today, Grace wonders if the dredgers have recently been at it, creating an even soupier slurry by stirring up the silt from its unstable bottom before dumping it at sea.

'You know Charlie, I wonder how my little girl self ever swam these grotty waters. But I did, lots of times. Fished too, but I only ever caught slimy eels and I couldn't wait to throw them back. So squirmy. Yuck! I'd scramble barefoot over the muddy rocks, squishy mud between my toes. Wonder I didn't cut my feet or break a bone. Huge river rats would scurry in and out of the crevices in the bank. Have you ever seen them? River rats? They're as big as cats.'

'No. We only seem to get mice at the farm.'

'You don't know what you're missing, Mr Alton. Quite the experience having rats strolling around your kitchen.'

'Quite the experience I can do without,' says Charlie.

'I played pirates with Marcie, my neighbour. We'd uncover treasure as we plundered the shoreline, finding jetsam from careless river pirates, something precious from the mainland. Where it all came from was part of the great mystery, you see: an old bottle, a discarded fishing reel, a shoe or hat. Once we even found six ancient-looking coins. They obviously came from an elusive treasure chest which just *must* have been lying in wait somewhere for our sole discovery.' She's enjoying evoking her memories now.

'Having such an interesting river near your front yard? I could almost be jealous,' says Charlie, his voice low.

'You sound jealous. You said you'd tell me more about the farm. I want to know everything, including the hardships.'

'Okay. Hardships, there are many.'

'It can't be that bad, can it?'

'At times.'

Grace fears this wonderful man may be trying to put her off. 'Here's a history lesson for you. Way back in 1797 Macarthur and Marsden first imported Spanish merino sheep to Australia. Those guys pretty much started the wool industry here, so I blame them for turning me into a pastoralist. If there were no sheep here, I'd be, well, who knows? The sky's the limit, isn't it?'

'I heard John Macarthur's wife Elizabeth played a big part in its establishment. Wasn't she a co-founder?'

'Wow! You are a clever girl, aren't you?' Charlie looks genuinely impressed. 'Were those first explorers Landed Gentry? Dad reckons my family probably descends from them, whatever that means. Convicts aren't we all, really?'

Grace blushes about the compliment and Charlie's frivolous comments of the connection to Landed Gentry, knowing they have that in common.

'I want to know about your family, Charlie, not about famous explorers.'

'I don't mean to sound ungrateful, but sometimes I feel that farming is my legacy of tricky business. We're so reliant on things out of our control.'

'You mean like the weather?'

'Yes—the weather, and other things. The wool glut in the United Kingdom during the war years could have been really bad news for the farm.'

'Was it?'

'No, but it was worrying. Our wool was still snapped up, and the floor price is rising steadily, and that's obviously good for us.'

'That all sounds positive,' offers Grace.

'Yes. But the 1944/45 drought was a shocker. We were so close to culling stock. But I'm happy to say that we managed to maintain running the farm without losing a single beast. I'm proud of that.'

'Farming is tough. I realise that. It's life and death at times.'

'Sorry if I'm making it sound like hell on earth. I don't want you thinking it's all doom and gloom. Let's talk about the good aspects of the dear old farm.'

Charlie raises his eyes to the sky, tapping his chin. 'Nah, there's nothin'.' Shakes his head.

Grace smiles, punches him in the arm, determined to lift him from thoughts of dark times.

'Okay. But promise me you won't think I'm a sook.'

'Promise.'

'Truth be told, well, one thing I can't get enough of is watching the new Spring lambs. Such energy, so playful. I guess I love animals, pure and simple. And despite the hardships encountered by every farmer that ever tried to tame arid or flooded land in Australia, I actually love farm life.'

Grace drops her eyes, feeling a little envious of a lifestyle that sounds surprisingly real and solid, despite Charlie speaking of hardships. Like Charlie, she has her own demons but they are inside of her. Every day she wrestles with self-doubt since that terrible day with Plasticine Man, even though deep down she knows she did nothing wrong. She also feels guilt about her lack of commitment to anything much, let alone nursing. Could Charlie be her ticket to freedom at last? Someone to help her ease her mind?

'We certainly have that in common—caring about animals I mean,' says Grace, fidgeting with her skirt as she practises a smile. She raises her eyes to face him with the best she can give.

'You must be a good person, Gracie, and you really must see the lambs.' Charlie's face reddens. 'Geez. Here we go, sheep again!'

'Perfectly natural. I would be worried if you didn't like what you did.'

'Gracie, can I have a word with you, and can I be frank?'

The thought that Charlie will never be Frank momentarily brightens her mood.

'I'm not going anywhere, Charlie,' she says, hoping he'll notice the double entendre.

He gazes at the river, takes deep breaths.

'I'm a farmer. Despite Spring and the lambs, the conditions are often dry and dusty. The land is flat. The most exciting thing that happens there is when the mail finally gets delivered. And the flies are a terrible curse. The rabbits can be unimaginably pesky, foxes too, but they haven't yet driven me to drink. Heavens, I'm not making it sound very pleasant, am I?'

'Not really, but—'

'But I'm happy there, it's home to me,' says Charlie. Grace takes her own deep breath.

Charlie examines his hands. 'Well, thing is, I haven't had many girlfriends. To be honest I've only had one and she wasn't very nice, so I guess I haven't had much experience with women.'

Her heart pounds, fearing he's about to ask her about boyfriends. 'But Gracie, this last week and a half, with you, have been the happiest of my life. You see, in my head I've been trying to figure out if it's just because of the places, you know, Brisbane, being all new and different and exciting, and the win of course. But then I picture us—you and me together in places that aren't exciting, and I still see us as being happy.'

Her gaze fixes on the skies as she tries to hold back stupid tears.

'Well, if you're, well, keen on me too, I'd like you to come with me to see the farm, and stay for a long time, like, er, forever.'

'Are you asking me to marry you, Charlie Alton?' She blurts out, the river casting its spell. Silence. Sudden horror for the runaway words.

'Well, yes, I guess I am.'

Relieved. Overwhelmed. Her moods all morning have been going up and down like, as her father would say, a bride's nightie. Suddenly, she realises she has Charlie where she wants him. 'Really? But Charlie, you still haven't told me how you really feel about me.' She can say the words but can't look at him.

Cradling her cheeks, he turns her face to his. She struggles free, wiping away tears before replacing his hands, and returning her gaze to meet his.

'I know it's sudden, but I feel I already love you Gracie, already more than anything in the world. It's crazy really.'

'It is kind of amazing. Listen Charlie, I'm clumsy and you may find that I'm a bit crazy myself ... but you make me feel more, well, steady. I love you too, nice boy,' she manages. Words she thought she'd never feel safe enough to utter.

'Well go on then,' she teases light-heartedly.

'What?'

'Propose!'

He takes her hands in his. 'Grace Love—will you marry me?'

'Yes, of course I will.'

Through a smile, he kisses her with a passion to stir up uncharacteristic little waves on the sleepy river. She can see them! The powerhouse whistle blows like a thousand brass bands, causing them to dissolve in mutual laughter. If jacarandas were blossoming today, hundreds of the cupped flowers would dance down upon them in tender adornment, like tiny fluted glasses. And they would be filled with champagne if the heavens could muster it. Cheers!

They celebrate with coffee. Grace stares silently as Charlie works his spoon around the inside of his delicate porcelain cup, mixing in milk to whiten the dark brew, from a set Grace almost didn't bring for fear of breakages.

Instantaneous. Such a dramatic change. Never the same again. She diverts her gaze, lest she drown in its pale sadness. The uneasiness ignited in her makes no sense. Her shudder beckons Charlie to wrap his jacket around her, but it doesn't warm her or curb the sense of foreboding which now grips her. She must not let Charlie sense her sudden change of mood.

What is *beyond* trying to tell her?

Chapter Fourteen

New South Wales, 1949

Twenty-year-old Izabella and thirty-five-year-old Joe are having a pretend marriage ceremony. Izzie knows her parents would never approve the bond. Her father has always insisted their only child marry a nice Hungarian boy, like her Greek mother did. Perhaps she'll marry a nice Greek boy, but she won't marry an Australian boy—no question about it, no choice. Yet even Izzie is not sure about Joe, and it's not because he's Australian, it's his manner and his habits. Spending a lot of time with him lately has cemented her decision. Today she'll try to have fun, and she can if she forgets the details. She soaked her black curls in olive oil the previous night, leaving them lustrous. She's wearing her good white dress—a girl must look her best on the big day. Against the sheer fabric, her golden olive skin appears darker, more exotic.

They sit on a large, smooth rock overhanging a creek—Izabella's toes just dipping into the cold water; Joe's entire calves are submerged, he is much taller than she is. Giggles spring forth when the four feet splash, turning calm water turbulent. Fat water drops leap up to smash against the rock, creating black patches on the grey sandstone. Wet now too, the pair jump in to make a decent job of it.

Her dress balloons around her small frame, its white cotton cloudy in the tannin-stained water. She looks like she's bathing in milky coffee.

They climb out of the water to sit back onto the rock. Joe's hat sits dry on the grass beside them. He lifts it and presents his new 'wife' a scarf from underneath it—pink, orange and aqua, the colours of dawn and dusk.

'It's from Italy,' says Joe.

'That the country where we sailed to Australia! Thank you, Joe. Very pretty beautiful.'

She cocks her head back and holds the scarf up to the sun. Smiling, she drapes the material across her facial features, squinting her large eyes as she views the sun's powerful light. She then holds the scarf away from her face and examines it thoroughly, admiring its embroidery edging, its detail. She rises and hangs it over a branch of a coolabah tree to dry, where a slight breeze appears to give it life. Runs back to sit with her husband, gives him a quick kiss.

'My little gypsy,' says Joe.

She reads to him from one of the English books she was given on the ship, trying to improve her language. Whenever she looks up to him, she can't help thinking he is bored. Doesn't he realise she loves to learn?

Although she acquired some English in Budapest and then on the ship en route to Australia, there's a gap in her education caused by the war she's determined to fill. She wishes dearly she could fill the gaping chasm caused by missing her school friends, but keeping busy helps set her mind on other things. She's very keen to learn the English language, to the despair of her parents, who've neither embraced twangy Australian nor its 'culture' since arriving months ago in the great southern land. Izzie can't fathom why her complaining parents aren't embracing their new, free lives in this strangely rugged yet beautiful country. Having once loved her home of Budapest passionately, when the city came under the horrors of war, she was thankful to leave. She prays some wounds have healed there, yet she's beginning to see potential here, despite her living conditions.

Or she was, until she was floored by the news …

Suddenly becoming impatient, Joe kisses Izabella's mouth. She drops her book. He's always too rough with her. Having withstood the dip, her red lipstick has transferred to Joe's lips. She laughs, with a bitterness she wonders if he can hear. She touches her mouth then points to his comical visage. He turns away, rubbing his mouth harshly.

'Why I want us to get married today you think?' Izabella says in her broken English, serious now.

'You just want a big wedding night, hussy,' says Joe, smiling, grabbing her.

Not understanding his last word, she pushes him away and continues, 'I want a pretending wedding. Is all we can do.'

'What do you mean?'

'Sorry, but I not see you again, Joe.'

'What the hell are you talking about? You make me do this stupid bloody wedding ritual and then tell me this? You crazy wog!' Shouting now.

'Don't call me that! You, you always mean to me anyway. Why you care if we not see each other?'

'I'd miss this.' He grabs her breasts. 'And this.' Yanks up her dress, almost ripping the flimsy material.

Straightening her clothing, she places her hands over her plump stomach, skimming both hands over its surface in a circular motion. Somehow, she's not fearful about his reaction to what she is about to tell him. Deep down she hopes he'll run away in fright.

'Look at my tummy. Fat. My baby is yours, Joseph. Apa, my father, say he send me away to have baby for other family he knows who can't have child. I not even know them, but he is friends with other family. They are going to take baby away, Joe! No-one else to know about it, father say to me, cross, so cross. What can I do?'

'Me name's not fuckin' Joseph! Hang on, what did you just say? You are really carrying my baby? Don't kid around about something like this, Izabella. Don't mess with me.'

'Why kid around, as you say?'

'Let me get this clear. Your father wants some strange family to raise our child? I thought you told me he was going to be working away for five years.'

'He will be, yes.'

'Then what the hell does he care if you keep the baby? He won't even be around here for the fireworks.'

'Fireworks? What you mean? When my father away he may get people check baby not here. I cannot think what to do.'

'I tell you one thing, if you decide to go it alone, there are people out there who would target your baby. Look at what the government is doing to the Aboriginal people—takin' kids away from their parents. Do you think they'd care about you?'

'I more worried for my father, what he does. How can I have this baby? You think I want to bring shame on my family? To curse them?'

'So, that's how you feel about it? About me? A curse?'

'Nem. No, that's not what I mean. I'm scared, Joe.'

He stands and moves to solid ground where, head bowed, he scuffs his feet, wearing down two semi-circles of grass to dirt in front of him. She stands to face him.

'Do you want the baby, Izzie?'

'Yes!'

'Do you want me?'

She looks down, says nothing. He raises her chin and considers her with something like hate in his eyes.

'What if I tell you that I want you to bear my children? To have my son?'

'Oh, my Jesus, Mary and Joseph! I told you when we met that we no future. But you not let me go. And you start your drinking.'

'Don't you start blaming me, bitch. I didn't get meself pregnant.' He combs his fingers through his hair. 'Now listen, seriously, run away with me, Izzie. Fuck your parents.'

'How you say that? What kind of man are you? They love me more than you do. They *love* me. They have pride. Family pride.'

'Don't say such shit. I'm warning you, Izzie. Come away with me now. You know what? I've decided I want *my* baby. Yes, *mine*. I have as much right to it as you do.'

'But I have no rights, so it seems.'

'You don't in my book, no. You either come away with me, or I'll set the cops onto you, the whole lotta ya.' He slurs his words, as though he's already downed his fifth whiskey of the day.

Izzie is confused; there are only three—soon to be four—people in her family, not a lot. Or does Joe hate everyone new to Australia? 'Cops? Police? For what? My *Jezus*, my family's never hurt you.'

'Not yet. But I can hurt them, Izzie, make no mistake. And I can hurt you too. I will hurt you if you take my child, both of you. Think about that. I have friends in high places.'

'What you mean, in high places?'

'You'd better just hope you never find out.'

She wonders if his friends live on a hill, like from where the army took aim on Budapest. Are Joe's friends' soldiers? She's never been more terrified in her life.

Chapter Fifteen

Grace knows her parents will have prepared themselves for their daughter's heartbreak, but it doesn't come. Grace fails miserably to keep a low profile at home. She's a little too quick to laugh, to offer help, to jump to attention. Her daily moments are filled with singing and dancing along to the radiogram or playing upbeat tunes on the piano. Can't help it.

Connie takes the large wooden cover off her old Singer sewing machine, banishes herself to the sewing room. She has decided to give her daughter space and Grace can't help but wonder what her mother knows. Grace is lost: wanting, not wanting her reassurance—a little big girl. Day after day she listens to the rev of the overworked motor, often peeking into the room, regarding her mother's profile, her greying hair, sagging bosom. As her mother determinedly works the lever, Grace notices her right leg is pinched, enclosed too tightly in a compression stocking for her arthritis, the oedema spilling over the top of the hosiery. Grace's heart breaks for a beauty aging naturally, tumbling towards death.

'Mum, what are you doing in there?' she ventures.

'Protecting you from yourself,' Connie answers cryptically. She stops what she's doing, turns to face her daughter and beams a smile that says, 'don't worry, all will be fine'.

'Are you alright, Mum?'

'Good as gold, my darling daughter, just like you.' She turns back to the machine, immersing herself in her outlet.

One evening, sitting in the lounge room, Grace is filled with anticipation. When the phone rings, its bell loud and insistent, she nearly topples from her chair. Once, twice, and she's just about to run to answer it when George shakes his head and rises with a huff. He takes the receiver around the corner into another room. She's not game to look at her mother but can feel her stare as Grace sits shaking her leg. Within a couple of minutes her father returns and hangs up. Too quickly. Did he hang up on Charlie, or vice versa? She has no need to worry; the grin on her father's face tells her what she needs to know. The Loves spend the night celebrating the engagement.

'I never had any doubt this would happen,' boasts Connie as they sit in the lounge room sipping tea.

'Yes, well of course *I* was the one who put it into his head.'

Grace is aghast. 'What are you talking about, Dad? Funny, I thought it had something to do with *me*.'

'Well, I just mean—when I explained to the lad on the phone that we were having such troubles with you since he left, how you had been moping around the place after him, useless as tits on a bull.'

'What? You didn't!'

Fails to keep a straight face. 'I didn't.' George explodes in laughter.

'Wouldn't put it past you! Anyhow, we were unofficially engaged when I came home.'

'Oh really? Without having asked our permission? That was rather presumptuous of you, darling daughter,' says Connie.

'It was only ever a formality, wasn't it? A courtesy?'

'Yes, I guess so, but an important one.'

Connie sneaks off and quickly returns, holding in her arms two white garments—one raw silk and one tulle.

'Grace,' she ventures—flushed, flustered. 'I guess it's about time I gave you these. Would you care to have them?' Her words are ceremonious. She holds a bridal gown and veil, white with gold trim, towards her daughter, as though presenting a sacrifice to the altar. 'If you don't like them, not to worry. But at least try them on?'

All that sewing, day after day, night after night, for her. Just for her.

Grace reflects on the timing: *She knew before I'd told her I would be marrying Charlie.* Overflowing with love, she runs to her relieved mother and hugs her, crushing the fabric in the process. Connie desperately pushes it to one side.

Darling Treasure, a wonderful thing has happened. I have met your father and we are soon to be married! I'm writing this from my childhood home in Norman Park in Brisbane, and after the wedding, we'll move to Charlie's family's sheep farm in Pig Peak, New South Wales. I know, it's a funny name. But I need to tell you that I'm bursting with excitement about marrying Charlie. You will understand when I tell you that he's the kindest man I have ever met. Grandpa and Grandma think the world of him, too. This is the happiest time of my life so far.

But all things come at a cost. As you know, I have a gift like the one I think you will have. Sometimes I see things that haven't occurred yet or may have already happened—important things. We understand each other, you and me, and I don't want to trouble Charlie about them because he's so excited about marrying me. I still can't believe that's true, me getting married I mean, but it is! Years ago, I heard some distant gunshots. They were disguised as an explosion during the movie I saw—'Rebecca', and another time, as door knocks. The shots came from very far away, and now I know the location was somewhere near where I'll be going soon, the Alton farm. Your father has shown me photographs of Pig Peak, and the landscape dotted with distant hills looks exactly like the area I visualised years ago when I heard those terrible jolting noises. I felt people being shot in that place. It was excruciating, like I had to help but there was nothing I could do at the time.

I'm not sure what this means, but I think I'll find out soon. Like I've said to you before, not everything in life is within our control, but you can use your gifts wisely. I can only hope that when I get to the farm, to our new home, that I'll be able to right some of the wrongs that may have already happened in that place. Or is the horror waiting to pounce like a thief when I get there?

Chapter Sixteen

New South Wales, Early 1950

Angrily—fuming since finding out about the pregnancy really—her father had sent Izabella off on a train to a far-away hospital: his 'sensible' plan. Once there, she lay on one of the ward beds—sweating in the heat of a scorching summer, shaking, fearful of the unknown horrors awaiting her. She knew there would be many. A room of terror. Izzie formed part of a line of beds containing young women carrying babies in their rounded bellies. Like her, most of the girls had 'BFA' scrawled on their files and above their beds, which Izabella soon learnt meant 'baby for adoption'. Crying, or compliant and still, each girl seemed certain of the fate of her child—to be given away to strangers.

She and her mother had made their own secret plans: Izzie would return home from hospital as soon as possible after she'd had her new baby. She just had to make sure she didn't sign the adoption papers in hospital. At home, the three of them could live uninterrupted, in harmony—at least until her father came back from his work, but that wouldn't be for years this time. By now, her father would have left home again for work far away. He left the day after she'd arrived in hospital, satisfied he'd sorted out the important business of getting rid of Izabella's baby before he left. At home, they'd have to be careful. If anyone came to their shack, getting nosy, Izzie and the baby would have to hide.

But now, in the hospital, Izzie's main concern is how to escape with the baby, for them both to get back safely to her mother.

The first contraction hits achy like her period, and each successional pain increases in duration and intensity. Izzie has tried to stay still and quiet, but the doctors and nurses recognise the signs of early labour. They tether her to the bed. A nurse tries giving her a needle, but she fights as much as she can, like a crazy animal, resisting, growling in defiance. She'll show those bastards. She'll defy them and the place, its order and sterility. She'll defy the cruel and calculating nurses and doctors. This isn't fair. Where is the justice in having a baby taken from its mother?

'Watch out for the barbiturate-wielding nurses,' warns a young blonde from the bed next to hers.

'I not understand,' says Izzie.

'You a wog, are ya?'

That derogatory term. 'Pardon me? I am from Hungary.' The words on her lips hesitate, sounding so unlike the confident phrases she had practised on the ship to Australia.

'Is that overseas somewhere?'

'Yes. Somewhere very, very far away.'

'So, you're a new Australian. I went to primary school with some new Australians. They smelt like garlic.'

'What about the barbit? What you say?'

'Just warning you, that's all. That needle that bitch tried to give you'— the girl points to the top of her arm—'they'll try to give ya needles to make ya sleep, to make ya forget things. Sometimes it's better that way, ya know, to block things, but I s'pose it depends on what ya got planned. I been looking at you. You look like ya got something up yer sleeve, pretty girl.'

Izabella doesn't have anything up her sleeve, but she does have plans. Having resisted one needle, she would any others. Just has to remain alert. But she feels her body and mind slowing with each hour, and it's more than exhaustion. She must have been given something, some kind of medicine. Perhaps it was hidden in the water they forced her to drink. She remembers someone dangling paper and pen in front of her face. Her head shaking no, her screaming at them to take them away. The scary thing is that she can't remember if she signed it or not.

She's known all along she would be keeping her baby. No Joe anymore: he abandoned her when she told him she was giving her child up for adoption, when she told him she wouldn't run away with him. And she was glad about that now: she would not let her baby grow up with a drunken father. No strange family 'friends' either, the ones her father said would adopt her baby. They would be none the wiser; she and her mother would somehow ensure they never saw the baby. She doesn't have to worry about her father in his absence—he who had forcefully ordered her to give her baby away.

On her way to hospital, she'd taken note of the whereabouts of the station and which train will take her back home. But it will be a long, tough walk through bushland to get to the station. At least her mother had given her money for the return ticket.

'You need to know something, sweetie,' warns the blonde girl. 'You've no chance of gettin' outta this place with your baby after you've had it. I seen it too many times—girls beggin' for their babies. They never take no notice. Once it's born, they'll take the baby and you'll never see it again. Reckon they must take 'em to some secret nursery in some locked- away corner 'cos none of us never hear babies crying.'

Izzie is struck with visions of evil doctors performing dastardly deeds in some kind of twisted laboratory, murdering infants—their starched white uniforms splattered with the shock of red newborn blood. Is that what happens to them here? All the babies? She shudders. She had intended to labour in hospital, then hide somewhere for at least a week to allow the couple, her father's friends, to cool off. But if she does this, if she gives birth in the hospital, she will probably never get to see her baby. She'll have to leave immediately.

Impatient to make her escape, she's waited tensely until the staff have gone to dinner to make her move. With the help of the blonde girl to whom Izzie had quietly confessed her plan, frantically they manage to untie the straps used to secure Izzie to the bed.

As Izzie rises from the bed, her waters break. Unperturbed, she pads her way outside, squelching in the spillage of amniotic fluid. Walks straight out of the hospital, so easily it's laughable. Prays she'll get home in time, before the baby comes. There, her mother will surely help her with the labour, or what is left of the labour ... How can she do this alone? Izzie does not make it to the station in time, having stumbled disoriented through thick scrub in darkness, avoiding the road in case of getting caught.

The contractions have taken hold in the wild, the child set free from detention now ready to misbehave. By the time dawn breaks, her broken waters have ceased their flow.

The heat of the morning has excited cicadas into a screaming frenzy, their strident buzz filling the air. Magpies warble long and loud, failing to silence the insect pests. Izabella tries to concentrate on the bush creatures, their droning, their instincts and behaviours—to focus on normality, the natural way of things.

It does nothing to lessen the pain.

Chapter Seventeen

The late afternoon heat is incessant, but the cicadas have given up for the day; the bush finally quietening to a low din. She's laboured for as long as she believes humanly possible—hour after hour, pain after wretched pain, beads of sweat clinging to every inch of her body. Izabella lies down in surrender.

'Izabella! Izabella!' She thinks she hears the faint commotion of doctors and nurses screaming her name from miles away. Would they be searching for her now? Would they set dogs onto her? Or men with guns? She must get moving. All she can manage is to drag her way through the virgin bush on hands and knees, oblivious to the deep cuts and scratches that are forming on her body with almost every move.

She smells roses, her mother's perfume. It is with her and with the bush; in the air, infusing every tree, every plant.

An elderly woman seems to appear from nowhere, stealthy in her approach. She must have heard Izabella's cries of pain. In the fading light her eyes look kind. She could be her mother; she may not be. Gently, she wraps her soft arm around Izabella's shoulders. The girl gives no resistance; she and her baby need so much help now. The woman soothes Izabella with cool water that, too, has appeared from nowhere, welcome and relieving in its refreshment.

They lumber, on and on, past giant ghost gums and through a pathway lined in tall stalks topped in messy red flower hats; they gleam in the fading light. As the humans pass by, the flowers stand to attention, their show reverent in anticipation of what is to come.

The dark shadow of pain is indescribable, agonising in a way she has never felt before, never wishes to experience again. The baby's head is weighing heavily on her vulva and she feels an irresistible urge to push. Izabella decides she cannot take it any longer.

'I think the baby comes! Mummy!' Finding her voice, her shrill cries are so loud that they scare the last of the remaining birds from the highest branches, to fly far away from the drama unfolding below. As the sun disappears behind the trees, the temperature plummets.

Finally, finally, a plump baby, smothered with a layer of protective white grease, drops into its little green bed, followed by a thick blue twisted cord, the pathway to the mother, the life giver. Room to stretch now. Exhausted, Izabella collapses to the ground overcome with laughter and tears. She hardly notices the delivery slip of the placenta.

'*Egy fiu!* A boy! Tripp—the traveller,' Izabella informs her helper in Hungarian and English. Both women have tears in their eyes.

Izzie notices a Boobook owl perching above them on a wattle branch. Its rounded yellow eyes blink languidly at her. It then focuses on the sky, alerting Izabella to the moon and the Milky Way casting white light on the scene below. The owl hoots as Izzie lifts her head and smiles up at the welcoming blanket of stars. She almost gives a hoot herself.

The woman helps Izzie wrap the baby in a cloth. She takes them both to a nearby shelter, where mother and son relax on a woven mattress. Imbibing the calm atmosphere, Izzie nurses her newborn who wolfs down the first nutrient-rich colostrum.

Flickers of flame reach out from a container on the floor near the bed. The smoke is perfumed with some special concoction of herbs. Izzie inhales deeply; the gentle aromas of nature feel healing, surely helpful to her recovery. Firelight picks up red and gold flecks in the baby's curly black hair, the gold shine to his olive skin, his eyes twinkling like Christmas lights. She's relieved and happy about his appearance; her son looks just like her, nothing like Joe.

Having slept and rested all of the following day, Izabella prepares to leave, to return with Tripp back to her mother, knowing her father will be away by now.

'Who are you? Why you help me?' says Izabella.

'You need help. I help.'

Izabella reaches out and clasps the woman's wrinkled hands, appearing lined in wisdom, seeped in history. Izzie feels a mysterious depth radiating from her. What are her stories?

'Thank you, thank you. I have no words. You are my angel,' says Izzie.

A reciprocated smile. A train whistle blows a tuneful note nearby.

Frantic now, Izzie shakes her finger towards the sound.

'Track. Over there. It'll bring you to the train,' says the woman, nodding towards the sound. Izzie looks towards the invisible station, then back to the woman who has herself become invisible.

Was the stranger ever even there, or with her at all? Has it been her mother all along? Sniffing at the air, her mother's perfume—which has lingered since the woman's first appearance—is no longer apparent. Soon the smell of sooty coal will intrude on her. Izzie smiles down at Tripp wrapped snug in a blanket, placing a finger in his mouth which he suckles. Yes, her baby is certainly real despite nothing feeling real lately.

They make their way hurriedly to the station. If Izzie's mother wasn't the elusive stranger, she will help hide Tripp when she meets him, won't she? Having had time to think, will she be angry with what her daughter has done? Not having given the baby to her father's friends, how will they explain that when her father returns? No, she won't be there for that. She can't let him see Tripp—God knows what he'd do to him. To her. Perhaps even to her mother.

She will hide him if she must. She's hidden before, lost before. She won't lose her son.

Chapter Eighteen

East Brisbane, 1950

The little Anglican church in East Brisbane is stuffed with November blossoms of delphiniums and daisies, Loves and Altons. Grace is as nervy as a Chihuahua in snow. Her mum's little helper—brandy—has done little to settle her, and as she sits sweating in George's Vauxhall she feels like escaping. Parents of bride and groom look chuffed, and to the relief of Charlie and Grace they seem to like one another. Charlie's sixteen-year- old sister Kitty, on leave from boarding school, looks pretty but petrified, in a pale gold organza gown, her long blonde hair coiffed up in a bun, clutching a basket of daisies, befitting the flower girl that she momentarily is. Charlie looks dapper in his morning suit, although anything but natural. Jimbo sneaks a peek at Honey, dripping off the arm of what looks to be a prissy US marine; his face suddenly changes to one of sucking a lemon. Frank looks woeful, but still hopeful Grace will realise what she's missing and come running. He sneaks her the type of look one shouldn't lay on a bride, unless of course you're the groom. Marcie, who Connie insisted 'really ought to' be bridesmaid, appears thrilled with herself, exuding an air of haughtiness as she glides down the aisle. She does do a fine job of keeping Grace from tripping on her train.

    Clicking cameras capture every move, especially when the couple finally crack smiles. After church, they drive to the small reception at the house of the Love's, looking forward to a night of dance, champagne and canapes. The wedding makes the social pages of all the Brisbane press, befitting such an occasion.

―※―

After the hullabaloo of the wedding celebrations, Grace escapes upstairs for some much-needed time to herself, to the bedroom of her childhood which won't be her room after tonight. Still in her bridal gown, unwilling to let the magic end, she reattaches her veil and stands at the mirror surveying herself. Glances down at the empty dressing table. Late last night she carefully packed up her little porcelain animals, explaining the situation, gently prepping them for the long trip to the farm. They'd be sure to fret terribly should neither be able to talk to her or one another, all wrapped up.

She sneaks a peek back to her reflection. Then takes a good, long look at herself in the dress her mother painstakingly assembled and decorated for her. After a huge day, she's surprised she still looks respectable. Her gold shoulder-length hair has held its bun, thanks to a multitude of pins; her make-up hasn't run but her lips have lost their gloss; her dark blue eyes are still sparkling, perhaps a little too much due to the swig of brandy and four glasses of champagne she consumed.

Blinks several times to clear her vision. With a twinge of guilt, she realises that she hasn't really looked at the dress until this moment. Her mother has somehow attached, no, embroidered, strands of the most luscious shimmery golden fabric, the likes of which Grace has never seen, around the outline, the seams of dress and veil.

Staring at herself in the fading light, her outline seems to glow, casting her as a strange and almost holy apparition, encapsulated in fine gold light, electric, pulsating with the power of it. Letting go. Letting herself be mesmerised by what she's seeing, she beams at her reflection and slowly raises one arm up, in Lady Liberty victory, Libertas—the Roman goddess, in a silent toast to independence from all she has ever known, and sheds tears of pure joy with a touch of heartache for her mother who's just like her, for her family she'll soon be leaving.

So—her wedding, her bridal gown—this is what *beyond* was hinting at the night she was getting ready for Cloudland, the night she met Charlie!

And dearest Mum, you brought me to this moment. I think you have the gift, too!

Here's to silent pacts.

During the wedding reception, whenever she could steal a chance, Grace tried to ply Charlie with alcohol. And now the moment has come. Wearing a pale pink pin-spot cotton nightie, she lies in wait for her new husband to do the deed. She knows this moment is the reason for the nerves she has failed to calm all day.

She's locked away this part of herself for such a long time, a part of herself which since meeting Charlie has been begging for recognition. Aching for him for so long, dreading this for so long. Such cruel irony. Charlie appears at the foot of the bed wearing only boxer shorts, grinning like a Cheshire cat. Too terrified to return his infectious smile, having gone through the scenario so many times in her head, never coming close to the solution of what to tell him, she gives nothing away.

The alcohol hasn't dimmed his lucidity, nor his manhood. She doesn't want to but thinks of the man she thought of as a car, with the Plasticine nose, who tried to steal her childhood, change her biology, her chemistry.

Not a boy. Not really a girl. Never a woman. Will this make me a woman now? Charlie soothes her little cry, covering her face and neck with tiny kisses.

Afterwards, as her new husband sleeps, Grace lies awake, willing a new start.

Chapter Nineteen

Luxuriating in the post-wedding euphoria, the newlyweds rise early in preparation for the day of driving ahead. The family hurriedly finish packing up Grace's possessions and strap them onto the back of the Chev truck, which Charlie had driven to Brisbane from the farm for today's purpose. Grace is overdressed for the journey ahead, for her remote destination. The Alton clan, Jimbo included, has taken an early train, the first of several on the long journey back home to New South Wales. Charlie, Grace, Connie and George stand awkwardly near the truck. Unconvincing, Old man Stubbs from next door pretends to be doing nothing more mundane than watering his gerberas.

'Nice day for it,' he offers George, who grunts in return.

Marcie comes bounding down the road. Wraps the newlyweds in unnecessarily long hugs.

'I'll miss you way too much, poppet,' she says through tears and snot, loitering around, unwilling to get out of there.

Grace presents her with a faint smile then stifles a yawn.

'Okay, let's get this show on the road,' says George, never one for sentiment, particularly when it emanates from Marcie.

'That's your cue to leave, Marcie,' says George, never one for tact, either.

'Oh—right then.' Put out. 'Have a safe trip. Write lots. I'll miss you,' says Marcie.

Another smile, barely there. But I won't miss you, thinks Grace, feeling slightly ashamed of herself as the frumpy girl shuffles back to her house.

She glances at the old family Queenslander which appears to look down on the young couple, perusing the scene, smiling as much as it can manage whilst carrying the legacy of a few chipped verandah posts. Not her home anymore. A pang of sentimentality competes with lingering feelings of fear and disgust caused by Plasticine Man. He did leave his stain.

George and Connie fidget as they prepare to say their goodbyes. Connie looks as though she's anticipating acute loss which her daughter fears will be nothing short of primal. Ties cut. Snip, snip.

'Well, this is it then,' says George. Flustered, having nothing else to pack, nothing more to distract him from the inevitability of this ending.

'Promise to come back to see us whenever you get the chance, won't you?' says Connie, her voice breaking with the desperation of a baby bird not trusting it will ever get another feed.

'Yes, we will. We'll get up here to see you whenever we can,' reassures Charlie. 'Though I think it's your turn to visit us next, Mrs Love, you too of course, Dr Love,' adds Charlie, said without really contemplating the enormity of such a journey for these two quite frail, aging people who are comfortably set in their routine existence.

'Sounds good, son. And for goodness sake, stop calling me Doctor Love. I'm your father-in-law and I certainly don't want to examine you!'

Charlie blushes. 'Okay then, Dad.' Eyes fixed on the ground. George reaches into his back pocket and presents his daughter a Box Brownie camera.

'Here, this is so you can send us some shots of the back of Bourke.'

'Thanks Dad.' She gives him a tight hug. 'We won't quite be at the ends of the earth. Promise to send you some nice ones.'

'I'll miss you every day, darling girl, *every* day,' Connie says, wiping away what Grace can imagine will be the first of her mother's tears today, smothering her daughter in a too-tight hug.

'I'll miss you more, Mumma,' says Grace, pulling away, retrieving her breath.

'We'll miss both of you, won't we George?'

'Mmm, yes, well, enough of this bullshit. You'd better get on your way. Make sure you make lots of stops and keep the tank topped up. Look after our little girl. She's all we have.'

Charlie glances at Grace and they both turn to George, who has turned away to study something in the distance.

Charlie starts up the engine. George turns back to the couple, an arm around Connie. Grace winds down the window as they slowly start to reverse the vehicle out the driveway.

'Grace–KYLTG!' George yells to her.

'What was that?' Charlie didn't catch George's words over the chug of the engine.

Grace's first reaction is horror. How could her father joke about things like this? After what she's been through? But that's his way now. So, she looks at her father and smiles, both father and daughter ignoring Charlie. She screws her eyes up, shakes her head and laments, 'Oh Dad, you're a worry.' Wry smile.

As they drive away Charlie ventures: 'So what was that all about?'

'Totally inappropriate,' answers Grace.

'What is?'

'Secret code.'

'Oh, come on. Spill the beans.'

'Well, if you really want to know, KYLTG means, wait for it, apologies in advance. Keep your legs together. See, told you. Very bad. He's been saying that to me just before I go out for the last couple of years. Mum was horrified at first, now she just laughs it off.'

'Like you do?'

'S'pose so. There's no stopping him. Probably not the best instruction for a new bride though.'

'Probably not.' He smiles, grabs her right leg and squeezes it tightly.

'Get off! I'll naturally have to do what my father tells me to do. I am, after all, goodness personified—the veritable good girl.'

'Not if I have anything to do with it!'

Charlie laughs heartily, Grace nervously.

'Sorry to change tack, but by the way, I can't see them visiting us,' says Grace.

'You never know, Gracie, stranger things have happened.'

Grace unzips her handbag and shows the brand-new Box Brownie camera to Charlie.

'We're going to have to use this. It's going to be a lifeline.' She chokes back a tear, quite aware of her fluctuating moods.

'Well, we're just going to have to make a life that will be irresistible to you and your parents. I do hope you'll love your new life, Gracie. I hope you'll find everything irresistible. I want that for you, more than anything in the world.'

'The thrill of a new adventure!' She gives his arm a little squeeze, then puts her head out the window, trying to think like a dog—clawing at the exquisite freedom held on the breeze, but unavoidably just hoping the wind will dry her tears.

Chapter Twenty

Pig Peak, New South Wales, 1950

Treasure, I want to tell you about when I first arrived in Pig Peak. I've been a bit concerned I may have worried you in my last letter, about the gunshots. I didn't mean to do that, and as I said, we can always try to fix things that may be broken. Well, anyway, the day your dad and I arrived at the farm, I was unsuitably dressed in shift, heels and Mum's cloche hat; town clothes in the countryside. The heat was smothering. But the vastness and clarity of the azure skies … It was as if someone had pulled back the curtains on those skies, laying bare a glorious panorama of unabashed nakedness. No place for the agoraphobic, Treasure—what a sight it was!

I found myself spinning, twirling like a dancer, on pointes in my Mary-Janes (they're a type of shoe) and I was barely aware of my dizziness, my disorientation … my near fall. My shoes soon wore a fine powder of red dust. My eyes wanted to squint more than I would allow them, unwilling to miss one square inch of the full circumference of horizons around me. Some distant hills were edged with ragged trees, like they were cut out with an unsteady hand using a blunt pair of scissors. Some horizons came to an abrupt linear halt in the distance. The long flat plains were dotted with black squiggles of more untidy trees—trees so unlike the exotic varieties pruned to neat sterility in suburbia. In every direction there was a glorious display of land and sky.

I thought about the little urban squash of life back in Brisbane, where the aesthetically bereft live happily in trenches dug out between buildings, the tiny glimpses of exposed sky tantalising only those who dare to dream of more. I've always been one of those dreamers and I'm sure you will be too, Treasure. Beaches have always provided me with the best vantage points to appreciate the sky, but the panorama and clash of colours I saw that day: terracotta and green on azure to almost cobalt-tinged blue, was so different, so exquisite, and I became instantly enchanted by a strange new intimacy that suddenly awoke in me. That place. This place. My new home. Our new home.

Straining my neck, I smiled knowingly at what my dad, your grandpa, calls a mackerel sky. The sky looked like a giant fish composed of little cloud scales. The poor critter jumped too high, seduced by the treacherous beauty of the skies, getting stuck in the crosswind. I shook my head at that, thinking I must have looked rather like a stunned mullet with my mouth wide open. It's no wonder the fish jumped—looking down the only water I could see was by way of trickery—a mirage shining wavy wet on the ground, despite Spring barely having sprung. I felt more than ready to fight the elements, and whatever else was to be thrown at me.

A twinge of pain alerted me to a blister on my foot. I unbuttoned my shoe to examine the damage through my stockings. My reverie, like my blister, was broken.

Grace soon learns that the Alton farm sits on several thousand acres. The property borders the eastern side of the Europa River. As well as Charlie and his parents—Al and Edith—and little sister, Kitty, who's away at boarding school, the Altons have employed a migrant family. When his wife died, Marco—the drover and general hand—came from Italy to the farm with his three boys—Mario, Cappi and baby Paolo.

And now, a new roustabout has appeared at the farm. From day one, Grace immerses herself in its day-to-day chores. Charlie's parents soon tell her she's indispensable. With only one daughter to gauge 'what girls do', they watch in awe as the little city girl takes on watering and feeding the livestock and dogs, checking on the new lambs—making sure the dams' udders are producing enough milk, moving the last of the season's first time lambers and their lambs into the protection of the jugs. Al has built a series of pens following the season he discovered a dead lamb, starved to death by its dam whose udders were riddled with mastitis.

One morning, not long after their arrival, Grace stops Charlie in his tracks. 'You haven't kept your side of the bargain.'

'What bargain?' asks Charlie, looking worried.

'Shearing.'

Back in Brisbane, Charlie had agreed to let Grace shear a sheep. 'Oh, come on, that old chestnut? Thought you'd forgotten about that by now.'

With the help of Marco on Blaze the colt, and Buster and Flash—the sheep-herding kelpies, Charlie rounds up a few shearlings and shows Grace how to shear sheep. She even manages to flip the sheep onto their backs to get to their underbellies—a most undignified procedure for the poor beasts. Still, once the shock of the shears wears off, they soon jump to their feet. He looks surprised by her finesse but doesn't give much away. She wishes her father could see her now.

So proud is she of the first of the many fleeces she vows to shear, she makes plans to spin the wool and knit Charlie a jumper. She'll dye it a pale grey, add some red stripes around the V-neck and hip-line and present it like a trophy to her new husband. So, he'll never forget her talents.

As Grace begins the task, she realises she'd rather be shearing.

Charlie was right about the lambs. They're the most marvellous little creatures Grace has ever seen, jumping in sanguine innocence around their bucolic home. When one moves, the others follow suit. She wonders if their commitment extends to the abattoirs, if they lead one another to their deaths. She feels guilty about her carnivorous ways, yet pleased these ones should live long, happy lives. Leaning over a paddock gate with Charlie, Grace stares at each lamb in wonder.

'I see now what you meant about the new-born lambs, bouncing around like rubber balls. Look at them, wagging their tails 'til they're almost dropping off. Brimming with excitement, so carefree.' says Grace.

'They only stop frolicking long enough to suckle from their weary mothers,' says Charlie. 'They're merinos. We chose them because of their unique wool—soft and fine, yet strong. We run a strain called Peppins. When I was a kid, I tried naming them but ran out of names. Of course— with so many sheep … Anyhow, I started with names like Baarnabas, Baarry, Baambi. After a while they started getting names like Koala, Lion, Fido—absolutely no connection whatsoever to anything sheep-like.'

'How confusing for the poor little things, I guess, well maybe.' Grace breaks into a smile as she pictures Charlie calling out to them with their funny names. She takes a deep breath. 'Ah, Spring at the farm. It just feels so full of, oh I don't know, promise? Yep. That's it: promise.' Contented, she gives a sigh of happiness.

Fenced paddocks span further than the eye can see, each one scattered with a sprinkling of sheep and lambs, the mix of ages and sexes determined by seasons. Several lambing jugs and stables for the two horses used for mustering have been built nearby the main house—the homestead. Around its perimeter, Edith has planted gardenias, jasmine, roses and spring freesia bulbs, dispersed amid magnolia trees, ensuring the family are enshrined in fragrance and colour throughout the year. In the middle of the garden sits a black painted wrought iron bench to entice the weary in need of some perfumed ambience. For the hungry there are fruit trees, and a well-tended vegetable patch lies to the right of the house, busily producing the next abundant crop.

The homestead is a cream-painted blackbutt structure with tin roof. Like an amputee Queenslander, it sits low with only two steps up to a verandah which spans the entire front section. The squeaky front door opens directly to the kitchen. Adjoining that is a modest cedar-panelled lounge room with coffee table, gramophone, fireplace, and a piano which Edith used to play. The house has four bedrooms—one presently used as a store room, one by Edith and Al, and one by Kitty, when she is home.

Sitting a couple of hundred metres from the homestead, Marco and his three children live in a worker's cottage. Al has painted it a cheery welcome of butter yellow.

Charlie and Grace move in to another little blue wooden workers cottage near the homestead which Al originally erected a decade ago for a family of farm hands. Sometimes it's housed seasonal shearers.

In the short engagement period, Charlie's parents, Al and Edith, gave the newlyweds' blue cottage a good tidy-up. It's now furnished with a Genoa lounge and two matching armchairs, a laminated kitchen table, four wooden chairs, and a double bed. The laundry will need to be done at the homestead; Grace quickly realises. Edith has purchased some new cotton bed linen, a lace tablecloth, floral curtains, an ornate gold and crimson Chinese rug, and bits and pieces for the kitchen: crockery, cutlery, bowls, saucepans, as well as new kitchen appliances: a mix- master and kettle. Upon testing the refrigerator and little cream coloured enamelled electric oven with stove-top, Al has declared them to be in good working order. With two bedrooms, a living room, kitchen and bathroom, the newlyweds are overwhelmed with the leg-up they've been given. They're particularly excited about their newfound privacy, and that privacy is about to become more so.

Charlie takes on a greater role in the running of the farm, and Grace appreciates his desire to appear a capable farmer for his new wife. She helps whenever she can with the chores, at night collapsing exhausted in bed with the likes of Du Maurier, Lee or Tolstoy before falling into a dreamless sleep. Unless Charlie has other ideas.

Al and Edith have taken a step back, and Charlie reckons they've surprised themselves, realising that they enjoy life when it's laced with a touch of leisure. With Kitty back at boarding school—when here, she always tends to take up so much space and time, says Charlie—they've been using the opportunity to encourage Charlie to show his stuff. As an only boy, he says one day he'll be taking over the farm, and as each day passes, Grace can see his parents becoming more confident about the prospect.

Only a few months after Charlie and Grace arrive, Al decides the time is ripe to make 'big plans'. And so, Al and Edith, with a big push from Al, Grace notices, decide to travel around Australia, in a caravan.

Now, they are convinced that this scheme of theirs isn't fleeting, according to Edith. Al's been threatening to buy a Teardrop, little more than a bed on wheels. Edith hopes it's tongue-in-cheek. She explains to Grace she's spent an inordinate amount of time researching all manner of these creatures with her husband, 'and this is what he comes up with!' Today Al has travelled into town to secure 'the purchase'. Edith didn't go with him, knowing she'd be unable to curb her distaste for the small appendage, knowing she'd see something she'd like, and Al would refuse to buy it.

As the women share a cuppa in the kitchen, Al phones Edith from the dealership. Edith is complaining loudly about the sounds of traffic and people in the background. Upon hanging up, she's red in the face. Fans herself with her hands.

'This is what my hopeless husband, sorry Grace, this is what my husband said: "Hi darling. How shall I put this? Well, the chap here, a very nice chap indeed, has shown me a little corker of a van. It is not quite what we were talking about, but it's such a great deal. It's so compact that it's sure to be a breeze to carry, and of course, it's comfortable. And, drumroll, it has a *double bed!*"

'"Hang on, take a few steps back," I said. "What do you mean by *compact*, dear husband of mine?"

'"I mean what I say. You won't even know it's there," he said. Was I meant to be reassured by this? I wasn't.

'"Just you wait, Edie," he said. "We're going to have the trip of a lifetime!"

'I told him that it sounds like the memories will have to last us a lifetime, because it'll be the last trip we ever take!

'"Oh, ye of little faith. Trust me," he said, just like that. And that was the end of the conversation. Oh, that man *infuriates* me sometimes!'

Later that day, when Al drives home from town, towing a new van at the back of a new Holden station wagon, a nail bitten Edith is suitably thrilled. Following closely behind drives Marco in the Ford Truck. Al settled on a spacious Victorian Hawthorn, boasting five windows, a double bed, dinette, wardrobe and table, as well as all the cooking utensils and linen they could ever need.

'What you put me through,' says Edith, shaking her head and waving a finger at her husband, laughing, then hugging him with all she's got.

Seven weeks and two days after their son's wedding, the pair take off on their trip of a lifetime. He tells his son that he and his bride should move into the main homestead as soon as they get 'crowded out' of their cottage, obviously hinting at children. And soon enough, with his father's blessing, they are moving themselves and their most precious furniture such as the Genoa lounge to the comfort of a larger abode. Grace can't wait to start creating her and Charlie's own little crowd.

Chapter Twenty-One

Because Grace has totally disregarded her father George's advice to stay true to the code, the pair get down to the business of baby making. Sure enough, within two months of practice, Grace is pregnant. Five months gone and she is huge. Blue veins run rivers around her enlarged, hardened breasts, the blueness causing them to appear grey. Her nipples have turned from pink to brown. Her neck seems somehow thicker. She wonders at the amazingly straight line of pigmentation running from her flattened belly button to her pubic mound. She can cope with the constant strange metallic taste in her mouth and the aching joints, but worst of all, she's been vomiting since she discovered this little life force inside her, and it's sapping her energy.

Today, Grace is so sick and weak she's convinced Charlie to accompany her to Doctor Malloy's rooms for her second check-up. Charlie waits as Malloy guides his elephantine wife into the consultation room. Doctor shuts the door on Grace's hopelessly awkward, shuffling husband who looks greatly relieved he hasn't been asked to join her. Anything doctor-related and Charlie usually does a runner.

After a few minutes Malloy opens the door. From the examination table Grace can see that her bag of nerves had just settled down to an ancient *Australian Women's Weekly*. Malloy beckons Charlie inside where he plonks him on a chair near a wall.

Grace is draped in green and knows she must look like a school project papier mâché mountain. Malloy takes another inordinate amount of time palpating Grace's womb. The wall isn't holding Charlie still. So, Malloy, becoming impatient with the wriggling figure in his peripheral vision, gets him over to where the action is. He thrusts the ear tips of a stethoscope into Charlie's ears, placing the chest piece over the area he has been examining.

'In your esteemed opinion, Mr Alton, what is it you hear?'

Charlie looks like he's waiting for the punch line. Have they got it all wrong? Grace cannot conceal a smile. Charlie listens obediently to the jackhammers at work inside his wife. 'A heartbeat?' What the hell other answer could he expect?

'Incorrect, Mr Alton.'

Charlie looks shocked, then blankly from one to the other, as the conspirators shoot mean smiles at him, waiting. For goodness sake, thinks Grace, put him out of his misery!

'You're going to have a busy household,' announces Malloy.

'Well yes, we will,' says Charlie. Grace just knows he's thinking Malloy is stating the obvious.

'Congratulations Charlie. Your wife is having twins.'

'What? How? Wow!'

Charlie looks vague, pleased to be sitting down for the remainder of the consultation. Grace can see he's somewhere else, probably only catching the occasional wave of Malloy's stresses such as *overexertion, rest and health.*

Charlie helps Grace into the Ford truck, set for the drive home to the farm. A minute of stunned silence is thankfully, for Grace's sake, filled by Charlie.

'I always knew you were a good sort, Gracie my darling, but my Lord, this takes the cake!'

'So, you're happy, are you? I wasn't sure for a while in there.'

'Twins. How did we manage that, eh? I've never felt so alive!' chortles Charlie. He sits up in the driver's seat, back straight as a board, beaming a smile as big as the outback. Bringing his wife home. Then unsuccessfully trying to put her to bed for months.

Chapter Twenty-Two

Malloy told the couple they can continue having 'relations', rolling the word around in his pursed mouth with distaste; his disapproving look changing to delight when he noticed Charlie and Grace's shocked faces.

In bed, settling down for the night, Grace lies thinking that *beyond* is tricky and unpredictable. She never expected this—twins—but she's excited, so is Charlie, and they can't sleep.

He kisses his wife tenderly. The lamp throws a dull gold glow, and neither of them moves to turn it off. Meeting his gentle tongue with hers, she pictures frisky little cave animals. He pulls back, stares at her with a question there he can't articulate, she's sure of it. Frames his face with her hands, gives him a kiss through her smile. She lets him explore parts of her she's thought disgusting for so long. There's a compulsion in his double breaths. She feels his rapid heartbeat; looks like Charlie has his own baby kicking from inside his chest. Her arousal helps Charlie as he moves inside her. No need to worry, Charlie would never hurt her, or the girls in her womb, and she just *knows* they're girls; trusts they're safe in their watery shelter. He's egging her on towards somewhere she doesn't know—she only knows she wants to go there with him. Moves match in urgency, love, lust. Trust. He dares then begs her to let go, to come with him to some elusive, magic place. Hearing him like that: primal, animal, child—knowing she has caused it, has done this to him. At some point, she realises she has crossed over an invisible barrier and couldn't return if she wanted. Particles ignite, charge, spark, find their willing conductor in her, and then comes a flood of exquisite pleasure, overtaking her, running through her, out of her, making her cry out in surprise and wonder at something she can't quite believe is real, bringing her to pulsate in gentle waves with him. She thinks to herself, so, this is what it's all about. Her relationship with Charlie has never felt more authentic. How could anyone love anyone as much as she loves her husband?

Afterwards—still, smiling, sated—they lay there holding hands, waiting for the gongs in their heads to fade to the cheer of faint tintinnabulation. Later as Charlie sleeps, Grace cries a river of tears.

It's her boy! It couldn't be a dream, it's so much more. Grace is in love with him, she feels it. He's a toddler now, sitting plump and intrigued on the floor. His chubby left hand encloses a fat brush as he rapidly paints the entire floor. His moves swift and deliberate, a huge impressionistic image of hills and sky appears, a Van Gogh *Starry Night* with a wider palette and subject matter. The central focus is a rainbow which adorns the sky. The boy takes her hand and ushers her aboard the kaleidoscope of colour.

He says, 'One day, we'll ride the skies together, Mummy.'

ROYAL PRIVATE HOSPITAL, DECEMBER 1950

'Champagne?'

'Yes, please Doctor.'

Doctor Malloy rummages around in his big old black leather doctor's bag and sneaks her a glass. An urban legend demystified, thinks Grace.

'Not *strictly* by the book, my dear, but I believe one small glass wouldn't hurt. Prescribed with care, to ease the nerves, a salubrious refreshment.' Knowing smile.

She'll take anything. She loves him at that moment. Looks longingly into his eyes. They're a strangely clear, pale blue, the transparency of shallow water above a sandbar. He would have been good looking in his day—still is, in a doctorly sort of way.

Feeling vulnerable and raw, she searches his eyes for some answers. Guzzles down the plonk as she waits for the next contraction to turn her inside out. They're coming in quick succession and she knows they'll only get worse. She wonders how anyone can live through this. Takes another swig of the nitrous oxide which is having no effect whatsoever. What a shock—this pain. She was never warned, not really. How callous she must have appeared to labouring women she had attended during her midwifery stint, never understanding the scope, the agony of parturition. No different from her.

Where is *beyond?* She wills herself out of herself, but nothing happens.

'Are you sure you want to continue with the labour?' His dumb words halt the beginnings of her out-of-body experience.

Does he have some kind of magic bullet to stop it? Stupid bastard.

'How shall I put this? You haven't progressed as we would have hoped.' The accusing look on his face turns her awe to ice. 'Let's get your husband in and we'll have a talk about it.' Malloy stomps from the room. 'Come in!' he orders the figure who has straightened up in his chair the minute he sees the doctor. Charlie jumps to his feet, peeks around the door. Malloy pushes past him and, having taken his rightfully superior position in the room, ushers him in, abruptly.

'Darling, please, I can't take this anymore,' Grace begs her husband. Her voice is small.

'What has happened?' Charlie asks the air.

'Nothing, nothing,' says Malloy. 'Well, that's just it, in fact. We've X-rayed, and both babies are in the birthing position, heads down, however your wife's cervix hasn't sufficiently dilated over the past eleven hours. Only one inch. She's *stuck*, if you like, and your *children are stuck.* Your wife is tiring and suffering quite unnecessarily. More *pertinently,* the babies' heartbeats have lost some *potency.* They are becoming *distressed.* A caesarean would be the more, dare I say, *humane* option here. I strongly believe that *now* would be the time to move her into the operating theatre and get these babies into the world.'

When he stresses a word, he does so in a lower octave, as if to darken the message and send the recipients into a spin. He's intent on hurrying things along. Becoming a tad bored, antsy. Never one for a scene, of course. Grace would like to give him a scene.

Charlie has been staring in awe and trepidation, as though just having realised his wife is really holding his children in her womb. Well, not for much longer by the sounds of what Malloy says. He grabs hold of his wife's sweaty hand. She squeezes it hard as another roll of agony overwhelms her.

'Well yes, absolutely,' says Charlie. 'Please hurry. Are you okay with this, darling?'

'Yes, for God's sake, get them out!' she shouts to the world just before Malloy chides him that there was no need to ask for his wife's permission, that there is no other option.

Malloy leads Charlie back to the waiting room, back to his little chair. The third wheel.

Grace can hear the doctor striding very importantly down the hospital corridor calling in staccato for the nurse, who comes running. Yes, Sir, no, Sir, three bags full, Sir. Sycophantic lapdog.

Holding her legs wide apart for the shave proves difficult for Grace, as her body is shivering in spasms, on the ride of each ever quickening, ever excruciating contraction. Her legs start to shake uncontrollably, in sympathy. In shock. Unperturbed by the labouring mother, the stuffy nurse carries out the procedure cynically. Failing to hide her annoyance, she strips those hairs down to their follicles with surprising speed and efficiency. Grace scans the clouds outside the window, searching for some other universe, searching everywhere in vain for her dignity. The rude surprise of cold water and sting of keen blade on soft skin pale into insignificance compared with the battleground her body has become.

She looks down at her belly: Four legs, four arms, two heads, limbs and heads pushing relentlessly out to the surface, stretching her skin to breaking point, a balloon ready to burst. They're taking up too much room in too little space, having a punch-up in there, like Jacob and Esau from the Bible. *Please don't let the antagonism between the babies continue.* No, think happy thoughts, an Irish jig, remember all the playful bed romps under cool sheets with Charlie—a distant memory now ... rising to the surface ... the babies ... She's going to burst. The brown line down her belly; that's where they'll cut. Is that why pregnant women get that line, to show the surgeon where to cut? Too incompetent to know where to stick the scalpel. She's being hauled onto a trolley and wheeled somewhere. Smells of ether, chloroform, death.

Life.

Two. Erin first. Fleur second—two minutes second. Thrown onto scales. Eleven pounds six ounces between the two of them. Erin a little bigger, stronger, Fleur seeming to possess more vim, judging by her screams.

Malloy dashes out. The boys at the country club await.

Chapter Twenty-Three

Girls! Of course, she always knew deep down they were girls. Where's her boy? Well, never mind. Next time. These girls will grow up strong and capable. Grace just needs to hold fast to her secret pact. Her protection will be their protection. If she doesn't court trouble, if she keeps quiet about her gift, nothing can go wrong.

The wonder of them. Fraternal twins. Two eggs, two sperm. Champions—the twins, and of course both parents congratulate themselves and one another. Charlie and Grace have been advised that these two cherubs will be no more alike than any other siblings, which suits Grace perfectly. She's always frowned upon parents who treat their twins as one child, dressed the same, expecting the same from them, showing a distinct lack of imagination. To say nothing of the effect it would have on the children. If her twins had been identical, she would never do that to them.

In silence, Charlie and Grace peer into the twins' nursery as they sleep soundly in their separate bassinettes. Grace imagines love silently bubbling out of every skin pore of the two proud parents. The potent mix of chemicals permeates the air around them. Unseen by these otherwise intelligent adults, the little capsules of joy float sneakily into the bassinettes. Sometimes the bubbles cause the twins to wake immediately, and they start to play with them. Both girls smile widely, gurgling, throwing their chubby arms around the air; Grace watches as they try to burst the little rainbow spheres.

Grace questions why the girls not only sleep well, but sleep at the same time, leaving their parents thankful for some blessed time to themselves. And whenever she or Charlie sneaks into the room, as quietly as possible, the twins wake up, and wake up happy, even when viewed from afar apparently unaware of their parents' intrusion. Is that normal? To be so at ease with the world? It's not what she has heard would happen. *Watch out for the commotion!* She had been warned. But what is this? What a delightful surprise! Perhaps it's all to do with the love bubbles.

Despite the synchronised sleeping pattern, Grace is constantly struck by the twins' individuality. Both are blonde. Despite her heft, Erin has finer features, and her mouth has been blessed with full lips and her mother's Cupid's bow. Fleur's mouth is a thinly-rimmed ellipse. While one could term Erin a classical beauty, Fleur has a rawness and honesty to her presence, and when her amber eyes—paler than her sister's—fix on someone, it's as if she's sharing all the secrets of the world.

When lying beside one another on the floor rug, the girls demonstrate their differences. Fleur kicks around in joyful bliss, content, albeit slightly hyperactive, in the moment. She seems quite assured of the certainty of her next meal, next cuddle, the next moment of attention from her mother or father. Erin is not so assured, more circumspect despite her bigger body. Even while lying in her cot, she appears to have the coordination of someone teetering on a cliff edge, unsure who, or indeed if anyone would break her fall should it happen. She's not a crier as such, neither of them is. But when the mood strikes, it's usually Fleur who sets them both off.

The theme continues as they reach toddlerhood. Light as air, Fleur's first steps arrive as a run, six weeks before Erin's. Her little body continues to skim surfaces as easily as if she didn't have legs under her torso which she needed to negotiate. Erin's gross motor skills, on the other hand, evolve steadfastly, without a smidgen of grit. When Erin does eventually decide to stand, Fleur sees her as a target to be pushed down, and so she does, repeatedly. It takes weeks before Erin finally manages to remain upright for long enough to take that first tenuous step.

'Erin has started playing the piano! She is *playing*, Charlie, she really is,' says Grace of the two-year-old girl. 'Well, this morning I was playing, and she toddled over to me, showing a real interest. I sat her down with me and, as usual, held her little hand in mine and she played,' says Grace.

'You know you've done that with her before, darling.'

'Yes, of course we have. But guess what?'

He looks enthralled at his wife's exuberance; she knows he wouldn't dare say anything to quell it.

'She played Chopin!' says Charlie, winking. Grace is smiling now.

'No, no, of course not. Grieg!' suggests Charlie playfully.

'Oh, stop that. As I was trying to say, she played "Chopsticks". One finger yes, but, by herself!'

'Chip off the old block. Where was firecracker?'

'She ran in, grabbed the piano stick and started trying to play chords on Buster's back.'

'Well, that's one use for it. I never understood the reason for a wooden stick covered in bits of rubber.'

'Mum says it's for playing chords. Anyhow, Buster was so tired, he just let her do it, the poor baby.'

'Probably enjoyed the massage, after the workout Marco gave him this morning rounding up the sheep,' says Charlie.

'I'm just so proud of our girls, Charlie. Fleur may be a bit more, well, lively.'

Charlie rolls his eyes at this.

'But she's *sensitive* Charlie. I just don't ever want anyone to put out her spark. I think back to how my teachers treated me when I ever voiced a remotely original thought. Well, let's just say I want more for her.'

'Don't worry about it, Gracie. She'll find her own way. She has the perfect mix of sensitivity and tenacity. Who could resist that?'

Four-year-old Fleur is decapitating all her sister's dolls. She's doing this because she's used her mother's lipstick to paint their faces, rationalising that she doesn't use make-up much at all, but now they just look horrible. She tried just twisting their heads around but found they could still stare at her if she turned their bodies around. The dolls' faces now look like clowns, and some of the lipstick is on their teeth, red like blood. Fleur is scared of clowns.

She throws the heads, some with real human hair, one made of porcelain which responds most disagreeably to the adventure, into the rubbish bin, banished to a grave of damp, dirty, limp peelings of choko, carrot and potato from the previous night's dinner. Fleur arranges the dolls' remaining anatomical parts, i.e. torsos and limbs, upright in a group of six gangling objects, sitting propped up by her sister's pillows.

She runs outside to the verandah, where she climbs onto the rocking horse, trying to take off, singing merrily to block the sounds of Erin's piano lesson in the lounge room. To her surprise, another sound, louder than the clank and clash of what she always considers to be wrong notes, reverberates the house, that of her mother screaming.

'Good grief, what on earth is that commotion?' yells Mr Potts, Erin's music teacher, towards the kitchen, sounding just a trifle more concerned with the interruption to the lesson than any other disaster that may have just occurred.

'Nothing, er, just a small cockroach,' shouts back Grace hurriedly. 'Fleur, FLEUR, can I see you in the kitchen, NOW?'

'Not fair, not fair, not fair!' Fleur shouts from the laundry, scrubbing the dolls' heads with a flannel as they bob up and down in a soapy sea. She thinks of her mother's words: 'It was wrong and cruel to take your sister's dolls and try to destroy them that way. I'm very disappointed in you, Fleur.'

She can hardly bear to look at their faces. Their eyes look horrid, as their eyelids, with and without eyelashes, open and close in the water. The piano is making terrible sounds now as she tries to drown the lot of them, holding them down until the bubbles stop rising.

Her mother has promptly removed the incomplete cadavers from Erin's bed. She checks on Fleur, to make sure she's done the job thoroughly before telling her to perform the re-attachment operation.

Later, when Erin returns to the bedroom, Fleur is there. She hasn't meant to be there, but her mother has banished her from the rest of the house. Disobeying her mother's instructions to confess to her big sister about the murders, she tells her that she's given the dolls a much-needed bath.

'Hmm, they're all pink!' exclaims Erin.

'I bath-ed them in hot water,' says Fleur.

'Where's Jemima?' asks Erin, looking suspicious of her sister, throwing around pillows in her search.

'She felled from the window. Sorry, sissie.'

Erin starts to cry at the tragic news. Fleur sniggers to herself. Big baby.

'Did you tell Erin you were sorry that you took her dolls, pulled their heads off and broke Jemima when you threw her in the rubbish bin?'

'Yes, Mum,' says Fleur. She figures that if her mother asks Erin and she tells her what she said, Fleur will just have to say that she's lying, just trying to get Fleur into trouble.

Chapter Twenty-Four

New South Wales, 1954

Fleet-footed, something evil skirts the edges of the half-built bush shack Izabella and her mother are attempting to make a home. Whatever is out there lays traps with shifty care, ready to snare, she just feels it. For Izabella, today's fears come not from the stifling heat—trembling though in its conviction—nor from her wayward son Tripp, her small, headstrong bundle of anger. This one has teeth and claws. She hasn't yet seen its face, and those traps, real or imagined, are set for a kill. Why is she feeling so tense?

She has an idea why: her father is due to come home next week. His capacity to hurt her or her mother terrifies Izzie, he's done it before. And Tripp? She can't bear to think about it. She just must reassure herself that he'll never find out about her son. What of her father's 'friends' who were going to adopt Tripp? Neither she nor her mother has heard anything from them since Izabella first brought Tripp home years ago. Did they find out she escaped from hospital with her baby? If they contacted the hospital, what would they have even told them? Perhaps they told them the baby had died.

She's determined not to be home when her father returns. He would never forgive her for keeping Tripp, for disobeying him, betraying his friends. Her mother agrees about her daughter and grandson leaving before he gets home, although Izabella worries how her mother will cope without her, without Tripp. Even now, so close to the time of her father's return, Izzie has no idea where they will go.

Still, several years after his birth, she fears Joe will find her and Tripp. She just has to keep telling herself that Joe has gone for good. He's probably fishing one of two rivers again—either the King Richard or Vicstanley—she tells herself, as he intermittently did when they were 'courting'. Here one day, gone the next. Unpredictable Joe. She's determined he'll never know about her keeping Tripp. She's not even convinced he ever really wanted the baby. And with all his drinking and selfishness, he would make a terrible father. She hasn't stopped worrying he'll pay her a visit one day—another reason why she must leave. But go where?

Izabella has been sitting outside on a woven rug, fretting over her niggling thoughts, sharing peanuts from the shop with her mother and son. Tonight, she plans to cook a damper and fry the eggs she collected this morning from their laying hens. Routine tasks. But she feels uneasy.

Not only Izabella feels uneasy—Tripp runs raggedly around her and her mother. Running with a sharp stick, he aims, throws and fails again to puncture a rug hanging to dry on a nearby wattle branch, screaming with each miss. The sun ignites the copper flecks in his dark, curly hair—just like hers—but today it looks like a small wildfire refusing containment. He's taken only a few bites of food. He picks up and tosses away his harmonica—not even his favourite pastime giving any of them pleasure or relief today.

Izzie studies him: the boy with no last name. Her father had even told the hospital Izzie's last name was something different to hers, to the family's. Her stolen child. She wonders what she's going to do about schooling him. He's a bright little bundle and she wants what is best for him. She knows he'd thrive in the company of other children.

Izabella yanks him into her lap, rougher than intended. She attempts to coo and sing in soothing tones, firmly tapping his leg to the beat, as much for herself as for her child, willing some peace.

'*Nani, nani,* my sweet baby *nani,*' she sings—translating the melodic Greek lullaby her mother used to sing to her, getting into the rhythm, the warmth of the song.

Tripp resists—his surprisingly strong little body twitches defiantly on her lap. He's tugging at her long dark waves of hair, poking her in the eye. They check his health; he seems well, but Izabella's patience has worn thin. She pushes Tripp towards her mother whom he adores, as he stridently, stubbornly fights the intrusion. Out of character for him.

She decides to walk with Tripp to the creek, hoping the bad vibrations don't follow them. But soon she's relishing the exercise and distraction of the fifteen-minute walk from the house, and she can see him visibly loosening up too, with each small step.

Izabella has learnt from Joe about the original inhabitants of the area. Mother and son occasionally stop to explore ancient drawings on the walls of shallow, umbratilous caves hidden under salmon pink sandstone overhangs. Messages on a *ganing* wall—a cave wall; profound in their simplicity. She knows the handprints were made by men, formed by spitting a slurry of white clay and water forcefully through pursed lips over hands and fingers—big and little; children were here too, long ago. Izzie is fascinated, as always, by the stories she knows must be embedded in the images. She thinks fondly of the woman who acted as her midwife— she often does. Her mother? Was she even real? If her angel was indeed flesh and blood, were these messages once created by her people? What do they say? Can they give Izzie advice?

There are grinding grooves here, where axe heads were made and sharpened. They find spherical cockleshells strewn in and around previously used middens. Tripp fingers them; Izabella imagines he likes their smooth coldness. Click, click, he taps two together. She clicks her fingers in accompaniment. Although her fears are still raw, sitting on the large rock from where she watches him, she smiles a little, letting this image of her happy son linger, please her.

They continue towards the creek. Tripp wears his favourite cap. She's brought with her the pink, orange and aqua scarf, the scarf from Italy, the only memento from Joe she has kept. She loves its sheer silk fabric. She used to carry it as a keepsake of Joe's safe return, but things have changed. The scarf has now become a pathway for her to escape to far-away Europe with Tripp close by her side. As Izabella anticipated, Tripp complains of walking. Wrapping the scarf around her head, she lifts her little traveller to her bosom.

A vibrating rustle of bush causes her to halt; the drum of her heart doesn't. Hearing it again, she alerts herself to its nature, smiles with relief, then stomps her bare feet powerfully. The revealing rhythmic swish through grasses of the startled eastern grey kangaroo eventually fades as it moves away. Tiny fairy wrens flutter and dart around a cabbage palm. Magpies cluster in overhead branches as though gathering for a performance. Izzie spots a tiny black and white bird flitting around another bush, its tail proudly erect and flicking. Staccato tweets. Surely this must be a willy wagtail, she thinks.

Arriving at the bank above the creek, Izabella surveys the jagged, eroded slope she needs to traverse in her bare feet to get down to the water. With her son in a tight grip, she begins her fumble down the bank, then loses control as she accelerates, almost overbalancing as Tripp lets out a squeal. She switches one hand from his bottom to grasp an exposed tree root which recoils them with a jolt, halting their plummet. Tripp sighs. Izabella's hand moves steadily down the smooth shaft which tapers off as it reaches the pebbly beach.

The black river stones are uncomfortable underfoot as they walk together towards the shallow section of the creek. Izzie ushers her son to sit down where water has partially immersed some of the rocks, and as he sits, it swiftly immerses his legs and buttocks. He splashes with glee. Standing upright, she stretches, inhales deeply, closes her eyes and listens to the tuneful tinkle of a pair of shy king parrots accompanied by the gentle trickle of water caressing the rocks. Steadying her breath, she extends her arms, stretches then curls thin fingers, as though summoning safety.

When she opens her eyes, she catches Tripp grinning up at her. She returns the smile, sits beside him in water a little deeper. Its cold assault makes her shiver as it rushes up to her waist, the skirt of her short dress now soaked. She fingers a couple of flat pebbles, scoops them up, stands and sets the stones skimming across the water's surface, creating an aquatic display of short-lived fountains—skip, skip, skip. Tripp squeals and tries to do the same.

'Come out further with Mummy, my dear little traveller,' Izabella says to her son.

Gathering him up, she takes him in to darker water, knowing darker means colder, but she's determined to push on, knowing their bodies will soon acclimatise.

Tripp hangs his arms around her neck. 'Cold, Mummy.' He shivers. His wet arms appear covered in drips of honey.

'I know it is. The water will feel warmer soon.'

She bobs her scarfed head in and out of the water just once, holding up Tripp's body to keep his head above the waterline. After a few minutes, she moves back to stand her son in shallower waters. They both sit. She unravels, then wrings out her saturated scarf.

Now for the best part. This is her ritual, their ritual when Tripp is with her here. Shaking water from her ears, she stretches the fabric out to its natural rectangular shape, then holds it up as an offering towards the sun. She lays the sodden fabric over her upturned face where it clings like wet paint. She inspects the tiny droplets caught in minuscule silk cages. They glisten and sparkle like another universe of stars against the aqua, pink, orange sphere of yellow sun. Each colour brings with it another effect, another mood to the wash of sky. She likes that she can view the sun this way. The scarf forms a lens to view the trees around her, a welcome reprieve for her own lenses which smart from sun and water exposure. She peels the material from her face, smiles at her son and passes it to him in an invitation to share the experience. He holds the material to the sun. They look through the scarf together.

Stillness but for the water. The sudden melodic notes of a bellbird. Izabella shuts her eyes and listens for more signs of life. 'Listen, Tripp. All is quiet except for the birdsong. So sweet,' she whispers, wishing the sweet sounds would blow away her innate dread.

Movement. Her eyes fly open. Something lingers in the bushes at a distance from the bank. She makes out a silhouette of something very large, something she knows doesn't belong there. As she focuses on the intruder through the water-weary fabric, her shivers creep back to capture her in a new revival, a new form—shock. Her first thoughts: *Must cover myself and Tripp.* Warily, she keeps the mask close to their faces, a veil of misguided protection, as if by dimming their own vision they can somehow become invisible. With trembling hands, she backs up slowly and attempts to ease the exposed parts of their bodies into the water, until all the thing could see of them would be two heads, one hatted—albeit both outlined too obviously behind the clinging wet scarf. Her eyes widen. Shoulder deep in the water, she looks ardently at Tripp, whispering to him in desperate tones to stay still.

As she suddenly realises how conspicuous they must look, a horrible snort and puff of steam comes out of the thing. It's a horse, with a tall man on its back. Knowing it's rare for brumbies to be out this way, she fears the worst. Is it a man from the Government? Could she be taken by authorities? Remembers Joe warning her their child could be taken if he wasn't there to protect them. Perhaps the man is from the hospital, still searching for their lost patient—one now two. Or has the family who wanted to adopt Tripp come to collect him? To steal him!

She reels in terror. This one has teeth and claws. Does he have a weapon? A gun? Lifting the scarf slightly, she sees its menacing outline alongside the man's body. The horse's muscles start to twitch.

Tiny insects whirr and flit in flight paths around the heads of Izzie and Tripp, worrying them to an extent that would normally send them fleeing, but she's hoping that in her stillness—their stillness, these strangers will view these animate objects as inanimate, curiously foreign but fixed parts of the landscape. Izabella shakes uncontrollably, and she can feel her effect on Tripp. But he's stoic in his stillness; her pride in him overwhelms her. He has learnt his lessons well. But why, in their harmlessness, can't this man just ignore them?

Sensing fear in the air, sick of the pretence of normality, the horse shies, rears and neighs. This causes the man to sit bolt upright and tighten his hold on the reins and his gun. He tries to calm the animal, whispering 'easy' repeatedly, stroking its neck and withers.

Both Izabella and Tripp are now startled beyond playing dead, flight responses enacted. They lose hold of the scarf. It catches the current downstream with the careless ease of a butterfly on the wing. She silently bids farewell to her favourite object. Tripp knows its importance too …

He squirms violently, breaking away from his mother then dog paddles to where the scarf floats. He snatches it, his hatted head bobbing above the water's surface, and continues to be swept around the river bend.

'No! Not the water! Get out and *run* back to *nagymama*! To Grandma,' she commands her son, realising he might be too far away to hear her.

She watches as Tripp is carried away on the current, floating out of view. She cannot even tell if he's made it to shore. She looks back to the man, whose interest appears to be with her. With death knell splashes she heaves herself to near the middle of the creek where the water is deep enough for her to start swimming. Feels like an animal about to realise the sting of a weapon.

The man slackens the reins and squeezes his legs tightly against the horse in successive contractions, until the beast tentatively steps down the bank and into the water. She's almost to the other side and has heard splashing, heavy breathing behind her; her pace doesn't slacken. The horse is making a commotion—neighing and snorting as the man shouts: 'Come on!'

Izabella wonders if the animal will continue to baulk, but suddenly she can hear the agitation of something swimming. Her breaths come fast and ragged as she drags her body up onto the bank and heads towards the thickest bush she can find. The horse hits the shoreline in shivers and shakes. Izzie watches from a bush as the man congratulates it, patting its neck as he urges it on to the crest of the bank. He looks around, can't see her. She can see them.

Izabella crawls through thorny scrub that rips her skin. She doesn't care because she knows there's no way a horse could get through the dense bush. Her plan is to stay close to the water until she can no longer feel the presence of the man on horseback. When it's safe, she'll swim back across the creek.

Knows she must get home in a hurry. Prays that Tripp has made it home safely. But then what?

Izabella could hear the terrible wails of her mother, even when she was miles away from home. The force of the first cry almost knocked her off her feet and with each successive cry, her body has since been trying to seize her up. The desperation of wanting to get home, the thought of what will soon confront her ... Bedraggled, she stumbles to the shack.

'He took Tripp! Save us, *Jezus*!' cries Izabella's mother.

She sits rooted to where she was at the time her daughter and grandson ventured out. What remains of the food has been strewn across a wide area around the upturned bowl. Her mother's ululation—calling for Tripp, presenting her empty palms to the sky in despair and defiance—arms and hands that are now bloodied and covered in scratch marks, which would earlier have clawed her grandchild so tight that it surprised and upset her. Before the inevitable snatch.

As expected, Tripp is nowhere to be seen. Not even acknowledging her mother, Izabella takes off in a run and heads towards the road; she believes it would be the clearest and most direct route for them to take. But she has no idea which way they have gone—the man, the horse and her son. She takes a stab at north. At last she finds indentations in recently softened earth which indicate the direction of travel, or so she hopes. Horseshoe prints. The kicked-up dirt suggests the horse and rider were in a great hurry. Thinking only of what has been taken from her, she starts running again, the run eventually turning into an exhausted stagger.

Chapter Twenty-Five

Her heart burns as it weeps. In a silent blur, a snake glides over Izabella's foot before disappearing into its bush camouflage. She's felt no bite; every part of her is screaming, has been for days.

'*Kigyo*!' Izabella yells a croaky Hungarian warning of the reptile to an invisible audience. A flock of cockatoos' scatter from the branches of an old ironbark nearby. They'd been making a terrible commotion, and she chastises herself for not attending to the signs of the attacker earlier. Where is her intuition? She gives a harsh laugh, mocking her stupidity.

It's her second day trekking north in search of Tripp. Though she may have lost sight of the horse tracks within a day, she hasn't lost sight of finding her son. Pictures him being whisked away on horseback, clinging to the paunch of the tall stranger; an unwitting passenger, his little face twisted in terrible confusion.

'Oh, no,' she whispers, noticing a bite mark on her ankle. Then louder, 'Worthless. Do what you will. Take me, not my boy.'

Izabella notices an imprint left by the snake—wavy, like the trail of impressions she left stamped on the straight road when her once stoic stomp became a crooked shuffle, disorientation hitting her even before the snake did. She surveys the two innocuous-looking puncture marks. Imagines a sliver of blood trickling from the wound, pooling in those imprints, the spill fashioning a stark reproduction of the snake that bit her—having spawned inside her, the birth of its offspring emerging languidly through the opening on her ankle. She shakes her head in an attempt to bring her senses back to reality.

Did she see bands on the snake? Can't remember but tries to reassure herself otherwise. Red-bellied black, or tiger? She's seen them in her book. She hopes the dark reptile was the former, less harmful one. Searches her mind for remedies. Viz. Water. She will try to find some, not knowing if it will help but suddenly desperate for a refreshing dip. It should be here somewhere; the nearby birds tell her so. She'd immerse herself in its coolness if she found some. Vows to keep trying.

'*Szomjas.*' The young woman licks salt from her crusty lips, exacerbating the thirst of which she complains. No water today at all. Hands on hips, she fills her lungs with a shot of hot air, shakes her head in despondence. Considers her wretched little package of body and soul, everything it's been through lately, everything and everyone taken from her. Too much stolen, too much to bear.

Izabella collapses in the red dirt. Surveys the shimmering sheet of mirage ahead, its mock of non-existent water. 'You lie to me. Always lie. Show me some water, bastard!' she screams angrily, wiping away her tears.

Her eyes blur. She blinks rapidly but it doesn't clear them. When she closes them, through eyelid filters the yellow sun turns orange. Orange is a colour in the scarf that Joe, her 'pretending' husband, gave her. Her limbs tingle. She can almost hear the fire crackle inside her. Needs medicine. Should rest. More importantly, she must find her son.

Fears she may not be going anywhere.

'*Fiu*! My boy!' She cries to the land, weeping now, raising her head and fisted hands in defiance. 'Where is he?'

Where is she? The girl forever displaced.

A buzzing blowfly niggles at her sticky eyes; she rubs them with her fists. Masses of wild mulga and banksia cloud her peripheral. Up ahead, the mirage continues to shimmer its reminder of the water she craves. It's now blotted by a dusty object which appears to be growing. The object is coming nearer. There's a noise coming from it, too.

As pain wracks her body, she drops head to chest, encircling her arms around her knees. Fearing death is coming to collect her, Izabella closes her eyes, sobbing quietly, willing herself away.

Chapter Twenty-Six

Pig Peak, New South Wales, 1954

Treasure, I'm telling you this not to alarm you, but because I'm suspecting that it was an important sign and I like to share these with you. This morning when I awoke, my bed was filled with water. It's confusing to be in bed and in the water at the same time. I was in a watercourse—a creek—with a beautiful young boy with darkish skin. He may have been mine, but he may not have been. I felt maternal love so acutely. I was floating on my back with the boy sitting up on me, his little legs wrapped tightly around my stomach, not trusting the buoyancy of the mattress. I couldn't help but smile at his acrobatics. He smiled back at me. Leaves deflected sunlight onto our rainbow-mottled skin, so we must have almost appeared camouflaged. Somehow, I could see the trees and both myself and the boy from above and at the waterline. The foliage trembled in the breeze— a breeze which was increasing in intensity. Suddenly, the boy was gone, swept up and away in a wave too ferocious to stop. My heart was pounding fiercely in raw terror.

 I shot my empty palms up to the ceiling. Everything was dry then.

Grace puts away her note pad and pen. Hasn't yet decided whether she'll let her boy read this letter. She'll try to distract herself from her niggling suspicion that *beyond* has something tricky in store.

 Okay, Sunday—a good dose of church is what's needed here,

considers Grace the day after the Fleur mishap. Grace is adamant her youngest daughter needs to respect the possessions of her older sister. As always, Charlie is dragged to God under duress.

The little Federation red brick Anglican church looks preened and puffed up today, bursting with pilgrims and pride as Grace leads her two unimpressed children to the second front pew. No fun, the children would be thinking, way too close and conspicuous for mischief. Grace is hoping for some meaty reminders about not taking the possessions of others. However, a formidable Father Murphy, at his anglicising best at the pulpit, asservates through mumbles something about landlords and low wages and disgruntled workers and the doubtful worth of money as the collection plate is passed around. Grace is nonplussed.

There's a boy, about the same age as the girls, running ragged around the pews. Grace peeks behind her in search of the parents, who appear to be absent. Something about him is worrying her, and it's not only his behaviour. Something unnerves her about his presence; she can feel bad energy around him. Pale skin, deep red hair, dark eyes …

At once, each family member spots a large spider, a huntsman, dangling precariously from an edge of a lamp positioned about a foot above Murphy's head. Looking as if it's about to drop at any second, covert smiles become less so as hands cover quivering lips and watery eyes. Charlie is smiling and examining his rough hands twisting in his lap. Little Alton eyes dart around the congregation looking for likely conspirators, but they're hiding well. Charlie and Grace don't dare look at one another. Even Grace is stifling laughter, despite her previous horrible associations with the furry creatures. Murphy's getting all worked up and raising his voice; the sweat beads on his forehead and top lip build relentlessly as his sermon builds to its climax. Suddenly, as if paying homage to a demented grandfather clock, he throws his arms around in orgasmic release, sending the spider into a tailspin to plonk onto his face. Murphy becomes even more animated as that spider just hangs on. This is too much for Fleur, her cackles now loud and uncontrollable.

The truck is filled with giggles on the drive home. Father Murphy had to retire early from the day's sermon; a spider having taken a penchant for his nose.

'The poor blighter,' says Grace. 'It was as if the spider was just waiting for the right moment to pounce.'

'I don't blame it,' shouts Fleur from the cargo tray. She doesn't really need to raise her voice—they can all easily hear each other with the cab windows down.

'Exactly, serves him right. I don't even think all the congregation got a chance to cough up into the collection plate. He'll be miffed about that,' says Charlie.

'We gave *money*, Dad, no-one coughed into it. Yuck!' states Erin. '

More's the pity. Shame old Murphy didn't heed his own words more often. I'd love to know where our money goes, they don't even clean the place,' says Charlie.

'We didn't even get to have conoomin,' says Erin, pushing out her bottom lip in a sulk.

Charlie chortles. 'Betcha Murphy wolfed down all the communion port when we left. Ha! Probably guzzled a year's worth when everyone left.'

'Next week they'll need to get a good collection, so they can replace it,' says Grace, smiling. 'What's that up ahead?' she asks, correcting her posture.

The further around the bend they drive, the more they can see of what is lying beside the road. Not what, who …

'Slow down, Charlie,' says Grace, 'I think it's a young woman.'

What a strange little bundle the family have discovered. Her tiny body rocks in its sitting position on the roadside. Sweating, mumbling to herself.

They take her to the nearest hospital. Coaxing her into the truck's cab has been a bit tricky, as it's only meant for two, but she's small. In the cargo tray, too nervous for frivolity, the Alton children are full of concern and shock; they would sit stock-still if it weren't for the bumps. Grace offers her water from a Thermos flask which she guzzles. She refuses to answer their questions. All she says to them is, 'I can never go home again.' Grace wraps one of her stockings around the girl's wound, watching as she fades in and out of consciousness: wavering, jolting, weeping, sleeping. The trip feels like an eternity for them all.

At last, upon arrival, Charlie races in and returns with two orderlies and a stretcher. The girl is taken away as the family is led into a waiting room.

'We can't treat her if we don't know who we're treating,' says a young nurse, with a silent *stupid*.

Grace glances at a worried-looking Charlie, knowing he feels as she does, wondering why they hadn't discussed this inevitable situation earlier.

'Well, what's her name?'

'Daisy,' offers Grace. 'She's our maid. We're worried sick.'

Charlie turns to the window, as do the girls. Not a blab within earshot.

'Well, you'll have to wait here while the doctor sees her,' says the nurse. Stupid nurse—no questions about her surname. Grace wonders if she'll cop it from staff later.

'That's fine. Just do all you can. She's very important to us,' says Grace.

Charlie looks as though he wonders what in Heaven's name they've gotten themselves into. He paces like an expectant father as the girls sit munching sandwiches a nurse has given them.

'We're going to have to take her home with us, you know that,' whispers Grace.

'Of course, I do. But you do realise we're going to have to report it.' Charlie whispers too, sternly.

Their conversation is cut short by a white-gowned doctor who prances into the waiting room.

'Mr and Mrs Alton?'

'Yes, that's us,' both say in concert.

'It looks as though Daisy was bitten by a tiger snake. A particularly nasty bite. It was extremely fortunate indeed that you brought her here. We have given her anti-venom and if she keeps responding as well as she has, her full recovery is expected.'

Smiles light up the room.

'You'll be able to take her home in a couple of days.' The doctor stares at Izabella's short and threadbare dress, shoeless feet. 'By the way, you may like to consider her attire in future.' The doctor drops his head, peering over raised eyebrows at the overwhelmed family.

Chapter Twenty-Seven

1957

For the last three years, Izabella has spent her nights quietly sobbing in her room. She doesn't think the Altons even know. How could they understand that for her every day is meaningless? This is not her home; she has no home. She's told them she comes from Hungary, but that's all she's revealed about her past life. How could they have any idea about what living in an occupied country is like?

Sometimes she thinks she should tell them about Tripp. But why would they help her find him? They want her here; they tell her every day. She may even have broken the law by taking her son away from that couple. Did she sign those papers? Maybe, maybe not. Perhaps she really is a criminal. But Tripp is hers, how could that be stealing? He may be with those 'friends' of her father by now, in collaboration having organised the boy's abduction. Achingly, she wants to leave, to search for her son. She fears he must think she's deserted him. Where is he? Sometimes she sneaks outside, sits under a tree in the cover of darkness, rocking, moaning, hurting. So far from her son and her mother. Imagines her mother back at the shack. How much has she told her father?

She can't stay here at this farm. She can't return to her parents without Tripp. She couldn't return with him if she found him—she just couldn't face her father with her boy.

Perhaps she never deserved a son.

The Altons have had a productive number of years on the farm. Naturally, two world wars and The Depression negatively affected wool prices, labour and demand. But recovery was relatively swift. They found themselves in the middle of 'riding the sheep's back' with skyrocketing wool prices through 1950/51. The United States decided it wanted Australian wool for their soldiers' uniforms fighting in the Korean War, which added to demand for Alton wool. But by 1952 the bubble burst, or at least deflated somewhat; returns on prices dropped to half of those received the previous year.

The next few years were trying. But Alton fleece was consistently high quality, and the farm had built up a good relationship with the wool classers. During this time, Charlie employed fewer shearers, and the two families put in long hours, working like the clappers just to get through.

For several years now, Grace has been feeling rather let down by *beyond*. The vision of herself and the boy in the creek though ... Was it her boy?

When she first arrived at the farm, she lined up all her china animals on her dressing table, having been lovingly packed and carefully transported from Queensland. She positioned them in a similar configuration to how they were at her parents' home. This was to achieve the best view of them as she lay on her bed, quiet and alone. But the menagerie fell painfully silent when it left Brisbane. And for all this time, no matter in which position, in which type of light she places them, she just can't seem to rouse them into lucidity from their long hibernation.

She's beginning to worry she has lost her gift— the ability to communicate with *beyond*, to receive its messages. And as marvellous as her life has become, she misses its magic, its excitement, the flying. Is it because she is too old now? She doesn't *feel* old. Does it think she doesn't need it anymore?

Perhaps Grace is no more special than anyone else. Perhaps it was foolish of her to imagine otherwise.

Chapter Twenty-Eight

The girls are in their second year of primary school and the daily pattern has become predictable. Izabella rises early each day to help get them out the door. Always with Erin's assistance, she cooks the family a breakfast of rolled oats, eggs, bacon and toast—unless it's the weekend, in which case it's also lamb chops from the local butcher, not from their stock. Izzie makes the girls' lunches of Vegemite spread and lettuce sandwiches—the lettuce limp by lunch break. If they're lucky, leftover roast beef sandwiches, although it's rare to have any leftovers in the Alton household. Erin judiciously packs her school bag, checking each pencil and sharpening the ones that fail her strict standards. Fleur wolfs down her food, having slept in, stashing what she thinks she needs into her bag, on the rare occasion she thinks about it.

'Thanks Izzie!' shouts Erin.

'Yeah, thanks,' mumbles Fleur, sometimes having to be prompted by Grace.

'Have a nice day,' says Izabella.

'Thanks, I will. You too!' says the ever-eager Erin.

Fleur's silence indicates she can't see the sense of replying.

As Charlie waits to drive them to school in the Chev truck—Erin sitting up straight next to him—he sees her patience tested as she waits for her 'hopeless' sister. Mario, Paolo and Cappi climb up back. Their wait for Fleur generally incites an argument over some trivial matter such as whether the cricket bowler really hit a leg-before-wicket, or who stole the last pikelet from their fridge.

'Pull yer finger out, Fleur!' yells Charlie, starting to sound more like Grace's old man than she thinks he would care to know about.

Like one of Pavlov's reactive dogs, Fleur responds by bounding out to the car, all flailing legs and arms, slamming both the front house door and the car door behind her, and usually getting something school- related stuck in each of them. She sits deadpan, shrinking her body away from her sister, bored witless before the day, or even the truck, gets going. Grace has started to drive too, courtesy of Charlie's patient tuition, to the shock and horror of some community women, such as Erna MacIntosh. Grace does the drive home from school, as Charlie and Marco are still working at that time of afternoon.

After school, Erin races in, unpacks her bag: lunchbox, drawings, flowers and such for Izabella and her mother. She grabs a bite to eat, studiously completes her homework then helps the women with chores and dinner preparation.

Fleur often brings home notes for her mother: *Fleur forgot her hat today. Fleur was talking in class today. Fleur repeatedly hitched up the skirt of her uniform today. Fleur was chewing gum in class.* Her report cards are starting to contain descriptions: *petulant, puerile, impertinent, churlish, easily distracted, must try harder, lacks commitment ...*

'For goodness sake Fleur,' begs Grace, 'just tell them what they want to hear!' She laughs to herself having just heard her mother's voice. She's been thinking of her mother a lot lately.

'I was looking at the girls' homework today, Charlie. Well, I almost had to drag Fleur's from her, of course. Do you realise they're learning exactly what I learnt twenty years ago? It's like taking a trip back in time.'

'Facts will always be facts,' says Charlie.

'Yes, that's true. But, with all the discoveries yet to be made, why do people spend half their lives, well, some stupid ones spend all their lives, learning what their predecessors and most of the population already know? I know our girls won't be like that; they'll want to learn the secrets of the universe for themselves. But I have a feeling some unfortunates think their first ever original thought on their deathbeds—the sudden shock of the thrilling brain wave causing them to sit up, terrify their nurses. I've been on the receiving end of this too often, Charlie. Their weepy eyes mad with fervour as they shout a determined but abstruse 'Eureka' or something to that effect before the inevitable fall into stiff and grey.'

'Beautiful imagery, Grace,' Charlie smirks, 'I think it's called life and death.'

'But I want life to be better, to uncover its treasures for the living. Is that so wrong? I just know there are answers everywhere; we just need to learn how to read the language. We need to pay more attention to our senses.' An impassioned plea.

'You're a complicated girl. Who else would put up with you?' Laughs. Grabs her in a tight tickle.

'You wouldn't have it any other way,' says Grace, giggling.

One day the girls both happen to have the day off school; Erin because of her asthma—a condition she's had since birth; Fleur as she has a mild head cold, having managed to cajole her mother into letting her escape the drudgery of school for the day. Grace worries about Erin's health a lot and today is one of those days. But Grace is starting to curse herself for letting them stay home together. She has foolishly put both girls into Erin's room, to keep a close eye on the pair, but she hears them arguing, and that usually means they are getting better. Then again, it's more so Fleur shouting so Erin could still be crook.

When the room quietens, Grace opens the door a fraction and peeks in at her daughters who are both lying on their beds. Fleur looks as though she's trying to sleep, turned to the wall, having coloured in her book and Erin's; both lie open on her bed. Erin has turned to the opposite wall, still wheezing.

'Can you please get me a drink of water, Fleur?'

'Can you please get me a drink of water, Fleur? Ring the bell for Izzie. She's with Mum I think,' says Fleur, who rarely instructs Izzie to do anything for her own self.

'She's in the laundry.'

'Well, get it yourself,' orders Fleur, dispassionately.

Grace quietly closes the door; creeps then runs to the kitchen. Erin rises and shuffles to the kitchen where she greedily drains a glass of water.

'Feeling any better, darling?' Grace is sitting at the kitchen table, wool and crochet hook in her hands. 'Damn. Sorry Erin, I'll never get the hang of this.'

'I can show you, Mum. Maybe not today. I feel horrible, and Fleur is being mean to me.' She holds a hand to her chest and coughs.

'Do you want me to say something to her?'

'No thanks, Mum.' That's Erin. Probably worrying about the repercussions, the wrath of her sister. Head bowed; Erin takes herself back to the room.

Every day, Grace receives niggling information that tells her the girls aren't getting on. She despairs they may never really get along.

Chapter Twenty-Nine

Mid-summer. Charlie has had an exhausting day with Marco and his boys, helping mend paddock fences. Erin has had asthma all day, which is starting to ease up for the time being, until the late-night onslaught. Grace had hoped to spend the day in the garden but she stayed indoors to keep an eye on her daughter, except when she did both school runs in the truck. She loves driving, but lately the school pick-up is tiresome; by the end of each day she feels like she's run a marathon. Tries to keep quiet about her woes.

'We're going to have to dip them early,' says Charlie as he turns in bed to face his wife. Grace knows his concerns about the yearly arsenic plunge dip, fearful about the damage it does to the waterways.

'Some've the sheep have been scratching themselves on the fences—wool everywhere. I noticed some have dags too, which could mean fly-strike if we don't do it soon.'

'Good thing this didn't happen before the shearers and classers did their bit,' offers Grace, trying for a bright side.

'We should do the shearlings too, just to be sure,' says Charlie, effectively ignoring her.

'Everyone'll pitch in to help, you know that. Why not let the girls have a go at it? They drive me crazy every time you go out working without them.'

'Well, they can help with the rounding up, I guess. The boys can help dip. They're used to it. I don't want the girls anywhere near the plunge. I'll get the stuff tomorrow and get things organised.'

She wants to say to him: And what if the girls were boys? Would you let them then? But she knows the answer and her logic tells her to be thankful the girls won't be involved in dangerous work.

Grace simply grunts as agreeably as she can manage. She hopes he'll stop talking, and he probably will now, because his banter at night usually revolves around answering her questions. She's deathly tired; hopes she'll have the strength for what lies ahead.

Cranky at not having been part of the *real* action of sheep dipping, Fleur sneaks out late the following morning, collects the hose and two small bottles: one Mercurochrome and one cochineal. She couldn't find the antiseptic yellow stuff. She fills the plunge tub with water. As she pours in the tincture, she rouses, 'They don't even look like they've been bathed!'

Then, suddenly realising she won't be able to lift any sheep into the tub, she fills the buckets and lugs them one at a time to the nearest paddock. She pours the pink mixture over as many sheep as she can, rubbing the wool of each one efficiently to make sure it sticks. She announces, 'much prettier in pink', over and over until she's done, or rather until the tub has been emptied. She'd do the whole bloody lot of them if she could.

Fleur jumps, as Erin appears by her side.

'How long have you been watching me? I nearly died of fright!' Panting, hand to heart.

'Looks like you've been dying alright. They're more like yucky purple than pink, Fleur. Don't you think?' she teases, scratching her chin.

'Wodaya mean? No—they're *pink.* They looked too dirty before, anyway.' She sticks her bottom lip out in a sulk.

'What do you think Mum and Dad will say when they see these strange looking little purple woolly jumpers?'

'Pink, not purple! Well, they need to know I can dip just as well as those silly boys can,' says Fleur.

'And oh, they'll be *so happy now*!' Erin says.

They both stare at the defilement. The stain has taken on the sheep thoroughly, and it is more glaring than Fleur expected. She begins to realise what she's done.

'*Don't tell,*' she hisses, the words barely catching up with her thoughts. Stares solemnly at her sister.

'Course not,' reassures Erin. Quick grin.

Fleur doesn't believe her. But then a pang of guilt hits her as she realises, she's never given Erin reason to do anything nice for her anyway.

Erin dobbed on her sister. There would have been no mistaking who dyed the sheep anyway, Erin reasoned to Fleur and her parents. Charlie received more than passing glances as he drove through town with a truck laden with five pink sheep, en route to a farmer with the right chemicals and equipment to strip their coats back, restore them to their former glory. Fleur sat up front with her father, guilty as charged, unprepared to confront the man and explain what had happened, as Charlie had insisted. She didn't think it would come to this. Amid tears, she confessed her sins to the farmer, as her father had asked her to, and watched on shamefully as the men huffed and puffed their way through washing and rewashing the five miserable, perplexed shearlings.

Chapter Thirty

Izabella polishes Grace's dressing table every week. Despite the stillness in the atmosphere, again it's coated with a film of red dust. She carefully removes Grace's hairbrush, comb, mirror and collection of china animals. Spaces them out on the large bed so as not to break any.

A blue and green scarf is draped over a bedpost, reminding Izzie of the day she draped the scarf Joe gave her on a tree branch. She tries ignoring it, but its pull is too great. Its colours are that of the sky at night, not of the rise and set of sun like hers. She loves colours so much, not the grey of her old clothes and scarves. Her eyes dart across to the open doorway. Tentatively, Izabella lifts the scarf from its perch and carries it to the window where she holds it up to the light. She's ready to escape.

'Could you make sure you get all of the dust? Izabella? What are you doing?' Grace has appeared at the doorway.

'Sorry, ma'am.' A mumbled response. Head lowered, Izzie quickly returns the scarf to the bedpost, hurrying past Grace, determined to be anywhere but there.

Grace never mentions the episode again.

She is in the kitchen, cooking the Australian way, as instructed by Grace. No herbs and spices: no flavour. Why? Izzie misses the spicy goodness of Greek and Hungarian cooking—before the war came, before all food lost its flavour ... She also wonders why this family thinks that every object, even every person must be cleaned inside and out with strange products. Sometimes with water, sometimes with a rag, or a puff or a pill—a different product for each object—living or non-living; it's all the same. Doesn't seem to do them much good, she muses sardonically.

Last week, she noticed an unusual bottle on the kitchen table. She picked it up, opened the tight lid, smelt the eye-watering concoction and sneezed. Looked at the picture of a sheep staring at her from the label. Smiling to herself, she shook her head in disbelief; not even the animals can escape the cleaning.

Izzie thinks of her time at the Alton farm. She does her best to settle in, but she knows that it will never be her home.

When she first arrived, she was led to a nice room, where she slept for two days. When she faced the family, she electively played mute. Wouldn't speak, couldn't speak. What would she say? That her son had been taken? The son she wasn't meant to keep? *Tolvaj.* Thief. That she may have been about to be taken, too? She has little idea of where she is living now. She had little idea of where she was living before being taken to the farm. The only thing she knows is that she cannot return home, with or without Tripp. Without Tripp ...

Soon after Izabella's arrival, she overheard Charlie speaking with the authorities on the telephone, then talking to Grace afterwards about the conversation. Charlie said that none of the hospitals had reported a missing patient, and seeing Izzie had no identification with her, it would be best for her to stay at the farm. Izabella suspects no hospital staff would want to admit to an escapee anyway.

She knows her mother wouldn't have reported Izzie missing. Reporting would have meant contacting her father, and all hell would have been unleashed once he'd found out that Izabella and Tripp had returned and stayed so long in the shack with Izzie's mother without his knowledge.

Izzie had always intended to leave home before her father's return from the power station, and her mother knew it; she was almost at ease with the plan. They were unsure how this would happen, or where Izzie and Tripp would go. But disappearing the way she did just before his arrival home was not her plan. Her mother must have known that Izzie had left in search of her son, yet effectively vanishing from her dear anya's life with Tripp, the little boy who knew his grandmother from the time he was born, who she loved so dearly, is heartbreaking for Izzie. They had not discussed how to explain Izabella's disappearance to her father. How did her mother handle that? How did her father explain things to his 'friends'? No baby for them. Or perhaps they had another baby by now and Izzie's was long forgotten.

She tries to speak only English with the family. When she slips up and babbles in Hungarian, on rare occasions Greek—so little Greek did her father permit her mother to teach Izzie—Erin and Fleur laugh. Sometimes they encourage her to keep going, to continue speaking in her home language. Izzie plays along—rolling her tongue, widening her eyes, gesticulating theatrically—just for fun.

The Alton family is nice. Charlie is quiet and kind. Erin is obedient, always helping around the house. Izzie likes Grace. Izabella thinks Grace is pleased to have someone to help inside, because she seems so much happier when she's outside. Izabella likes Fleur a lot; Fleur has spirit.

Izabella is relieved they never probe about her past life. Early on she told them her real name—her Christian name—and they seem happy to call her by it. She thought at first that it may belong with her old life, but she soon realised it was the only thing she had left.

Her body is comfortable. She has health, nutritious food, clean clothes. Her employers treat her well, as they would a welcome guest, she imagines. She tells herself she's a lucky lady and is careful to present a grateful façade. In fact, she *is* grateful for the kindnesses afforded her and she has grown rather fond of the family.

But the family are not hers. Her life is an act. Sometimes she thinks she should be dressed as a clown, a harlequin—a character from the girls' books—because her performance never wavers. A puppet perhaps, like the ones she saw as a child in the Budapest markets. Oh, how she loved the shows! But her performance conveys more sadness than jocularity. At night, she prays for closure, but reliable Izabella is always called for an encore. Another curtain call, day after day. She dances around uncomfortable conversations, silences, like the good ghost that she is. She wonders at times if these people can even see her, really see her.

Izzie is puzzled by the person she sees reflected in the mirror, understanding her duties, not her mission. She thinks back to her long sea journey from Europe to the bottom of the world, how standing on that deck she vowed to wear only bright colours in Australia. And here she is, dressed in white every day. Does lack of colour equate lack of heart and soul? She feels as blank as she looks.

Her language is sometimes muddled, with weighty gaps. The vibrant stories she once shared with her mother in and of her home country, have been replaced with trite and pedestrian chatter, save for those smuggled moments with Fleur, who has some understanding there. Fleur lends her books, helps her to read, even though Fleur tells her she doesn't particularly like reading. With Fleur, Izzie feels she can almost be herself.

But each day's monotony dampens her spirit further—chip, chipping away. She calls this her afterlife, not quite purgatory in the Catholic sense, but for Izabella this is a spiritless existence. At night, in her dreams, she escapes to a place of belonging. She understands things could be a lot worse. But it pains her greatly imagining what has happened to Tripp and her own mother, and everyone back in Hungary she loved and lost. Wonders if they would even recognise her now.

Recently in the newspaper, she saw black and white pictures from Maralinga country and heard the words of the Tjarutja Aboriginal people—according to Fleur. Izabella saw pictures of huge, strange clouds rising as the result of something that had destroyed the land. Atomic tests, Fleur told her. The visions reminded her of the bombs in Budapest during the war: screeches, explosions, dirt and dust. Izzie was terribly concerned for the people caught up in the horror back then, just as she worried about this latest event in Australia. Although Fleur tried to reassure her that most of the people went away before the startling event occurred, Izzie knew some of them would not have escaped. How far away was it? The fear of anything having happened to Tripp out there …

Patiently, passively she bides her time. The pervasive hunger never quells, *never* quells. And she can neither comprehend, nor explain the emptiness. So, she is quiet—a quietness which has so far gone in her favour here at the farm homestead, in terms of how she is viewed here. She knows the family sees their Izabella as a marvel—clean, conscientious, kind, a problem solver, pre-emptive of any household disaster and nursemaid to the sick or wounded.

She sometimes recalls her time with Joe before he started drinking not long after they met. They used to fish together; that was something they shared. Perhaps she did love him, just for a short while.

She will never forget the day her world turned upside down, the day Tripp was taken from her. He's the one she misses the most.

Chapter Thirty-One

1959

Grace hasn't had a period in seven weeks. Day by day her excitement builds. At thirty-two, so long since the birth of the girls, she thought she had little chance of falling pregnant again. But there is no mistaking the lethargy and nausea that now grip her.

'Darling, we need to talk.'

'Sounds a worry. What is it?' Charlie prepares himself by taking a seat at the breakfast table.

'Do you think we could use another boy around the farm?'

'What? Why? Do you have your eye on someone?'

'Well, put it this way: We'll both be keeping a very close eye on someone soon.'

Charlie is getting twitchy, shuffling around, his leg starting to shake furiously, the leg which two minutes ago was folded harmlessly over the other one.

'You're kidding me!' cries Charlie. 'You're upset.'

'No, not at all. It's just, well, we're not in our twenties anymore, are we?'

'So, you think I should hide away for months?'

Charlie gives a chuckle. 'No, silly sausage. It's wonderful news. We'll just have to put the girls into one room.'

'Oh, they're going to love that! We'll keep him in ours 'til he's old enough for a single bed. Then he can go into one of the girl's rooms. Then naturally, he'll have his own room later.'

'Hmm. Have him in our room, will we just? You're getting very protective of this one, and he isn't even born yet!'

Charlie feigns anger, Grace hopes it's feigned. She thinks he's probably happy at the news, but secretly worried about any bedroom action he may miss out on due to the appearance of a new tenant.

'Ha! You said he!' says Grace.

'Did I? Slip of the tongue. By the way, what makes you so certain it's a boy?' asks Charlie.

'He's a boy.'

She knows. The boy of her dreams. They are really coming true.

She asks Charlie to take her to Dr Malloy. The doctor calls her 'near geriatric', and sadly, she can detect enjoyment on his face as he calls her that.

If I'm geriatric, what's he? Gruff, pompous bastard.

Charlie returns with the mail from the post office and something unexpected, a small package for Grace. It's from her mother—unusual, as the only correspondence Connie sends on a regular basis is letters. Grace carefully cuts the string and opens the brown paper wrapping, wanting to preserve all traces of her mother. Photos. Photos from a roll of film she had sent her mother over a year ago, to get developed in Brisbane. Wiping back tears, she stares intently at the black and white shots: the girls in their school uniforms—first day, Erin playing piano lost in a symphony of sorts, the four of them on the verandah surrounded by pots of blue hydrangeas, Charlie and Grace shearing, Marco and his family. No Izabella. Grace realises she hasn't even told her parents about her and doesn't know why. She feels acutely ashamed.

Attached is a little note written by her mother saying she is okay, which Grace knows doesn't mean much, as Connie has severe arthritis. Both parents are missing their daughter dearly and can't wait to see their grandchildren again. When the girls were three, the family road-tripped to Brisbane. They played up the entire time and Charlie swore 'never again'. Connie says that Dad is now president of the bowls club. He thinks his daughter has finally lost the plot—shearing sheep and working like a 'real' farmer—a man, Grace understands his meaning. Grace wishes he could see how well she works here. She screws up her mouth at her father's words, that old tug of never good enough. Then she traces each pen mark lovingly with her perfectly fine finger—knowing the scratches were created by arthritic digits. There is another photo inside the folded letter—her parents in their swimming togs, or *bathers* as they are called in other parts. They're sitting on the beach at Surfers Paradise, beaming for the camera. On the back, George has written: *What you're missing.*

Grace wishes her parents knew what they were missing, too. Hurriedly, she writes a letter, remembering to tell them of the pregnancy. Hopes they'll get this mail, hoping they haven't left their sand and sea paradise yet.

Chapter Thirty-Two

1963

He's arrived—the boy she has always wanted, the one she knew she would one day bear.

From birth, which for Grace meant an elective caesarean as Malloy refused a 'trial of scar', Teddy had two shell-shaped ears which showed promise of the magnificent unfurling of two large cabbage roses. Sure enough, they blossomed, but the result was not aesthetically appealing as predicted, not in the slightest. Two large aural receptacles emerged either side of his head, looking like inverted snail shells. He was the perfect poster boy for pinning, and this task was attended to eventually at a time when the surgeon thought, but wasn't quite sure, that his ears were mature, or at least in a dormant phase.

Teddy also had the misfortune of being born with skew-whiff, 'wandering' eyes that eventually resulted in a 'lazy' left eye. Throughout toddlerhood, the lad was lumbered with an eyepatch over his normal eye to strengthen his weak eye. This disturbed the boy greatly, as wearing the patch made it difficult for Teddy to see clearly. Constant collisions with animate and inanimate objects were starting to wear thin on the boy and those around him. Of course, Erin did her best to jolly him up and provided an understanding shoulder when it all got too much for him. Fleur thought the whole situation was hilarious. She started to call Teddy: Dead Ted with the pirate head, Dead Ted, sometimes simply Head or even the more unfortunate Dead for short when she was impatient for his attention.

Teddy is three and she's still calling him names.

Grace wants to hold onto Teddy for as long as possible before years of schooling take him away from her. She loves the time after lunch, when she spoons his little warm body against hers in her double bed. Before their nap, Grace reads to him—Teddy's voracious appetite for books rendering nap time shorter than it should be. Enid Blyton's The *Magic Faraway Tree* is his current favourite, another is A.A. Milne—*Winnie the Pooh*. He recites 'Happiness', a beloved Milne poem, to her every day lately, marching horizontally to its beat as he lies in bed, pretending to be John in great big waterproof boots, making her heart soar. Hard for her to wait for him to finish before grabbing him and planting giant kisses on his face.

Teddy entrances everyone with his innocent cheekiness. When he smiles with his mouth fully open—which is what usually happens—his little tombstone teeth appear, caught at different stages of bud and bloom, which makes any audience unavoidably smile, no matter how upset they may be with him at the time. Whereas another child may be self-conscious about having crooked teeth, when he's in the mood, Teddy is more than happy to let anyone nearby check out the wildness of his oral garden. Grace wonders if he'll end up with a gap between his front teeth like hers; the girls haven't inherited it.

Grace often watches on as Charlie sits Teddy on his shoulders, as though he can't wait for his son to grow taller than he is. Sometimes he positions him so he can walk upside-down on the ceiling, much to the boy's delight.

At other times, Charlie takes him to the garage next to the main house. For Teddy it's a secret place with tools and strange metal parts under car bonnets—a place Charlie would never take the girls. One day, after filling the truck with petrol and oil at the service station, Charlie brought home a present for Teddy—a small blue Matchbox Maserati. Teddy fell fearlessly in love with it.

To the girls, Teddy is their plaything, albeit often a wriggling, non-compliant plaything. When he was younger and smaller, he fitted perfectly in their dolls' pram. And when he didn't anymore, they still stuffed him in—his fleshy limbs and tummy spilling over and under the girls' makeshift restraints. Just like him really, Teddy is never one to be tied down. Even as he grows older, the girls still parade him around like prized stock. Erin nurtures him with love, food, comfort. Grace is sure that Fleur views him as her sidekick—the foil she would never find in her sister.

On many occasions, both Grace and Erin feel the need to pull Fleur up about her treatment of Teddy. Grace thinks she is forever extending her brother beyond what he's capable of doing. But the little chap never seems to mind, even when one of her ideas brings him harm or trouble. One day, Fleur pushed her brother down a hill after she'd buckled him carelessly into their go-cart. The machine toppled over and Teddy fell from the vehicle— resulting in a nasty bump to his head.

Against Grace's wishes, Fleur took him to the river to teach him to fish. A fishhook impaled his eyebrow, leaving a scar he would always bear. Obviously, both Grace and Charlie were furious on both counts, especially regarding the fishing exploit, considering his previous eyesight problems, let alone his young age. But Grace must admit that he seems to wear his scar as a badge of honour. Little bugger.

Teddy never blamed Fleur; he adores her. The more she pushes, the more alive he seems to become. Because he is just like her: restless, guzzling up life's delicacies—the excitement of the adventure and the next big thing always eclipses any minor inconvenience that often happens, such as injury, pain. In Fleur's eyes, she's helping him, introducing him to the real world. Isn't Fleur, she rationalises to her mother, in fact doing them *all* a favour? By extending Teddy? Because afterwards, after every minor accident, when he convalesces, what perfect opportunities there are for Grace and Erin to practise—extend upon even—their own renowned nursing skills, just like Florence Nightingale. Fleur is a terror.

Although Teddy has been challenged by his eyesight, his curious, wild spirit is what draws him to Izabella. She tells Grace she reminds him of a boy she used to know. Grace was part curious, part shocked when Izzie told her this, as it was a rarity for her to speak of her past. When Grace probed her, she clammed up.

Izzie seizes the chance to claim Teddy when she can, so, thinks Grace, she must have loved that little boy from her past. Izzie teaches Teddy how to throw a rubber ball through an old bicycle tyre hoop— attached at just the right height to a tree. Standing with his back to the target, he focuses his upside-down eyes then tosses the ball through his wide legs. Teddy helps her make cakes, and she teaches him to blow a gum-leaf so well, it makes the dogs come running every time.

'I can't believe how lucky we are, Charlie,' reflects Grace, one evening when they have some precious time together.

'He's a darling, that's for sure.'

'They *all* are. Erin mothers him terribly, do you notice?'

'She'll make a wonderful mother one day.'

'Yes, she will. Need to keep an eye on firecracker though. She'll lead him astray, if she has her way.'

'Partners in crime already, those two, despite the age difference,' Charlie smiles widely.

Early one morning, the stillness was broken by the rattle of a vehicle negotiating the dirt road to the homestead. Charlie opened the door to his parents, looking dishevelled and thinner but happy. They had come to meet their grandchildren.

Although Grace could see the initial hesitance in the children, especially Teddy, their grandparents soon won them over, to the point that, one week later, when they set off for the next instalment of their journey, there were tears all round, especially from the children.

Grace is feeling bigger, buoyed not only because she's added a couple of inches to her girth, but also from the visit. She only wishes her own parents could meet Teddy.

One cloudy day, at three-and-a-half years of age, Teddy decides he wants to paint. Only too happy to accommodate because her son is grouchy and bored, Grace uses sticky tape to attach large sheets of butchers' paper to the kitchen walls. She dresses him in an apron, gives him a big paintbrush, a pallet of paints and a glass of water for cleaning.

His mood changes. 'I want to draw you a picture. A beautiful one. With gardens and flowers and pink for you.'

'Well darling, that sounds just like a picture that Mummy would love. Remember to paint only on the paper; it's too precious to waste.'

She knows that leaving Teddy to his task is a little risky, but she believes in the worth of his creative expression, and that it's for him to learn some responsibility.

Grace takes herself to the lounge room, turns on the radiogram and listens to her favourite ABC program: 'Blue Hills'. She finds it hard to concentrate, hearing furniture being moved about in the kitchen, but she forces herself to stay where she is. When the program finishes, she rushes to the kitchen to see Teddy's masterpiece.

The boy has moved the table and chairs up against the wall. He has removed the pieces of paper and spread them on the floor, joining them with sticky tape to form a large rectangle that almost covers all available floor space.

Grace starts, her breath coming fast and shallow as she props herself against the doorway lest she collapse. Her sweaty hand moves to steady her jumping heart. It's her son's interpretation of Starry Night with all the colours and the sky and the hills and the rainbow, and Teddy smiles as he looks up from his artwork, holding his thick paintbrush in his left hand, reaching his other chubby hand out to usher his mother aboard.

He says, 'One day we'll ride the skies together, Mummy.'

Chapter Thirty-Three

1966

Guy Fawkes Night, or Cracker Night, as it is more commonly known. Erin and Fleur are nearly sixteen, Paolo is eighteen, Mario and Cappi are twenty—never too old for this ritual. Charlie has upheld it every year, much to the delight of the kids and pretend resignation of Grace. Having invited Marco's boys to the homestead this afternoon, Charlie brazenly left a huge box of firecrackers open on the lounge room floor. The sight of their dangerous and exotic treasure inspires the children to make plans, some of which get lost in the excitement.

Six-year-old Teddy has been assigned to Erin, but Grace keeps an eye on proceedings. Teddy has been the first to go for the most violent crackers, and the Double Bungers are swiftly snatched from his chubby grasp by Erin. She suitably gives him the less deadly task of poking sparklers into the lower section of the paw-paw tree, but she keeps a motherly eye on him in case he pokes anything else with them.

The kids drag the box outside along with some Redheads matches and empty previously gold-topped milk bottles Grace has pre-emptively left in the kitchen. The girls nimbly dissect the clusters of tiny crackers called Tom Thumbs, but some are left on their stringy vines for more whiz-bang explosions. Cappi and Mario attach Catherine Wheels to the lattice fence. Each child places one skyrocket into their assigned milk bottles. The excitement of wondering where they will land, and the next day finding something that has *flown*, is palpable.

Stage 1 complete, they build a six-foot Guy Fawkes from sticks, old shirts, pants, string, newspaper and straw. Far from pleased at his completion, he appears sceptical on his perch. Nightfall and the poor little bugger is lit. Gloriously haloed in sparks and smoke, he appears almost biblical as he melts and shrivels, rapidly losing his clothes and more crushingly, his dignity. Adding further embarrassment to his predicament, the boys have thrown some sheets of Tom Thumbs onto his fiery grave and he flinches with the quick succession of each determined pop. Teddy wonders out loud how many Tom Thumbs it would take to kill a person, or a guinea pig, his brow furrowed deep with worry.

They ceremoniously light their skyrockets which whistle as they fly haphazardly across the valley. Catherine Wheels whirl their pretty rainbows into the air. The lower half of the paw-paw tree looks impressive.

When Grace retires to bed with a headache, the kids beg Charlie to let them go to the river. He acquiesces—thrilled by the children's excitement. He gives Erin a strict instruction to look after her little brother.

Saving the best until last, the kids smuggle several Double Bungers to the river. They set off three on land. But Marco's boys know underwater explosions are so much more satisfactory than the land variety. Fleur goes first, her fingers trembling as she lights a cracker and quickly throws it into the river, resulting in a dull boom and rumbling whirlpool. Paolo reckons if Fleur can, so can he and achieves a similar explosion. When exploded, thick smoke and the waft of gunpowder remain in their wake. Teddy says he is concerned about all the shell- shocked fish down there, biting his nails to the quick. He is ignored. At Erin's request, Cappi lights her cracker but she panics and throws the squib on the ground—its loud, bright blast causing her to scream. Cappi guffaws and offers her another, which he again lights, dangerously prolonging the hand contact. The couple appear mesmerised by the reflected glow in one another's eyes. Just in time, Erin gives a forceful throw, banishing her cracker to the river. It just reaches the water before it explodes. Mario and Cappi have more elaborate plans. Bending their crackers in half to almost breaking point, and holding the ends, they ignite the bursting-with-gunpowder middles. Shards of golden sparks erupt from their mangled weapons which they throw away just in time.

Grace smells gunpowder. All she hears of the festivities are three loud bangs. Double bungers, for sure. The explosions make her jump. Each blast infuses in her a terror that once hung thick and stagnant in the air somewhere around their property. Somewhere nearby, she knows it. It's the same feeling of dread she experienced when she heard Plasticine Man's door knocks, when she was startled by the screen explosions while watching *Rebecca*. More stark reminders of gunshots. But it was more than gunshots all along, wasn't it? Something more sinister ...

The death she dealt with during her nursing years never felt like this, never really made her feel anything much but relief if she was honest with herself. This is palpable. It has substance. It is the sound, smell and feel of death.

The following morning, the children roam the paddocks, trawling for spent skyrockets. Teddy worries out loud whether sheep may have been stabbed when the spears crashed down to earth the previous night. Fleur puts her arm around him and reassures him otherwise. Erin and Cappi linger in one of the paddocks for a long time, engrossed in each other's company.

'Are you two *coming*?' shouts Paolo as all but Erin and Cappi make their way back to the main house with their prizes.

'Go ahead!' yells Cappi, a little too quickly. Erin looks shocked, then shyly turns away from the boy.

Fleur dawdles towards the house, occasionally kicking up stones, cow pats, tumbleweeds, dirt—unwilling for them to get away with anything they may plan. When convinced she's out of their sight, she hides behind a large tree and peeks as they approach.

When they go in for the kiss, Fleur runs towards them, chanting: 'Erin and Cappi sitting in a tree k-i-s-s-i-n-g.'

Erin bows her head and lumbers back to the house, leaving a lost-looking Cappi to try to compose himself. Erin refuses to speak to her sister for the remainder of the day.

Chapter Thirty-Four

1967

The family sit uncomfortably in the Chev truck on the drive to church, apart from Izabella who never attends. Their discomfort is exacerbated because the road—snaking with the windy river—is comprised of pebbles. They cross the archaic sandstone bridge: a familiar landmark on and around which the children have explored extensively. Its sight momentarily distracts them from the perpetual rocking of the car—as each child silently recalls the adventurous times they have shared there.

Determinedly armed with makeshift tree branch rods, the children have caught bass and yabbies from the stoical old structure. The fishing ultimately failing—jam jars have become collection chambers under the bridge for tadpoles, frogs, dragonflies and fish.

Once they sighted a death adder slithering along the muddy riverbank, causing them all to flee screaming. Weeks prior to this sighting, Fleur had skimmed a whip snake hiding in one of the farm's orange trees when she was picking fruit. The latest reptilian appearance prompted her to warn her siblings of the evil in the whip snake's gaze, its tiny forked tongue, that unlike a whip snake, a death adder is *deadly*. As Fleur's own eyes glinted menacingly, flicking her tongue towards Teddy who recoiled as though he was about to be bitten.

When the river runs low, as it has been lately, they take their sieves—Grace's old throwaway kitchen strainers—in search of gold.

So far, the quest has failed. Today in the back-cargo tray, the kids make big plans to rectify the situation. Grace can see them in the side-view mirror and with windows down she can hear every word; she trusts she will know when to pounce.

Grace watches Fleur as she nudges her sister and says under her breath, 'Okay, so I reckon we should try along the riverbed near Robinson's land. We haven't been there before, and I doubt anyone else has either.'

'Perhaps there's a reason for that?' counters Erin, rolling her eyes, picking up and continuing the whispering cue.

Grace begins to twitch, as does Fleur. 'Don't you get it? Untouched land. Do you have any idea of what we might find?'

'That's exactly what I'm worried about, Fleur, not knowing what we may find.' Puts her sister in her place.

'It's just a bunch of doughy old cows and bulls. How could you be scared of them?'

'Don't be silly, I'm not scared of common old cattle. It's the unknown I'm worried about, and something that *is* known. Old Robinson's got a gun, and not just a gun but a semi-automatic machine gun! I've heard he's shot people and not only that, he shoots anything that moves. It wouldn't be a smart idea to go there at all,' warns Erin.

'Must you always be so, so old?'

Erin engrosses herself in trying to make out detail in the smudge of bush outside the truck.

Teddy, slow on the uptake today, yells: 'Wow! Can we go see the gun?'

Grace decides to move, twisting around to stare them down.

'No! I don't want any of you going near that place, and in fact, I don't want you to go near *anyone's* private property. Teddy, you need to know that not everyone is kind like your father. There are bad people out there, and when they have guns, well, goodness knows what can happen.'

She's heard nothing but worrying information about Len Robinson. Years ago, Charlie told her about Robinson having discovered some males fishing the river from his land, at a time before he turned his property into a small wheat farm. Apparently, he just went crazy and started shooting. Got all three of them. Someone said they were gypsies of sorts. No-one originally reported it; the Alton's opposite neighbours said they heard shots but thought Robinson had been felling pig or 'roo. If they suspected otherwise, they kept it to themselves, perhaps in fear of Robinson's retribution.

Several days after the shooting, some poor bugger was swimming downstream and came across one of the bloated bodies, floating amongst the alligator weed. A search party found the other two bodies—one, a child—upstream, not far from the old bloke's land. No charges were laid; it was widely known that the police superintendent was related to Robinson.

She remembers a follow-up story from Charlie a few years ago. 'You wouldn't credit it Grace, but Len Robinson is back employing workers now, has been for a while now, and I use the word *employing* loosely.'

'What? How can the authorities allow that? How can he be trusted after that terrible time? My God, Charlie, he killed those people.'

'It's criminal, I know. Robinson said he had been scarred by the mishap that happened on his land. Says he doesn't want anyone feeling it's an unsafe place. Says he feels he *owes* them. He may feel that way but he doesn't show it. I've heard he's made his workers build their own dwellings out of scrap metal and canvas. Gives them just enough supplies to keep them out of mischief. He might not even be paying them any money, that's what I've been told anyway. Reminds me of the 'canvas and tin' stations up north.'

'What a rotter. How on earth does he get away with it?'

'Friends in the right places, I expect.'

'I can't seem to get over what he's done in the past. It's horrific.'

'Just let it be, Grace. Nothing we can do for those poor buggers anymore.'

'So, we just let it go and never mention it?'

'It's for the best. The last thing we need is for that old bastard to be after us.'

Grace knew Charlie was probably right not wanting to antagonise Robinson. Despite his bravado, Charlie is a pacifist who stews over any confrontation. But she couldn't stop her flush of anger, and she knows she will always prefer action to any form of injustice.

'Has he employed Aborigines?'

'A few, I think.'

'Most can speak English now, right Charlie?'

'Probably, yes.'

'How did they learn it?' She knew the answer.

'Years ago, it was probably from the missions, where they lived after they were removed from their parents. They were schooled there. Lots of them go to regular school now, don't they?'

'I'll bet that in so-called regular schools they'd be segregated, treated differently to white kids. And why are our schools *regular* anyway? What about *their* languages? I wonder if any of those mission kids remember their birth language, or even speak it now.'

'Maybe. Maybe not. I don't know, Grace.'

'At least they can vote now, not only if they served in the forces, like used to be the case. Didn't all of Australia's citizens always deserve a chance to vote?'

'I guess. I don't know. Stone the crows! Why don't you ask the pollies?'

'The politicians? Why didn't the pollies ask them? Perhaps they may even have liked a say in the running of the country we took from them.'

'We didn't take it. We *share* it with them.' Charlie raised his brow, sarcasm apparent.

'Oh yes, they want Australia's first people to assimilate, don't they? If you can't beat 'em, join 'em, but only if it is on our terms. Dog-tag the ones they think may be of use. Harking back to the war, do you realise that thousands, of Aboriginal men volunteered to serve in World War II, and they even fought in the first war at Gallipoli? Trackers served as far back as the Boer War. My dad told me all this. And another thing, they certainly didn't return to accolades.'

'At least they got to vote,' he shot her a wry smile.

'Stop it, Charlie. Dad said when some of his mates enlisted, they had to say they were Maori or some such—denouncing their Aboriginality.

When they returned from war, they couldn't get war pensions. Do they still get chased out of RSLs—as if they were never soldiers, never even involved? Returned Services League of Australia my foot. And imagine coming home to Australia from war to find your children had been taken? It's so unfair.'

After a silence, Charlie offered, 'Surely the government has always had good intentions, don't you think? I really hope so. You know we may think differently to many mainstream Aussies, don't you Grace?'

'Perhaps. I hope not. Perhaps people just don't know the truth,' she replied. 'But if it's true that people don't care… Well, I've never been one for the masses, anyhow.' She shot him a slim grin.

Obviously stewing, Teddy eventually asks, 'Is Mr Robinson a bad man, Mummy?'

Grace tries to sound in control. 'I'm sure he has some good qualities, everyone does. But I don't want any of you going near enough to his land to find out one way or another. When people think they're being trespassed upon, well, they sometimes shoot first and ask questions later. Shoot them dead!' Her voice betrays her.

Grace suddenly thinks back to the time Plasticine Man came to her room, the three gunshot door knocks, the explosions in *Rebecca*, and the detonated double-bungers that affected her so acutely on Cracker Night. It was Robinson shooting those innocent people! She just knows it.

'But if a person is shoot dead, how can they answer questions?' asks Teddy.

'Shot. Well yes, that's right.' Flustered. 'Now, let's just have a think about what we're going to pray about today.'

That shuts them up, momentarily. But Fleur and Teddy dart their little eyes at one another knowingly. Fleur must realise Teddy is keen, and Grace just knows she'll make sure he won't forget about it.

A rare silence befalls the captive passengers as the Chev truck continues to traverse the riverbed, and Teddy takes a good look at the huge gums and paperbarks reflected near perfectly in the still water. The reflections make the trees appear to have doubled in height. Due to the long years of drought, the water depth has fallen and what is left is near transparent on the surface due to lack of agitation. As Teddy looks down into the water, Grace imagines that he's wondering if there's another world under there, and are those bird reflections looking up, or looking down on them? Grace knows Teddy's thoughts because she's wondering about it, too.

Chapter Thirty-Five

Summer has hit early. The humidity is high and so are Erin and Cappi, especially the boy, who has been finding feeble excuses to see Erin whenever he can lately. But Erin too is becoming captivated by the boy with the piercing eyes and dimples that appear either side of his mouth when he smiles, like a movie star. And his voice? So rich and exotic. Most of all, she's flattered by his attention, finding it novel. They sit together outside on the wrought iron bench.

'*Ciao, mi chiamo* Cappi. That means, Hi, my name is Cappi. Now you try.'

'*Ciao*, um, I've forgotten.' She's flustered by his deep voice, his close proximity.

'*Mi chiamo.*'

'*Me chiarmo.*'

'*Mi chiamo* Cappi.'

'*Mi chiamo* Erin.'

'*Perfetto!*' He smiles, giving a satisfied sigh.

'*Perfetto!*'

'You will soon be a true Italian girl!'

'I think my parents may have something to say about that.'

'Why? Don't you think we Italians are good enough for you precious little Altons?' Erin wonders why he has said this with so much venom.

'Hmm, let me think about that. Well now, come to think of it, you *are* merely hired help.'

He looks away, sniffs, and Erin wonders if he's hurt by her careless, cutting words that she covered with a thin air of flippancy. When he turns back to her, her head is bowed. She's realised the effect her words have had on him, but also the meaning she couldn't even hide from herself.

'Oh, come on Cappi. You know you'll always be my friend.'

'Your humble servant Cappi. Is that it?'

'You're not so humble.' Punches him in the arm, trying to cheer him up. If she's true to herself, she could easily let him be more than just a friend.

He grabs her and kisses her longer and harder than necessary. Erin suspects the kiss was a way to get his point across, vent his anger. Is he wondering if she'll ever respect him enough? Hoping that one fine day she'll see the way it's meant to pan out?

'Hu-hum!' Fleur announces loudly, then clears her throat. Startled, Erin and Cappi turn to face the girl who has suddenly appeared directly behind the bench on which the pair are huddled tightly.

'Well, well, just look at you two lovebirds. Hey Cappi, you have lipstick all over your mouth,' Fleur announces as Cappi uses his hankie to wipe away the invisible make-up.

'Ha, got ya! All I have to say is: First comes love, then comes marriage, then comes Erin with a baby carriage.' Fleur has performed her chant with her hands firmly over her hips, wiggling them to the beat. Does she realise how ridiculous she's being? How ridiculous she looks? She's acting like a child.

'Oh, GROW UP!' Erin glares at her sister, embarrassed by her, hoping one day she'll simply vanish off the face of the Earth.

Fleur sneaks into Teddy's room at 5am, sits on his bed. He groans as she digs her index finger into his ribs.

'Wake up, Teddy.'

'Huh? What?' he says loudly, rubbing his eyes, pivoting his little fists.

Fleur places her right index finger to her lips. 'Shush. Don't wake the others.'

Teddy sits straight up in his bed, wide-eyed and excited now. Fleur notices how cute he looks in his flannelette pyjamas with the sailing boats on them.

'What are you doing, Fleur?' He yawns, then smiles and blinks.

'How would you like to go on a little adventure with me?'

Teddy becomes animated, clapping his hands. 'Yay! To find treasure?'

'Yep—lots of treasure. Here, I'll help you get dressed. There's just one thing you must promise me—that you won't go near the water. Promise?'

'Yep.'

'Okay. Let's get you ready.' Fleur jumps off the bed. 'Now, where are your boots?'

'I want my car. I'm not going without my car,' Teddy states, grabbing the little blue toy from under his pillow and pushing it into his pocket.

Soon they are making their way towards the river, to the secret place Fleur rationalises has been forbidden to them for way too long.

Chapter Thirty-Six

Late 1967

It sapped Grace's strength getting the family ready for church this morning. And she understood that the terror and sadness she had experienced the previous night would remain with her for the rest of the day.

She had slept fitfully. When she finally dosed off around four in the morning, the dreams started. The usual rollercoaster type had her in full flight until they darkened into something more sinister. She knew it was night because it was dark, and the skies were full of stars, many stars. Suddenly, and very curiously, they all started moving in unison, to form an arc directly above her head. All she could think of was that this was a very ungodly move. Then stars started to drip down upon her. The gentleness of their descent was deceptive; they were burning—fiery red rock missiles that turned the ground molten as they landed. They would surely melt holes in her if they struck her body. Ineffectually ducking and dodging, she knew it would be her turn to be hit soon.

The heat has been ruthlessly building since sunrise, resulting in a tired and listless family craving cold drinks with ice and longing for no more exercise than what's involved in lounging under the electric ceiling fans. The price tag for these recent luxurious purchases was exorbitant, taking Charlie several weeks of stewing before committing his wallet. He's had them installed in the lounge room and bedrooms. They've had great results in keeping the children home, especially when the destination is unpopular, such as on a day like today. Grace knows the church is lacking in such luxuries and knows the children are aware of this. But despite the pleas of protest, she can't believe she's managed to cajole her children here this morning.

The only thing she's feeling chuffed about is the transfer which hasn't involved any manual handling, not that she's ever been hands-on with any of them in a pushy way, but the heat is making her cranky and today's manoeuvre could easily have pushed her to the brink of some serious rough stuff. A longing to pray for her family, and of course for the elusive rain, has drawn her to church, and she's advised her children to echo her prayers, believing the adage of safety in numbers.

The crushing heat equates a church half full. The sanctimonious, therefore forgiven ones have stayed home, legitimising their absences as they legitimise everything they do. Those who aren't sure, including the Altons, have dragged themselves here, and they're secretly hoping to score some extra Brownie points being in church on a stinker of a day like today. Murphy seems to know about this and is looking decisively petulant. Someone has fully opened all the windows, but the result is fruitless—no air circulation whatsoever.

The children shuffle around as their sweaty backsides make wet patches on the pews. Grace tries not to shuffle around—she's stuck to the seat anyway—but she finds the stillness excruciating. As if a small shift in position would have any bearing on the heat anyway, but she's a little more animated than she would like. She's still embarrassed after her trip on the welcome mat that unceremoniously announced her entrance to the aisle, turning a 'shit' into a more respectable, but unconvincing and loud, 'Shall we sit here, children?'. This outburst, along with its corresponding near somersault resulted in a collective turn of heads in her direction, to Grace's horror.

Charlie has wisely opted out this morning, telling Grace he'll be de-leafing guttering in preparation for the impending rain. They'll be pleased to get some clean water into the water tanks. She knows he'll lie for a while under the fans. Doesn't blame him. But Charlie is always glad for an excuse to wag church; he finds Murphy ridiculous.

She remembers recently when he called the minister 'The Munster', after Herman Munster from the telly. She has a private giggle over this; his bulbous forehead and awkward gait would enable him to convincingly body double Frankenstein's monster, too. Just add a couple of bolts and hey presto. But she'd never tell the children; their mimicry in church would be unbearable.

Ethel the organist is hitting more wrong notes than usual—her sweaty fingers sliding off the ivory; all is forgiven in this heat. Ignoring each wonky faux pas, the congregation choruses about the Lord God making all things bright and beautiful. Fleur appears unconvinced, blasé; she's seen ugliness, or at least heard of it. She covers her mouth in a yawn, then uses her pincers to grab hold of the teeth-secured chewing gum and artfully extracts a long strand. Her tongue performs some top-notch circumnavigations as she sucks it back in before another go. Grace darts her as ferocious a look as she can muster, mouthing a perfect *No* to her incorrigible daughter. *Of all things, chewing gum!* Teddy looks on, probably wishing Fleur would sneak him a packet of the fresh stuff. She pokes her tongue at him and—realising he's got Buckley's—frowns, drops his head and continues to fiddle with the little blue Matchbox car hidden in his pocket.

The congregation is producing a rancid atmosphere of bodily fluids. Wheezes and coughs come thick and fast from Erin. Murphy is a human sprinkler, sweating up a disgusting storm in a ray of sunlight beaming from an open window, spray dispersing with every move. Either enjoying himself or trying to rid his sweat, he shakes his body in some strange dance with every word. His spiel today focuses on famines and pestilences and great signs from Heaven.

Grace can feel the signs from both Heaven and Earth acutely today, some for reasons she cannot place. She's twitchy and thick in the head and fears it's not just the humidity that's getting to her. Perhaps it's *beyond*, and if so, what will it reveal? She shudders, wiping her brow for the umpteenth time.

All at once she feels like an outsider, like how a refugee must she supposes—an immigrant thrust into an inhospitable landscape. Out of place. Sometimes Grace wonders how anyone could choose to live in Australia. Wonders why she was originally excited about coming to Charlie's farm. She now knows this area as a place that too acutely showcases the continent's often-troublesome moods.

Did Izzie actually choose to come to Australia, of all countries, in all its aridity? Was she warned about its harsh conditions? Does she, like Grace, hate this country on days like today?

The eyes of both mother and daughters are inexplicably drawn towards the teenage altar boy sitting to the side of the pulpit who is staring at the three of them. Judging by the length of his legs, he's tall. Handsome and brooding, blue-tinged skin pale like wax. Deep red hair. Eyes fit to burn holes in a person. She's seen him before. Having found their reciprocating target, the girls nudge one another, stifling giggles. Grace, too, is spellbound. Not stunned by his good looks, but because from her perspective, on a shelf behind him sit two tall lit candles—limp and bending away from one another in the heat—and they appear to be growing from either side of his head. Glowing red not only from their candle wicks, it illuminates his entire countenance. Grace feels as though she's staring at the devil himself.

Shaking from the encounter, Grace breaks his spell by directing the girls to the benediction. When Murphy finally finishes the reading, Grace sighs, and unceremoniously shuffles her brood outside—her haste making them almost cheer. Outside Charlie pulls up in the Chev truck, ready to whisk them home, and Grace feels relief like she's barely felt before.

The wet human heaps fall into the vehicle. Charlie would be glad he didn't have to wait for them in the heat, which he sometimes must if Grace gets caught by one of the parishioners. She's so hot and fed up, she doesn't even greet Charlie. She does notice he's dirty and sweaty, hopes he's been working. He gives the Chev truck a deliberate revving as they take off, showering a chatty Murphy and some elderly ladies in a shock of dust. Grace doesn't have the strength to chastise him, besides, she secretly approves. Also, it hasn't been a pleasant morning and she doesn't want to jinx the afternoon.

Sitting in the cargo tray, Fleur has fashioned a paper plane from her hymn sheet and is threatening to poke it into Teddy's good eye. Erin the pacifist sits in the middle, silent as usual, but she looks ready to burst. Grace knows she's been feeling unwell, too, which wouldn't help her mood.

'Mum! Fleur wants to hurt us with her plane!' yells Erin.

'Fleur, for goodness sake put that thing away,' pleads Grace. She keeps an eye on them through the open windows of the cab.

Complying, but not without with a huge huff, Fleur screws up the paper and tosses it onto the floor, where she sits on it to prevent it from blowing away. The little sardines settle down to a game of paper, scissors, rock: a game they've modified for the three of them, however the rules and outcomes are never the same, and often neither amicable nor fair. When the volume ultimately accelerates, Grace is quick to pull them up, fearing the ruckus will exacerbate Erin's asthma.

Charlie tries to lighten the mood with some conversation, a rarity for him when driving.

'Radio's saying we've got a whopper of a storm coming. You'll all be pleased to know that I've worked up a storm myself this morning. The gutters are now freed up and I got that dirty rotten gum branch near the house. Can't trust those gums for quids.'

'Yay Dad,' echo less than enthusiastic voices from the back.

'That's marvellous dear. Well done,' Grace manages before dosing off.

Upon arriving home, Grace is awakened by her own puzzled sigh actually having slept in the bumpy old truck, or was it the gentle Charlie nudge? Drags herself out of the car, as do the others. On cue, before heading to the house, the family stands staring at the dark western skies, anticipation mixing with trepidation. Accompanied by the mellifluous call of a whip bird are Erin's louder, rattly wheezes—her achingly tuneful notes giving the bird a run for its money.

'Yep, it's going to be a big one,' says Charlie, rubbing his hands together in expectation of something big happening, breaking the trance.

'You really must see to that rattly chest, Erin,' says Grace, ignoring her husband.

The gaudy allure of faux toffee sap glistens on nearby gums, playing tricks with Grace's mind and hungry tummy. Staring at those tall, bleeding trees, Grace's mouth starts watering as she dreams of lollies. Realises everyone must be hungry.

One tree is crying, incessantly—the eucalypt with gnarly, twisted branches. The family calls it, predictably, the crying tree. The sporadic rain from the previous few days has caused water to gather in its canopy, and now it spills from every branch. *But it didn't rain that much, did it?* Grace wonders if it's feeling sad and unable to buck itself up, or if something darker lurks in its show.

The family look insignificant on the vast, wide landscape—little specks on the long brown plains that they are. Insignificant perhaps in the scheme of things, but Grace knows they're each holding onto so much hope, for one another, for their livestock and property, in hope the upcoming weather event will signal a break in the drought the farm has suffered nine years, since 1958. Despite the showers over the last few days, a storm is what they really need. The languor crushes in until it is almost unbearable. Grace sees Erin trying to draw breath into her constricted air passages. Grace fears that soon there may not be enough air in the atmosphere for Erin to breathe at all.

The signs of a storm are all around them. Fluffy spun-sugar cumulus clouds expand rapidly, rising like a soufflé in a hot oven, just about rubbing out the remainder of blue sky. Organisms twitch in anticipation. Cicadas buzz earlier than usual in the stifling heat. Storm birds pave the way for the afternoon performance—nothing accidental about their tuneful peal.

Chapter Thirty-Seven

Grace is first to break the spell and move towards the kitchen. The old door has buckled with expansion from the humidity and protests loudly as Charlie pulls and pushes it back and forth, trying to open it. Even the house is complaining, she thinks grimly. Once inside, Charlie rushes to the shower, while the kids move to their bedrooms.

Grace scans the kitchen, thinking of the life moments to which it has been privy, as though today is momentous somehow. How many Saturday roasts has it seen? Memories of the family sitting around the old pink laminated table flood her psyche. How many games of Scrabble and Monopoly have there been, bringing them all together in funny little competitive groups? Laughing, shouting, challenging, loving.

Izabella must be in her room as the door is closed. She often retreats for hours at a time—although when she works, she works. Grace imagines she's collecting herself for the next onslaught of Altons.

Grace knows she should be excited about the storm—because it may mean much-needed downpours of rain—but she's rattled. In the still kitchen, Grace sights rows of determined ants scanning the wall. Ants: a sure sign of rain.

These little insect workers ritually emerge from, and return to, a small hole between wall and benchtop. As they scurry along on through the wall, some carry giant boulders of food on their comically athletic, teeny-tiny backs. Fretfully, Grace gives them an excessive dousing of Mortein insect killer before gathering them up in tissues and binning them. The strange clove-like tang of squashed ants' melds with the fly spray, lingering like death in the thick atmosphere. She follows up the mass slaughter with a good rinse of the benchtop.

The big human worker washes and dries her hands, then swiftly further busies herself making ham salads and lemonade. Before church this morning, she picked a pink protea from the garden, and it now sits displayed in a vase of water in the centre of the food-and-drink-laden table. The routine, which she's performed almost manically, has failed to shake her unease.

'Lunch is ready! Izzie dear, come join us at the table for lunch!' she yells louder than necessary, and the hungry family comes charging in, including Izzie.

Charlie is clean and dons' fresh clothes. Still handsome. But tiredness and cares show as deep wrinkles, as two vertical indentations of about an inch long between his eyebrows. To Grace, they seem to be caving in more so these days—worry lines, giving him a slight grimace. Wonders why he feels he must take them on— the world's worries. When they're all seated, grace is said collectively before tucking in: 'For what we are about to receive, may the Lord make us truly thankful. Amen.'

Grace glances at Izzie, her little head atop her white uniform. Her hands are tiny, and Grace is drawn to the callouses on her fingers— hard and rough-looking.

'Izzie, I noticed you moved all the pot plants from outside. Where did you put them?'

'In the shed. The storm would have taken them.'

Grace shudders. The storm would have taken them; she fears there's a darker meaning hidden in those words. She's being ridiculous.

'That's very good of you, Izzie. Now we just have to batten down the hatches and hold on!' Her attempt at mood lightening sounds foreboding.

Grace reaches for her daughter's hand which is cold to the touch, and a sneaky check of her pulse reveals it racing. Could be the result of the medication. PRN: take whenever necessary—a memory from her nursing days. She wonders why the medicine is not helping. Erin's asthma has been playing up all morning, which is another reason for

Grace's tetchy mood.

'Have you had your inhaler, Erin?'

'Yes Ma,' comes the dutiful reply in high, then low, pitch. Frustration evident.

'Since church?'

'Yes, of course. I don't actually enjoy being sick, you know.' Grace surveys her daughter with an objective eye, a medical eye. Still wheezing. She's picking at her food. Her face has assumed a pallid appearance and there is some blueness to her lips; not quite cyanosed but closer to it than she would like. Ever so gently, Grace lifts a strand of lank hair from covering Erin's eye, hooks it behind her ear. This ostensible move reveals her forehead to be cold. Grace sees and feels beads of sweat gathered there. Admittedly all the family are sweaty, but she's worried about her daughter.

'I think you should rest this afternoon, dear.'

'I'm planning to, Mum, if I manage to get any rest with this storm coming,' says Erin.

Grace is somewhat, but not fully, relieved.

After lunch, all but Grace retire to their rooms for a lie-down. Still het up, alone in the kitchen, Grace paces the room, rationalising her mood as due to the impending storm. A headache has now shown itself, so she takes a couple of Aspros. With more energy to burn, she sets to work cleaning the large kitchen windows, on both sides, inside and out. The others may be resting, but Grace is on autopilot. No rest for the wicked, she thinks glibly. She frantically rubs the windows with methylated spirits and a rag, until they gleam. Throughout this process, Grace tells herself the rain will undo her hard work, but she doesn't care. Hoping for a glimmer of an endorphin rush, she views this work as an outlet from her dark mood, one she can't shake. When finished, she sits at the table sipping a cup of tea, surveying her work.

Cup in hand, she walks to the window and places it in the sink. Outside the birds are chirping up a frenzy, frightened of the approaching storm, looking for shelter. She searches but can't see them, until suddenly a flock of welcome swallows darts perilously close to the house. Grace sees a small grey shadow heading towards her and automatically ducks in synchronisation as *smack*, a bird flies straight into the window pane. Stillness. Grace shuts her eyes, gripping the sink until her knuckles whiten. Eventually, she loosens them and forces herself to look through the window to the bird lying still in the dirt outside. Adrenaline competes with the drag of tears as she fills a glass with water, runs out the door, down three steps and splashes the liquid over the bird. It doesn't budge.

'Please let it be shock, please,' she mumbles.

Crouching down and not even feeling her now arthritic legs, Grace carefully picks up and cradles the tiny warm body. Its beak is stuck open. Looks like the little cork Punch doll she used to play with, and she remembers how her hand worked the mechanism to open and shut the mouth. She broke the lever, its mouth doomed forever to hang slack, suddenly appearing ghastly and never to be played with again. A trace of scarlet blood oozes from the bird's yellow beak.

'Oh no, forgive me, I'm so sorry!' Grace yells to the universe and collapses in heaving sobs onto the dusty ground. 'Dear little thing. My poor darling,' she whispers to the dirt.

Recovering enough to rise, she carries the dead bird and buries it under a tree. She knows full well that the dandelion she has placed on top of the upset dirt will be blown off as soon as the wind picks up. A token. The family will remain unaware of what has happened; Grace fears disclosure will jinx any chance of the day improving, fears the dark side of the always sibylline *beyond* will join the tribulation of this cathartic day.

Chapter Thirty-Eight

Erin has been jerking around on her bed, unable to get comfortable and relax. Half an hour ago, she inhaled another dose of nasty white powder from a punctured capsule, hoping it would stop the wheeze, but it hasn't. As usual, the white grit stuck to her throat on the way down, leaving a bitter aftertaste. Despite being loath to lie supine— lying on her back makes it twice as hard to draw a decent breath— her three pillows have diminished to one, and she lies staring at the ceiling. Having just dosed off she's awakened by a howling rush of wind followed by a deafening clap of thunder.

Charlie calls to the family. The sounds of windows slamming shut soon follow. Groggily, Erin pulls herself up and helps Fleur shut the bedroom window. As the girl's peer through the glass, another loud rumble of thunder vibrates the house. Simultaneously, a blinding snake of lightning cuts right through a nearby tree, blasting off a long section of its trunk to land somewhere in the yard—they can't see where but they see the wound. Teddy suddenly appears at the doorway and huddles up on Erin's bed, all nerves, yet grinning deliriously, devouring the unpredictable antics of the thunderstorm after an uneventful churchy Sunday morning.

The rain starts with slow plops of bulbous raindrops. The pace rapidly intensifies. After an hour of driving rain, ferocious thunder and lightning bright enough to illuminate a city, the gusty winds suddenly still, leaving only a gentle trickle of water dripping from the roof.

Erin opens her window for a clearer perspective, hoping to inhale some fresh air through her narrow air passages, fill her crumpled lungs. What strikes her most is the sudden vividness of nature's star-bright hues. The rain has washed away the grim blanket of atmospheric dust, exposing a clarity of colour to rival a Fauve's palette. The brazen sun casts luminous patina in crazy patterns on eucalypts against the retreating black sky. Pitted in deep pockmarks, the trunks of gums shine soft like green satin. Leaves glisten a little too fiercely—tiny light-filled canoes floating against a sea of pale washed-out sky. It could all be garish if it wasn't so beautiful. Steam rises from the sated earth. Distant thunder growls its last hurrah. Currawongs, storm birds and whip birds crack the high notes, competing for boss status, alerting the next world across the plains and far hills of what is approaching.

The back door slams. Erin knows her parents will be checking out back for damage and distressed livestock. The sun shines as though nothing has happened, but the adults won't be convinced; they're no doubt worrying about what they'll find.

Fleur and Teddy crave some action—a few fallen trees for them to climb over and stir up, or best yet, hailstones to toss. But there's been no hail, to their disappointment. Around the children, the petrichor casts its spell.

'Let's go to the river!' shouts Fleur louder than necessary to get her point across. 'We can watch it rushing.'

'To the river, to the river. Yes, we must!' shouts Teddy.

Erin coughs and wheezes in response.

Naturally, Fleur has launched this plot, knowing she doesn't have to try hard to snare her little brother. She gives a satisfied smile as he nods and grins, wide-eyed in anticipation.

'I don't think it's a good idea,' states Erin. 'It will be too powerful.'

'Well, we can go to Robinson's land,' suggests Fleur. 'The river has never broken its banks *there*.'

'Yeah, that's right, *never* broken its banks *there*,' parrots Teddy.

'Oh, and what if old Robinson is on the war path with his gun?' asks Erin.

'Well, we'll just tell him that some of our sheep have disappeared.

They may have.' says Fleur, surveying Erin's frown. 'Oh, come on Sis, come on.' She keeps trying. Broken record. 'It'll be fun, and we'll be back before Mum and Dad even realise we've been out.'

'Look, I'm really sick, okay? I don't think I can do it.' Erin is almost crying, choking on the words, panting. She feels she must look as pale as a ghost.

'Well, alright,' says Fleur. 'You stay here. We'll go. We're big and bad enough not to let anything happen to us, aren't we Ted?'

'You bet!' exclaims Teddy, looking from sister to sister as though worried he's neither big nor bad.

'Just don't dawdle, especially not around here, not around the house. You can look for the bits of exploded tree another time. We're on a mission, remember.'

'Like soldiers,' says Teddy, smiling, missing teeth.

'Pow, pow!' Fleur shoots her pretend gun at her brother who clutches his chest, falling to the bed.

Erin worries about going but knows nothing will stop them, and they will need supervision.

'I'm coming,' she whispers.

'Are you sure? You can always come back if you're too sick,' offers Fleur.

With this tenuous consensus, they don coats and boots and creep out the front door into the eerie aftermath of the storm.

'We all have to look after each other, okay?' says Erin. 'Everyone has to return safe and sound.'

Fleur and Teddy nod gravely, trying to look suitably responsible, then exchange cheeky grins. Erin is not happy.

Soft pink shimmers in the breaking sunlight. One fleshed-out boy of seven. Two sixteen-year-old girls attempt to take the reins of their slightly unfocused brother. Together they slop their way across the muddy ground and undergrowth towards the crumbly wet bank, the roar of water guiding them. The Europa River seems to have greedily slurped its jumbo- sized drink and now has indigestion; Fleur hears its gurgles just above Erin's wheezes.

Teddy pauses for the umpteenth time, purses fat red lips and blows another dandelion, scattering mini jet-propelled parachuted soldiers across the battlefield. Fleur has no idea how the delicate flowers could have survived the storm, or are these newly sprouted? Seems impossible, but the rate of new growth after rain always astounds the family.

'Did ya see them fly? Bombs away!' announces Teddy.

Erin looks pleased for the distraction. She stops and bends double.

'He needs a bomb under *him*,' mutters Fleur. 'For goodness sake Teddy, get a move on.' She yanks his arm harder than intended, resulting in a yelp then crumpled collection of boy limbs. He starts to cry and dribble as he rolls around on the ground holding his arm.

'Stupid girl! I *hate* you. I'm telling Mum!'

Fleur knows the threat won't eventuate. She prompts, 'Aw, come on silly sausage. You'll survive.'

Both girls help their little brother to his feet as he gives a whimper, wiping snot from his face. Erin doesn't bother chastising her culpable sister.

A murder of crows creates a cryptic line-up on a telephone wire. As the children approach, the flock alights, all but one. The rogue bird has made eye contact with Teddy. Black on blue death stare causes Teddy to stop, mesmerised. It opens its beak and produces a nasty gurgling click, then spasmodically turns its head to indicate a rainbow across the river. Teddy picks up its cue and spots the ridiculously colourful arc spanning the sky; its pull is magnetic.

Fleur decides to ignore this, striding with purpose towards the rushing river. Erin walks slowly behind, struggling.

'Fleur!' Erin's gravelly voice.

Fleur turns, walks back to her sister, soon followed by Teddy.

'Look, I have to sit down here,' Erin drops her body to the ground, butting her back against a wet tree trunk. Not the ideal position for inflating her lungs, but exhaustion overtakes her.

Fleur doesn't like the look of her sister; Erin is hunched over, and

Fleur sees her thin grey fingers sticking out like dead sticks from her coat sleeves. She suddenly has a flash of a skeleton propped against a tree, and shudders.

'Just don't be long, okay?' Erin says, gasping for air. 'And Fleur … look after Teddy.'

Chapter Thirty-Nine

The afternoon before the storm, Marco was called to herd the new lambers and lambs into the livestock shed. He worked on horseback, surrounded by two yapping, itchy collies, ever-ready for the thrill of the herd. It was a busy, often frustrating afternoon for both man and beast. Sheep are even more stubborn when there's a buzz in the air.

With the squall over, Charlie and Grace head to the shed. They take a good look inside and are relieved to discover all animals still in their shelter. But they're making one hell of a racket— testing their lungs after the danger of the storm has passed. The sheep are impatient to escape, wanting to check on more of their own kind.

Donning over-clothes of oilskin coats, rabbit fur felt hats and gumboots, the couple start up the Chev truck and slowly drive around the property. Checking fence after fence, they assess the condition of the sheep that have faced the elements. They locate most of the stock still standing under the shelter of trees, as they probably were during the storm. It's taking some time to dawn on the animals that they're safe to move now. As there's no leader, they all wait for the first to take the plunge.

Charlie hops off the truck at the gate, unlocks the heavily rusted chain, gets back into the vehicle and they drive to the next paddock where trees have been hit hard. Branches strewn across the grass; the place looks like a battlefield. Several sheep cower under what is left of the trees. One huge branch lies like a reclining giant in the middle of the paddock, nowhere near the tree from which it was ripped. At first, Charlie suspects the damage is from a wind tunnel.

Then they both see it: a huge ironbark stump sits alongside its severely pruned neighbours. The couple watches hypnotically as it smoulders, releasing fine dances of smoke from the gaping chasm of its wound, the lightning having pierced the giant straight through its middle. 'Lightning. Wouldn't believe it if you hadn't seen it, eh? Better to have happened here, although that strike near the house did some damage to that gum. We're very lucky to have escaped the worst of it,' says Charlie nervously, as though he's wondering what will be next.

Grace sighs, opening the truck's door. Hesitantly they both alight the vehicle and slosh their gumboots across the wet paddock to have a better look. As they move nearer to the massive branch, they hear bleating. What they find is two huddled sheep gathered reverently over a poor ram, crushed beneath a huge offshoot of the main branch. Its head has almost flattened into the ground—the impact having created a small crater. Inside lies a soupy bowl of blood, pieces of white brain and hairy skull in a spatter around what remains of where the head was once attached.

Grace shudders. 'No.' A mournful cry.

Charlie places his arm around her shoulder. Grace knows that he, like herself, would be feeling nauseous. Charlie has always tried to protect his animals from practices he finds abhorrent: the slaughter of bobby calves, the cries of the mothers for their absent offspring; the glare of huge cow eyes pleading as they're driven away to the slaughterhouse; the cruel practice of mulesing. His father Al always stringently defended his choices with any farmer who dared take him on, gladly tackling any of his shearers unopposed to mulesing. They're always kept particularly busy during a blowy outbreak, crutching each beast carefully. 'No bastard's gonna slice steaks off the arses of any of my sheep!' Charlie often reminds Grace of his father's words which now ring in her ears. Yet for all their care, this happens. Moments like this floor both Charlie and Grace.

Too distraught to deal with the destruction now, the couple shuffle arm-in-arm back to the truck.

'The children ...' Grace trails off, sounding weak and frail.

Chapter Forty

Three now two. Fleur continues her stoic stomp, guzzling up adventure— something that always seems to follow her. She knows Teddy will be following behind her like a little lost dog. Fleur is worried about Erin but not enough to stay with her.

To be sure, Fleur looks back to her brother. Teddy has noticed that the rainbow is across the river and he appears to be following it— detouring towards the riverbank. Fleur knows he'll be playing hide and seek, teased by the little flashes of colour appearing in the canopy breaks of the trees, like a movie reel needing a kick start. Fleur can almost feel his frustration as the colourful arc taunts him—retreating with each of his steps. She can imagine his thoughts: *I'll show the girls. It's right THERE and I'll reach out and touch it.* Caught up in the visceral pull of it, the exquisite attraction of the colour spectrum.

The landscape is changing. They're on a rough voyage in unforgiving territory. Trees are getting denser and taller; Teddy isn't getting any taller. The pretty beacon of the rainbow still shines heroically, so although Teddy is behind Fleur—she's seen him there—the direction in which he's heading is now her destination, too.

Within minutes, Fleur's haste has given way to fatigue. As she turns around, Fleur sees her brother's little red-hatted head where it was earlier, over the top of tall grasses, Teddy swallowed up to his shoulders.

'Hurry up, slowpoke!' yells Fleur. 'Typical,' she mumbles as she shakes her head, plodding on.

Fleur sees it—a heaving and alive thing of crashing water, dirty with bracken and stirred-up silt. Its waters nudge the bank. She makes her way to a tree about six feet from the turbulence, where she steadies herself against its trunk, not daring to move any closer lest the roar and rough waves overpower them.

Where is Teddy?

A sick thud suddenly strikes Fleur as she realises she hasn't sighted her brother for several minutes. Having earlier been hot on her heels she'd started to take his presence for granted. Glancing back, she sees the red hat in the same spot as the last time she looked ... and the time before.

Why is he still there? What is he doing? Is he hurt?

She tries to snap herself to action but feels stuck fast, under the river's spell, shocked by its untamed roar. Finally, she wills her body to move and lurches, pushes, trips her way back to find Teddy. Finds only the hat sitting atop of the grasses, out of place in its red colour clash against the brown reeds.

No, why hadn't she considered this before? He must have taken off his hat. It would show him the way back, just like Hansel in the story Fleur has been reading to him lately, the story he obsesses about.

She screams his name with what little force she can muster, over and over, breathlessly running in circles then tripping over her feet before racing upstream and down, ripping up the ragged flora in her mad path.

Until she stops.

What strikes her first is Teddy's little blue car—the one he always carries in his pocket. It is stuck fast in the mud on the riverbank. Her eyes move to Teddy who looks to have become a parachute. His hands extend from his white billowy coat like pale driftwood. Fleur has an urge to unhook the material which has caught on a tree branch, deep down understanding the futility of her wish. He must have come to rest there after careering around the river bend. The pummelling on his body is relentless in the slipstream of white water, making small waves over him, causing him to rock back and forth in regular rhythm. Teddy had failed to break his own fall as he ran towards the colourful lie, that spectrum of nothingness. And now, The Luna Park mouth of the rainbow smiles down at him horribly, belying the scene it frames.

Fleur stands frozen, yet giddy with adrenaline, managing nothing but breathing. Nothing is real today.

An overhead branch inexplicably magnetises her gaze and perched upon it she swears she sees the area's notorious ghost. She'd always heard it was nearby.

Chapter Forty-One

'What have you done to my children?' Grace implores Fleur as she watches her daughter's rain-soaked frame come towards her from the river— alone. Grace knows it would have been Fleur's idea to visit the river after the storm—always one to push the boundaries. With a pale blank stare, Fleur walks past her mother to her room. Erin returns fifteen minutes behind her sister.

The following day the wind has picked up, in a force hell-bent on showing whoever and whatever is taking notice that it's powerful enough to blow away death, reveal new life; what a convincing job it does. But Grace won't be conned and neither will the trees on the riverbank; she's sure of it. Having borne witness to the ordeal of a drowned child, they have accelerated their usual lilt to wave frantically and in unison; she knows they'd do so with or without the aid of a breeze. Their cries for help having fallen on deaf ears, they would have let out frenzied screams as they tried to uproot themselves, perhaps even fly to a safer sanctuary and start all over again. Even if the act itself didn't kill them, it would be better than living here, knowing what they know now. One tree has succeeded in uprooting itself, Charlie has told her, with half of its trunk and all its branches now submersed.

In the river of death, thinks Grace.

That afternoon when Charlie appears in their bedroom for an

uncharacteristic nap, Grace can see his telephone calls to the family have drained him. He sinks his large frame into the mattress beside her, causing the bed to buckle. He tells her he's located his distraught parents in Coober Pedy who fear they won't make it back in time for the funeral; nor will Connie and George due to Connie's ill health—shattered, they send their love and condolences.

Grace has her mind on other things. Feeling she has little left to lose, she makes her ultimate disclosure.

'I did this. I was so bloody ignorant. Vanity got the better of me and now Teddy is dead.'

'Oh love, whatever are you talking about?' asks Charlie, his voice cracking.

She sits up, stares down at him. 'I've been keeping secrets, from you and from the family.'

'You have enough to worry about now without thinking of anything else such as keeping secrets.' He sounds jaded.

'But you don't understand. All my life I've been seeing things, strange things, that usually predicted something good. Like I dreamt of a painting by Teddy, and he painted the exact painting in real life! Yesterday, things forewarned me of something bad about to happen.'

'I think we all get feelings like that, my dear girl, especially in hindsight.'

'It's more than hindsight though, more than feelings. It's real. I've always seen and sensed things that other people don't notice. Given signs, you know? And until now I've been proud of my sentience and prescience, if that's what I have. But I was vain enough to think that if I kept quiet, then I'd somehow be protected, *we* would somehow be protected. It was like I had the biggest and best secret in the world that I knew I had to keep or things would go wrong. If I didn't tell people about my premonitions, all would be okay in life; the magic wouldn't be broken. How stupid is that? I always said intuition is the most powerful sense. Then why didn't I act upon it, Charlie? True, I've always told myself that life can be unpredictable, but I think, I *know*, that some people can pick up on things more than others, and I'm one of them Charlie. Today? I know it was horribly hot and everything, but I just *knew* something terrible would happen. There were signs everywhere that I didn't act upon. I thought that if something bad were to happen to anyone, it would be Erin, with her asthma. She may be sick, but she is alive. But I had no idea our little man would not be with us again, ever again. After you all left the kitchen before yesterday's storm, a bird flew into the window, smack— dead.'

'You know that could have happened at any time.'

'Yes, but it didn't! It was yesterday, and I didn't do anything about it. I should have checked on the children, make sure they stayed inside and were safe before we went to check on the stupid sheep. I could have saved Teddy, but I didn't. I didn't. Save ...' Her words come in a jolt as she sobs.

'I've always thought that we're neither as big or as small as we think we are.'

'What does that mean?'

'Nature is big and invincible, as are our souls, both for reasons humanity doesn't understand—probably never will. Don't you see? Nature doesn't exist merely for our exotic pleasure like some impotent, aesthetically pleasant background to our big lives; it's our guide. When our deeds and associations are out of sync with where we should be, what we should be doing, that's when things turn ... nasty. We underestimate the knowledge hanging in the balance and flow of nature's life forms.'

'I can't see how your 'deeds and associations' have been out of kilter, Grace. And how were you to know that something bad was going to happen to one of the children?'

'I knew something bad was coming. I should have kept us all together for the day. We were checking sheep when we should have been checking our children, I know that much. And that dead ram was another sign! Sometimes I hate this place, Charlie, I really do. People aren't meant to live in places like this.'

Ignoring her last comment, Charlie says, 'Well, if it's true, if you have some kind of gift of foretelling the future, from now on you can use it to help people.'

She sees him immediately cringe at his insensitive remark. He reaches out a hand. A peace offering? Grace immediately rejects it, throwing his hand back at him.

'It's not a gift, it's a God-damn curse! I foolishly thought I was somehow special, in control. I never was.'

She looks to the ceiling and says quietly, 'Whenever we read together, I called him *Treasure*. I have letters for him ... He was always ... was always, *will* always be my Treasure.'

She collapses back on the bed in heaving sobs, neither of them touching one another.

Outside, the crying tree howls, almost drowning in itself.

When Charlie creeps out to the pastures early the next morning, Grace randomly opens one of her letters to Teddy from her gold box. She sniggers at the irony laced in the written messages from her little life in Norman Park—words that sound smug now, words that have come back to haunt her.

I believe that the trick of life is the unpredictability of it, and that unpredictability cannot always be waved away as somehow being related to what humans have or have not done or said. We bow to chance, fate, nature, disease, serendipity ... God. But I haven't had to battle any of these demons, yet, thank goodness, and a very large part of me can't help but wonder if I've somehow been chosen. If I just keep on doing the right thing, if I just continue to open to possibility. If I listen to 'beyond' and heed its advice, I'll be protected from all the evil in the world. I know that sounds a bit pompous, but I can't help the way I feel.

I decided long ago not to subscribe to many of the pretences or trickeries of adulthood, and I now find myself entrusted with secrets unbeknown to most adults, or I suspect that to be the case. As for pretending the human brain is the keeper of all knowledge, well, I can't, for I know better. The vanity of humans (sigh)! And so, I retain this perceptiveness of mind, or what I think is perceptiveness. Now I think I couldn't lose it, even if I wanted to.

Coming like an incantation on a breeze, I find myself welcoming the fervent whispers of my private ghosts as they continue to breathe gentle puffs of secrets and wisdom into my straining ears. I make sure I listen with all my senses—wide-eyed and attentive. Make sure you listen too, Treasure, because they will be talking to you! Those who have lost the battle are discomfited towards any such intrusion, for the breeze to them holds no language at all except for the occasional reckless roar, a logical vibration as the force of a current penetrates air between matter. For them it is nothing more than an inconvenience, an annoying assault to their senses, a harsh monochromatic filtering tool for the air we breathe and see through, blowing the day along.

But I can hear the secrets on the breeze, and I can see them. As a seer, I ride gently on that convoluted breeze. I am beginning to accept myself for what I am and what I suspect I will always be: a trusted harbourer of the secrets of the harbinger.

Charlie sets to work with ferocity, like a mad man, fashioning a preposterous little coffin in the shape of a car—not quite the Maserati of Teddy's dreams, but created with heart. Fleur watches on as her father chops and saws enough pine for a room full of furniture. He uses real tyres and metal hubcaps and he paints the whole thing blue, like Teddy's beloved toy car. Fleur is glad there are no windows because she doesn't think Teddy would want to see where he's going. Her father thankfully uses paint for that illusion.

Poor little Teddy—too young to get a licence but he'll be driving up to Heaven.

Chapter Forty-Two

The only time Erin can settle on her hospital bed is when the medications hit, allowing her to surrender to the blissful oblivion of sleep. Lucid, she lurches herself around, ridden with worry. Pneumonia, she thinks she heard someone say.

She has let her little brother drown, let him down. Drown, down, down, drown. She lets the rhythm of the words become a chant in her head. She knows she shouldn't sing-song about it; it's not a game; it's cruel, hellish. The dangers of the Europa in flood have always been well known to her, especially the strain put on it by too much rain in too little time after drought. God knows, her parents have rammed it home to her so many times. Erin thinks she may as well have given him up as a sacrifice, like in a film she once saw at the theatre when a virginal girl was thrown into a volcano. But for Teddy, the bastard of an ungrateful river took his life then spat him out.

Unworthy of happiness in this life, the stars have set her fate. From now on, she vows to be stoic, obedient, steadfast in her sufferance. As penance for failing in her caregiver role of Teddy, she now asks God to fork out the consequences she deserves. Not in the Catholic way—her disclosed sins should not be forgiven—but more like the fire and brimstone, eye for an eye, tooth for a tooth variety. Karma. She knows the deal; it's the way it should be. For her family's sake, Erin will return to be the good daughter. She'll do whatever it takes for them to once again have faith in her, be proud of her.

She missed Teddy's funeral, another reason to feel guilty. One week later, when she returns home from hospital, weak and brittle, she plays her piano more than ever before. To her appreciative parents, Bach and Strauss have never sounded more alive. To Erin, it's a show of desperation. Beethoven's 'Moonlight Sonata', and Tchaikovsky's 'Romeo and Juliet', break her heart with each new key change, another little death. Copious tears spill onto her fingers—whiter and colder than the ivory she pounds. The beauty is that she can hide and covertly implode this way. *Don't look at me, just listen.* Beauty often masks pain. And danger.

Erin remembers her little fingers covering big mother fingers as Grace played; the toddler sitting importantly on her mother's knee, caught in the sweet misguided conviction that it was she, Erin, who was playing—sometimes it was. And oh, the thrill of standing on Dad's feet as he waltzed her around the room to her mother's piano accompaniment. The princess swept up by her prince. Little snippets of dormant memory now coming suddenly and vividly, always featuring Erin longing to be a grown up.

She finds herself now, irrevocably, adult.

Cappi discovers Erin in the garden, relentlessly stripping gardenias from an increasingly bare, sad-looking bush.

'They're for Mum.' Erin examines the flowers in her hands. 'Pretty, aren't they? I have so little to offer her, certainly nothing that would help.'

'I wish I'd picked those for you,' mumbles Cappi, sighting her bundle of picked flowers then staring at the bush's stark branches.

'Why would you? Cappi? Why would you even bother?'

Reaching out to him with both arms, Erin's near fall turns into a reserved hug. Steadying herself, she nuzzles her head into his shirt, finding the curve of his collarbone. 'It's just too awful. Sometimes I think back to good times, you know? Like Cracker Night. And I wonder, will there ever be fireworks in the world again? How could anything brighten all this sadness? Oh God, I sound corny and pathetic, don't I?'

Cappi pulls his body away and grabs her cold hands, one of which crushes the heady-smelling flowers—rhythmically making fists—each squeeze releasing another perfumed waft.

'I don't know what to say. Is there anything I can do for you? Anything at all?' asks Cappi.

'No, nothing can help.'

'And are you well now? I was so worried about you, Erin. I don't think you quite understand how much.' He looks into her eyes, as though searching for life.

'Physically I'm healthy. All cured. Strong as an ox. Although I have no idea why I should have been saved that day. So much for heroism. I was useless. Bloody useless.' She detects fear in Cappi's handsome face. 'Look, I know you were worried about me, Cappi. Don't be, okay? You poor, misguided fool.' A faint smile. She then runs a dismissive finger under her nose. 'You're a thoughtful person Cappi, that's for sure. I'd better keep at this.' She resumes her work, continuing to rip what is left of the foliage from the shocked gardenia bush.

'Well, please know I'm always there for you.' He shuffles off, turning to her with a slim smile she barely sees through misty eyes.

Chapter Forty-Three

Grace looks at her man lying beside her: so tired and troubled, so uncomplaining and brave in his pain. Charlie always believed in her more than any other man had done, not that she'd known many men before Charlie, but she wonders how proud he is of her now, if at all; she can't bear to imagine. She remembers the time when Charlie first put his trust in her, or was it bravado? He made a vow to her he would later keep.

It was their first Sunday together. They lay on towels on the sand at Broadbeach, the shrill squeals of ratty children on school holidays making it impossible to nap. The winter sun was starting to sting her. Grace sat up, wriggling her toes around in the sand, searching for coolness.

'They say it's warmer in than out,' she said.

'I don't want to be any warmer than I am now, Grace. I'm hot,' said Charlie.

'You know what I mean.'

'Perfectly happy lying here, getting fried.'

'I have my togs underneath,' said Grace, trying to tempt him.

'Oh, you mean your swimmers? Well, I don't.' Not buying it.

'Surely you can just wear your shorts. They'll be dry in no time.' Her voice had a curt edge to it.

They sat in silence.

'You *can swim*, can't you?'

He looked out to sea. 'Is it a crime? Swimming has never been something I've felt the need to do.'

'It's something you could do for pleasure though, Charlie.'

'Hmm. Pleasure? No, I don't see the association. My grandfather once threw me into a creek full of reedy muck when I couldn't swim. Not good. Maybe that somehow scarred me. I dunno.'

She studied him as he looked around, anywhere but at her.

'When I was about seven, I was body-surfing with Dad,' said Grace.

'Well now, I'm enormously happy for you. Child prodigy.' Charlie's voice sounded harsh, not like him at all. He then shot her an attempted smile.

'Just wait. Mum was lying on the beach under our umbrella. There was a big swell in the surf that day.'

'And you rode the wild surf to the wild applause of the landlubbers who'd been biting their nails to the quick fearing for your safety.' It was as though he couldn't help himself, scared of where the conversation was heading. She recognised it as fear.

'And, Charlie, I got caught in a rip. Dad had ridden a wave in and I could see him get up and walk towards Mum on the beach. He wasn't looking back for me because I was always right behind him. I could see him moving further away from me, well I was really moving away from him. I wasn't that far out but I couldn't touch bottom. I think I was in a gutter and I was suddenly being pulled towards the south quickly. As I tried to get back to shore a dumper got me. A couple of underwater somersaults and when I finally got washed up near the shore, all I could think about was my next breath.

'At the same time, another girl washed up beside me. I could see her pink togs, sorry, bathers, under the water through the wash of the wave. She must have been dumped by the same wave. Suddenly all I could see were her legs. I think she tried to stand, but she lost her bearings and then she sat on me. She *sat* on me, Charlie! All of this before I'd drawn breath from the dumping. That wait, that sense of panic and helplessness, she was a big girl Charlie. Anyway, through a tangle of limbs, I finally managed to struggle free. I coughed up some water. My breath was *heaving*. She just stared at me, and me at her. I've never been so terrified in my life. I was so shocked; I never said a thing about it.' Her voice shook.

'But your parents must have known? They must have seen you.'

'I don't think they even knew it happened. After I composed myself as much as I could I went back and collapsed on my towel.'

'Sorry to hear that. What made you get back in the water? I assume you have?'

'Yes, I have. Many times. Just bloody-mindedness, I guess.' Silence.

'Tell you what Charlie, I'll teach you to swim if you teach me to shear a sheep.' I want to come back to the farm with you, Charlie, she wanted to say.

'Oh, come on, Grace. Shearing's men's work.' No doubt exceedingly pleased to have something over her.

'Are you saying I can't do it?'

'Sheep are really hard to manage. I just don't want you getting hurt.'

'So, you're saying I'm not strong enough? Well perhaps I just think you're scared to swim.'

'Don't be ridiculous!' There it was, she'd hit a nerve.

'Well if you're not up to it.'

'What? I am! Come on. Here and now. I'd probably show them all up. But if I must.' Charlie scanned the groups of children around them. 'Just not here.'

Grace giggled. Getting her way. 'I'll shear that sheep one day.'

'You're a minx, Grace.' Playful words with a sullen expression.

She introduced him to the safe waters of Currumbin Creek, when it wasn't too crowded. This saved face for Charlie who would not have wanted his manly body to be seen floundering about in a creek, of all places. Charlie quickly learnt to swim; well, perform a curious display of freestyle, breaststroke and dog paddle, but enough to keep him from going under. When he first ventured into the water, he was visibly trembling, but Grace coaxed him gently and steadily until he seemed to enjoy it, and then he took to it like a bird released from its cage. He enjoyed almost everything with her back then.

Charlie later confided in her that he'd never been more terrified in his life than when he went back into the water again as an adult. And he thanked her for giving him the strength to do it. But why did she do it? She dared him to do something he didn't want to. What was she hoping to achieve? So, what if he couldn't swim? Was it for him or for her? She blushes as she realises the episode may have been about control—hers over him. Now she's so fragile, she'd never have the cheek to dare him to do anything he didn't want to do. Those memories were from another time. A lifetime ago. Carefree times.

Why is she now thinking of this? Suddenly realises the connection to Teddy. The water. The terror ... *Focus on Charlie.*

Lately, Charlie falls asleep the minute his head hits the pillow. She knows he's as worried as she is about her and the girls and she's glad he gets the sleep he needs for the long days on the farm, but ...

He needs a good mate, a man with whom he can talk confidentially. Charlie has rarely heard from John and Honey, only via short letters. Pity about Jimbo. Despite his family's farm being in reasonable proximity to the Alton farm, he rarely visited them—once as soon as the newlyweds arrived at the farm, to borrow the Chev truck. On the other couple of occasions, he appeared embarrassingly jealous of the couple's relationship, mooching around, refusing to be included in anything they tried to organise. God knows, thinks Grace, I tried. Seemingly averse to the idea of giving her a decent go, Jimbo phased himself out of their lives. Charlie recently heard on the grapevine that Jimbo discovered that it was Charlie who paid his cousin Honey to go out with him back in 1949, and his pride just couldn't take it. So, the break- up in the friendship was never about Grace, as she had mistakenly thought for years.

She's not heard from or of Marcie, not that she's tried to contact her. But Grace reasons she's had enough on her plate to worry about any former fair-weather friend now.

She doesn't even have the strength to help her husband.

Chapter Forty-Four

Why can't Grace see Teddy, her Treasure, the boy she loved most, in or out of her dreams? He was always such an animated presence in her life, and they loved one another fiercely; she wonders why he hasn't visited her. Does he blame her for what happened to him? Will he ever forgive her? She knows there is no return; he's left them now for the place everyone will one-day return. Here, for now, she must do all she can to make amends for the horror that eventuated because she didn't heed the warnings. That's all she can do.

She writes:

My darling Treasure: I have let you down and 'beyond' has let me down. But then again, how can I blame an unseen force for something so tangible that I could have prevented? Why didn't I simply listen to the breeze?

Nature's life forms scream at all of us—wearily, for they have seen all this before— warning us, celebrating with us, her trajectory most drawn to those who are most receptive, for they are the seers. Warning us … Why didn't I heed my premonitions? Perhaps I was never meant to be a seer because seers would do the right thing; they would heed warnings. I know now I'm no more special than anyone else on this fragile journey called life. If I was, I wouldn't have been robbed. You wouldn't have been robbed; you would still be with us. I can only beg that one day you'll forgive me.

When Fleur returned home without Teddy that terrible day, Erin hobbling doubled-up far behind her— so sick she could barely walk— her mother just scowled at Fleur. She'll never forget that look of horror, of disgust, on her mother's face.

Her mother's words will haunt her for the rest of her life: 'What have you done to my children?'

She hates this place. Look at that sky! Screaming pretty at her in blazing clear blue, blatant and cruel—no absconsion, no penitence. Attention seeking, as a child would. Birds ring out the dead, some fall from the sky; is it the heat, or acknowledgement for the tragedy that has happened? Her eyes sting with her stare—the burning sun having failed to blind them—so she flips onto her stomach and dog paddles in the ochre dirt, clawing up handfuls of dust. Mum's mackerel from the sky in death throes. Head to one side, she lets her dribble, snot and tears hit the ground in a fleeting sea of grief before the heat kills her bodily fluids. She can't rid the stench of death.

Alarmed by the quiet commotion the dogs bark, sensing Fleur's presence. A small whirlwind swirl by her in a red fairy floss cloud, dodging her inert presence. She rolls onto her back again and sits up. Covered in red dirt, she knows she must appear rusted. Laughs at the irony; she feels rusted through. Fleur grabs more handfuls of the dust she has loosened and scatters it over her head in a feeble attempt to purge her sins.

Anything but beauty today.

Grace has fallen into herself like a deflated balloon, all definition gone. Crying has exhausted her thin frame. Her tiny mouse voice peeps out to show itself only when she feels it safe to do so. Shrunken in stature too, Grace has almost disappeared in the big-boned household. She thinks that would be alright.

Melancholy. It's a good word. Sadness overwhelms me. I've had a nervous breakdown. That's what Doctor Malloy has told me, and I trust his good word, despite his lack of bedside manner. He advised me to keep this diary and write down my feelings. I don't think it will help but I'll do what I'm told. I can do that. I have severe depression, apparently brought on by the loss of our beloved little man. Depression—the irony of that word. If the condition came with a flatness which rendered me devoid of feeling, I would embrace it, because I don't want to feel anything. What then, is this cruelly heightened self-consciousness and suspicion of people that engulfs me all about?

I fear that people regard me cynically now; I can see it by the way they look at me, speak to me. I'm distrusting those who once were dear friends, like Marcie, although I guess I never really did trust her. But it is breaking me to feel this way, to show anyone this face that is me but isn't the me I would ever wish to be, or wish anyone to see. I don't even recognise myself. Since the accident, and it must have had something to do with it, I not only distrust people, I no longer feel worthy of love. I'm scared of living but more scared of dying. How selfish is that? My precious child drowned, and his mother is too weak to do away with herself, to join him, to be there for him again. The thought of him waiting for me is excruciating.

It wasn't my fault and it wasn't Fleur's fault.

A moment in time, a moment in time, just like this one but nothing like this one. How does it feel to drown, to breathe water? How does it feel, not to be able to sate our most base and primal instinct? Does the adrenaline help us on our journey, or do we experience every shocking, painful and wrongfully inhuman water breath? Do we apologise to our bodies at the time? To our families? To God? Do our hearts truly break at that moment? Or does the commotion of the event cancel out that emotional response? Please God, I hope that's true. Do not have let him suffer, emotionally or physically. I cannot bear for Teddy to have endured any amount of pain or heartbreak like I now feel.

I've been advised to try to get back to a 'normal life' but everything is empty and colourless now. People have stopped showering us with dinners and flowers. The gifts in themselves meant little; the kindness with which they were given was ever more meaningful. Now, when they do visit, even though I don't want to see them, I sense only their dull acknowledgement of me, bound merely by obligation, custom, habit, as

I am not a pleasant conversationalist, having lost whatever spark I once had. I've obviously turned into something unpalatable, decrepit, to be dealt with and discarded post-haste. I suspect it makes them feel better, to be able to say they have spoken to unfortunate Grace—the vapid vestibule of no interesting surprises.

For me, communicating with the living has become intolerable. I know that elective solitude looks ugly to those having to witness it. I'm trying to put on a facade of coping for the sake of Charlie and the girls, but it seems the only people I can trust are my family; only they can truly understand. My dearest family. My heart breaks to think what they must be going through. Are they in as much agony, too? Of course, they are and I'm not helping them. Insularity, another ugly trait. I should be helping them, not the other way around, and the guilt I feel overwhelms my every waking moment, but I'm ashamed to say that it's not enough to rouse me from my self-absorption.

It wasn't anyone's fault. Was it mine?

Charlie doesn't know what to do. I heard him sobbing one night, turned away from me, probably wishing somehow the darkness would hide his muffled sobs. I thought I'd die of heartbreak. The burden he feels must be harrowing, wanting so acutely to help me and the girls. I think it would be easier for him if he had to look after our bodies only—to attend to our daily care practices, and not have to deal with our minds. He's good at nursing the sick like I used to be. I've seen the gentle way he has handled the children and the animals when they have needed care. Charlie, like Nurse Love was in her previous life, tries to calm the fractious moods of his patients, but I fear he's at breaking point, trying to hold all of us, including himself, together, trying to fight demons he cannot see, trying to heal wounds that won't respond to a lick of antiseptic and a shiny new sticking plaster. He's busying himself around the house to a ridiculous extent. Everything and everyone are shiny clean and we're all just wandering around like lost sheep.

As for people outside of our little cocoon, like the church people, I look for hidden meanings in their conversations with me. They're waiting for me to slip up, as I inevitably do, to utter the foolish foible which I know will escalate out of control, as it always does. Is this distrust I'm feeling part of the condition or can I now see something they think I cannot, thinking I'm too stupid to pick up on it, as their blank, far away eyes scan me in non-committal glimpses and throw words carelessly into the air around me? Words, only words, but words I obsessively sift through, analyse and theorise about until I discover the murderous clue, which finally proves that their intention all along was to cut me down. Told you so, and you know what? It works for them every time. So, it's best to avoid others at all costs.

Yet deep down I find myself craving the whimsy of their lives. I wish I could throw away lines to them as lightly as they do to me without fearing they'll be used against me as a weapon to shame, humiliate, belittle my being. I can almost feel my body shrinking with each new day.

That's the nasty trick of dealing with others—the repercussions. The pain I feel seems to have immersed itself as an inescapable part of me, but it's also being force-fed to me from others—the ones I don't trust, and they are many. Like disease attacking a body—receptive, without immunity—I choke on every painful word they utter until their hidden meanings metastasise and slowly destroy me, while the carriers of the slanderous words remain immune to hurt, seemingly growing stronger as they watch me fail. I think that even if I could tell them all I know; they wouldn't care at all.

Only the strong flourish in this world. I'm at a point where I can't tell if I've always felt this way. I must not have. I search my carefree face in photographs, but I can't remember those carefree feelings. The 'purple heart' pills the doctor prescribed give me sleep and help me with some semblance of routine existence. But when they inevitably wear off, and the ghosts return, as they do at the dawn of each day, I'm a mess again.

Chapter Forty-Five

Weekdays always make Grace feel a little brighter. Because of this dim conclusion and feeling slightly less encumbered since writing, she takes herself to Teddy's room. It's the first time she has approached it since the accident. Having had too little to eat and drink the past weeks, she is weak, faint, and almost keels over upon opening the door. She steadies herself by holding the door handle.

Inside his room, she rests on the unmade bed, next to the boy's teddy bear which lies limp, threadbare, moth-eaten, so loved ... He used to call it Freddy. 'Because *I'm* Teddy, not him.' She knows she'll have to clean out his things, some of his things ... *None of his things, my dear little precious angel, my Treasure.* Wiping back tears, she scans the room. Opens the top drawer of his dresser. All his little shirts and shorts. Quickly closes it. Middle drawer—underwear. Bottom drawer—books: *The Book for Boys, The Secret Seven*, comics. Limply, she flicks through the worn magazines.

Puzzles about some colourful, but faded, material which lies underneath the reading matter. Pulling the silk from its little home, she unravels it, discovering a scarf that is certainly not one of hers. She lifts it to the window light to get a clear view of its appearance, its mottled pink, orange and aqua colours. Some of the fabric has ripped. It would have been pretty in its day.

As Grace stretches out and studies the scarf in the light, *beyond* returns to her, making a last-ditch attempt to retrieve a friendship. The colours seem to be absorbing more light than the sun is giving, becoming increasingly vivid. A shape forms in the centre of the material—about the size of a human head, features taking shape as she stares. Dark curly hair, dark complexion, male. Her shaky hands drop the scarf as if it's on fire. It floats theatrically to the oak floor.

Beyond. Am I being punished for taking in Izzie? For doing the thing I always swore to hate. She has lost someone. I'm sure of it. Is it too late to help her?

Chapter Forty-Six

In her predictably bad mood, even after twelve hours of sleep, Fleur throws herself and other various objects around the kitchen. Grace asks her if they can talk. Fleur notices that looking at her daughter obviously makes her mother flinch and responds with a scowl.

Fleur can hear Erin playing piano in the lounge room which doesn't help her mood. Erin would no doubt have risen two hours earlier and already had her breakfast. So predictable, so sickening.

'What's the problem?' asks Fleur harshly, not quite yet having forgiven her mother for that cruel accusation the day of Teddy's death.

'Nothing to worry about at all. Well, I am worried about you, and you may care to believe that or not.' Grace's voice is broken, and she looks as if she's about to cry. Taking a deep breath, she continues, 'But that's not what I want to talk about now. It's Izzie.'

Fleur has had to strain to hear her. Her mother's voice shrank like her body seemed to on that horrible day. Fleur stares her piercing light amber eyes at her mother.

'Why, is she sick?'

Fleur is genuinely concerned about Izabella. What her mother doesn't realise is that Fleur is just as concerned about Grace, who seems to be fading before her eyes.

'No. Not at all. You seem to have a good relationship with her. Tell me, darling, do you think she's happy here?' She hasn't called her daughter *darling* since that day …

'I don't know. She smiles and talks more now, but I think she frets for lost time. She must miss her family. God knows what she's been through.'

'It's just, well, here.'

Grace presents from her apron pocket a faded and tattered pink, orange and aqua scarf. Fleur's body heats up upon seeing it.

'I found this in Teddy's room. Do you know anything about it?'

Fleur feels her face flush and is sure her entire body has broken out in a tell-tale rash. 'Well, I know it was Teddy's.'

'How? Come on Fleur, please, when did he show it to you and where did he get it?'

'It's just an old scarf,' replies Fleur, rattled.

'Please Fleur. If you want to help things, you'll tell me what you know.'

'Alright. He found it at Robinson's.'

'When did he go to Robinson's? You took him there, didn't you!'

Fleur ignores her mother's vitriol. 'Why are you worried about it?'

'Because I think it's Izzie's.'

Fleur knows some of Izzie's history, discovered through hushed conversations with her. How young, vivacious Izzie was frozen in time back when she thought she'd lost her home in Hungary in the war. Fleur fears there is much here in Australia she has lost, too. They just need to find out what it is.

After Fleur left the kitchen in a rush, having been interrogated further by her mother, Grace remained sitting at the table fingering the scarf, trying her best to summon the ghosts that surround it, get a sense of its history. So many questions. *Why did I see the vision of a young man? Why do I know so instinctively that the scarf is Izzie's? Perhaps we have both lost our sons. If I'd been more open with her, she may have confided in me.*

Later that morning, when Charlie enters the room, Grace pounces.

'Tell me Charlie, what do we really know about Izzie?'

'Hi Charlie, he mutters.

'Yes, yes, hello. Why are niceties so bloody important?' she snaps.

'What do we know about her, Charlie?'

'Well, you know the answer to that question as much as I do, and it's certainly not much.'

'I think there's a hidden story there, Charlie—a mystery begging to be solved.' Grace lifts the scarf from her lap and presents it to her husband. 'I found this in Teddy's room. After a bit of coaxing, Fleur confessed Teddy found it at Robinson's.'

'What the hell was he doing there?' Charlie has come to life.

'She told me they just wanted to see if there was gold in the creek. She was all apologies and I really didn't want to press it, considering what we've all been through.'

'Alright then, nothing we can do about it now. They found a scarf. So what?'

'Please don't think I'm crazier than you probably already do, but I just *know* it's Izzie's. I think she had a son. I think he may have been the boy who was killed on Robinson's land.'

'You mean the boy who was with the other two men? The fishermen?'

'Yes.'

'But how? Why would you think that?'

'The scarf has a connection to Izabella and a young man that I'm feeling so acutely, Charlie. Please believe me! Teddy and Fleur found the scarf at Robinson's. Teddy told Fleur he found it under a rock and that he loved its rainbow colours, even if it was faded. He even told Fleur that he was going to give it to me because it would help with something. Well, it didn't help him, did it? But perhaps it can help get justice for someone else. You know the only way to solve it, don't you?' baits Grace, waiting for her perplexed husband to take a leap of faith with her. She's never felt more agitated, yet somehow excited. Perhaps it wasn't true that she'd never put a dare to Charlie again.

'You need to question Izzie first, Grace, before we even think about involving that man.'

She is pleased her husband qualified his last point. She'd probably never approach Robinson on her own. Well, actually, she would, she'd march straight over there and confront him. But she wants Charlie's help. With all of this. Perhaps deep down she still is the girl at the beach, the one who taught her love to swim.

༺

Grace waits for her arrival back from feeding the dogs outside. Remaining at the kitchen table, she has placed the scarf on her lap, so Izabella can't see it when she comes in.

'Morning, Izzie.'

'Good morning, Grace.' Never people to stand on ceremony, there were usually only first names in the Alton household.

She can feel the weight in Izabella's voice. Suddenly she realises she hasn't even discussed how hurt Izzie must be feeling after Teddy's death.

'I went to look through Teddy's things this morning.'

'That's good, Grace, that you went in there, that you tidy up. He would want you to fix things in his room. He never liked to do that, did he?'

Grace smiles at her. 'No, not at all. Just a normal boy I suppose, really. He was a clever little thing. He cared a lot for you, dear. You were very special to him.'

'Yes.' She looks away. 'I think so. He like it when I play with him. It's always so sad when … when a little one goes to God. Sad when your boy leaves you.' Tears form in her eyes.

'Yes. It is. Too sad. We're all feeling it terribly. Look Izzie, I need to ask you about something I found in Teddy's room. It's not mine and I wonder if you've ever seen it before.'

Grace gently places the scarf onto the table, watching the woman's puzzled expression turn to shock. And Izabella's eyes roll as she faints—very slowly, very carefully collapsing to the linoleum floor, as though not wanting to make a fuss.

༺

She's been lying on the floor with her feet propped up on a cushion for several minutes. When she recovers enough for Charlie to position her on a chair, Grace makes her a cup of tea and tells her where the scarf was found. Izabella sighs and mumbles incoherently.

'Izzie dear, you don't have to talk to us about this now. Just rest.'
'But I must, I must.' She holds a thin hand to her face as she balances her elbow on the table, as though it's an effort to prop up her head.

'What is it, love?' Grace tries to comfort her as Charlie sits beside them looking flummoxed.

'The scarf. It was mine. My husband gave it to me.'

At the word *husband* Charlie and Grace exchange worried glances.

'But, can you be sure?' enquires Grace.

'Yes. Mine alright. I'd know it anywhere.'

'We didn't know you had a husband, Izabella.'

'I also had a … a little boy. His name is Tripp. You see, I lost my boy too, Grace. My boy loved that scarf. He knew it important to me, to us. He tried to get it back for me one day when a man on a horse came to the creek. Staring at us with evil eyes. I want him to go away. We were swimming, only swimming!' Crying now. 'Tripp tried to swim to it and the man, the man, he took him from me. My boy!'

Gripping her stomach, she collapses in tears, the outpouring as copious as that of the crying tree.

Grace wonders if it's her womb she's trying to clutch. Charlie glances at Grace in surprise and their eyes meet. She extends her arm around Izabella, and the women sit there waiting for the tears to subside, struck with the gravity of the situation in which they now find themselves. Charlie slowly shakes his head.

Chapter Forty-Seven

Sunday morning. At Grace's insistence, despite Charlie's hesitance, he acquiesces; they are on a mission. They drive the truck as close to the river as possible, through paddock after paddock, gate after gate until they reach the boundary between their land and Robinson's. Not taking the main road, they've decided to arrive on foot. As there's an area of uninhabitable, impossible-to-traverse bushland separating the two properties with no road access, the only way is by foot along the creek bed. From the pebbly bed, they'll locate Robinson's path and take it to his house. Charlie telephoned him earlier—surprised the old man would possess such a modern convenience—so Robinson is aware of when and from which direction to expect his visitors.

They aren't sure what they'll achieve by going there, but if there's any chance at all to stop him from treating his new lot of workers badly, they'll take it—anything to stop another murder. And of course, they hope he'll recognise the scarf, the only memento Tripp had of his mother. They hope their neighbour will cringe and confess. Charlie and Grace suspect the boy dropped the scarf upon the impact of the bullet, where it may have caught under a rock until their own boy Teddy found it. It was probably still with him when he was shot by Robinson, he may have been clinging to it in desperation …

It is mid-summer and the pair imagine Robinson's workers are busy harvesting his wheat, if they haven't already done so. From the creek-bed, they follow the path which has been cut between bracken, at the end of which lies a barbed wire fence and gate. On the horizon, they glimpse several workers peppered in the yellow fields. Much of the crop stands tall.

Just as promised, Robinson has left the gate unlocked for them. It creaks in alarm as they open and close it and tentatively make their way up to the ramshackle house. Panting, Grace realises she has faded physically, due to having been house-bound for so long, but her tenacity is sustaining her for the journey. She's after answers.

Two dogs start barking madly upon their arrival and leap towards them. The old man pulls up the scrawny, dribbling mutts with a couple of loud whistles, at which point they quieten, cower, whine and retreat to their broken-down kennel. Standing scowling on the verandah—hairy arms akimbo, chest puffy above a pot belly—Len Robinson's large frame appears the epitome of anything but welcoming. He extends an arm towards the house and the pair follows him, heads bowed and feeling unprepared for this encounter. The stench of Robinson's body odour is overwhelming.

'So, what brings youse to the Robinson mansion?' he asks in an abrupt cello tone. His tongue lolls against his bottom lip like a fat slug.

Grace scans the threadbare room, almost appreciating the irony of the comment. She can smell alcohol on his breath—whiskey probably— another smell added to the disgusting mix. And another smell cutting through it all. Oil? Petrol? Something to do with a car. She will not think of Plasticine Man. Her nerves are jumping.

She glances towards a hunched, timid woman with thin grey hair pulled up in a bun, back turned to her, busying herself at the sink. Noticing Grace's interest, with an offhand wave Robinson says, 'Oh, my mistake for not being polite.' He rolls his eyes. 'This is me woman, Dot.'

Charlie and Grace glance to one another. They didn't know Len Robinson was married.

'Pleased to meet you,' says Grace, extending a hand to the pathetic woman, who gives a half-hearted wipe of her wet hands on a dish cloth, then dampens Grace's.

'Pleased ta meecha,' she mumbles, to which Charlie gives a grunt of affirmation.

'Well Len, it's been quite a while since we last saw you. Wondered how things are coming along with the harvesting?' asks Charlie.

'Well, not that it's any of your business, but it's comin' along just fine and dandy,' says Robinson.

She can almost see his hackles rising in suspicion. Grace notices how small and burrow-like Len's eyes are, just like someone from her past, just like—

'So, Robinson, we hear you're employing new Australians,' says Grace.

Charlie rolls his eyes and shakes his head a little as if to say, typical of you, leaping before you look.

Len gives Grace a look of distaste, and still staring at her he cocks his head and says, 'Dot, looks like we have some business to attend to.'

The haggard figure shuffles from the room.

'What's it to youse?' His glare at Grace is unflinching.

'I'm curious: being new to the country mean they wouldn't know the things that have happened here on your property, would they?'

If Charlie's eyes were drills, Grace fears she'd find herself punctured.

Robinson's laugh is caustic. 'I tell you what Alton, that woman of yours sure has a mouth on her. You'd better do something about that. Anyhow, what exactly are you insinuating? You'd better watch yer step.'

'Just an observation,' she says.

Len is puffing, obviously getting riled, so Charlie changes the topic to another one Grace knows he dreads.

'Len, I suppose you've heard our sad news.'

'Hmm, yes, condolences to youse all,' he mumbles, still seething. 'Thanks. It's difficult for all of us. Before the little fella passed away, he found this on the boundary of our two properties and we were wondering if you knew anything about it.'

Charlie pulls the scarf from the pocket of his cotton drill trousers and presents it to the old man, who takes it, eyeing it suspiciously. Grace hopes Charlie won't say anything about Teddy having been on Robinson's property. Hopes the old bloke will crack. She wants to say: Here—look at this carefully. It belonged to the innocent boy you shot. The visitors stare at the ageing man intently, watching his reaction, waiting for any reaction. Len remains stony-faced and silent for a while, fingering the material. Feels like an eternity …

'Ha!' Charlie and Grace jump. 'That old thing,' He throws it onto the table. 'Belongs to Tripp—one of me workers, and believe me, I use the term loosely. Keeps it like a security blanket. He'd be miffed knowing it was missing; poor, sad bastard. Ties it to tree branches when I send him fishing like it's his little puppy dog. Slow as a wet week, that one. Always gotta keep me eye on 'im.' Rolls his eyes at Charlie.

Charlie looks as light in the head as Grace feels, so stunned at the words having just come out of his neighbour's mouth, his shock rendering him momentarily speechless. Eventually he manages, 'Tripp, you say?'

'Yeah, so what's it to ya?' he repeats, angrily.

Charlie and Grace dare not look at one another. They hadn't prepared for this— didn't have any idea he could still be alive. Grace knows they're instinctively reading each other's thoughts; they must get him home to Izzie.

'We know of someone who'd like to employ him. Name your price,' says Charlie.

Robinson's eyes widen. Takes a deep breath and stares out the window, appearing to weigh up the offer. 'Ha! Him? You're jokin'! If yer lookin' for a worker, you'd pick another one. He's a refo wog, but he's real lazy just like the rest of 'em.' His fist taps the table three slow times. 'Now, hang on a minute. Tell me why this Tripp fella is of so much interest to ya.'

'Let's just say it's a favour for a friend,' says Charlie.

'And tell me why I should do you a favour?'

Charlie fixes him with a steely gaze.

'Because I live too close to you, too close for our liking. We hear things, you know? Things you may not realise we hear about. I know of some little secrets you've been hiding here, about what you did years ago to those three fishermen—shooting them. One was merely a child, for God's sake!'

Grace knows the idea that the boy who was killed was not Izzie's son is still sinking in, but he was still an innocent boy.

'About the 'canvas and tin' scheme you've been running here. Hardly paying your workers, barely feeding them. But I'm willing to keep quiet about the whole sad, sorry mess, if we can come to an arrangement. You're a lucky man Len. Not only am I willing to keep quiet about your deplorable practices, I'm also willing to compensate you for losing one of your workers. Like I said, what's your price, Len?'

The large, overweight man hobbles over to the kitchen sink, clutching its rim until his knuckles turn white, then flies around to face them.

'Alright, give me fifty of your best lambs—and make sure they include some offspring of the ones that won that fancy prize up north.'

'What? For Tripp?' asks Charlie. 'You heard me,' states Robinson.

Grace catches her husband's eye, willing him to feel what she's silently saying to him: *You can't put a price on this, Charlie. Give him anything, anything he wants.*

But she can see him shudder in horror. His best breeding stock. Charlie must know this is worth it, that he and Grace need to put some things right, things now in their control. But they know also fear if Len did confess to them about the murders, either he wouldn't admit it to anyone else, or he has crooked police mates who have been protecting him all along and will probably continue to do so.

Charlie traces and retraces the cleft of his chin with his index finger.

'I'll give you thirty,' says Charlie, offering his hand towards Robinson's big, grimy paw.

'Deal,' says Robinson, without returning the handshake.

Charlie widens his eyes, looking not so much offended as surprised the man gave up so easily. 'By the way, why do you want them? He asks, appearing fearful now of the response.

'Mate's a butcher.' Robinson makes a production of licking his peeling lips and then exposing a strange collection of crooked brown teeth in a sick smirk.

Grace stashes the scarf into her pocket. She stands, and Charlie follows her outside. They can't wait to get out of this place. At the gate, Robinson presents Tripp to them, having pulled him from one of the fields. Grace can see fear in the boy's expression, yet a spark of something like determination. She recognises it as the same gleam she's seen in Izzie's eyes.

Finally unbridled, Tripp walks away from Robinson's, for the last time, through the creaky gate and onto the riverbank with the two smiling strangers. Tripp, Grace and Charlie—they all look up, drawn to a pair of huge wedge-tailed eagles cutting the brilliant sky in a glide of seduction above the tree-tops.

Len Robinson stands firm at his barrier, unmoved by the show of birds. In stillness, waving goodbye to his son.

Chapter Forty-Eight

Tripp follows Grace and Charlie through the front door. Confused and nervous, he hovers about, pacing foot to foot as he watches Izabella washing vegetables in the kitchen sink.

'Izzie,' Grace calls to the back of the industrious little figure.

'Yes, Grace?'

'We've found someone you may know.' Grace's eyes flick between Izabella and Tripp, with apprehension.

'*Anya?* Mummy?'

She drops her rag and clutches the sink as though afraid of falling again. 'Tripp?'

'Yes, it's me.'

It takes an eternity before she turns to face him, her face full of trepidation, fearing this is a very bad joke. 'It can't be. Is that really you? Yes? Oh, my child, where have you been? Where? Every day, every day I died without you.' Her words come melodious, quick and panicky as she fixes her hair and rushes towards him. Her eyes widen as she looks up to study his face. 'It is you. I know you! I know my son in a heartbeat. That smile. Look at that thick hair, just like your mother's. Wavy, black and copper like new cent pieces. Your eyes, same as mine.'

They embrace, Izzie's hands wetting the back of his shirt.

'Look at you. So handsome! My *Jezus*, how can you forgive me Tripp? Where were you? All this time, too much time!'

'I was working nearby. The scarf, your scarf. Grace arrived with … the man?'

'Charlie,' says Izzie.

'Grace and Charlie gave the scarf back to me, then brought me back to you.'

'How? I not know. So, confused.' She shakes her head. 'All I know is my love for you.'

Izabella's shock at seeing her ghost son has been swiftly dispelled. And Tripp's amazement and appreciation are near palpable.

Soon, the family say they have never seen Izzie so happy, so animated, alive—since arriving at the farm.

⁓

Izabella wavers between elation and despair. Could it have been near here that it happened, where Tripp was taken, in these waters? But she lived much further south, didn't she? And she had walked so far north on the days following Tripp's abduction. She's confused. Could she have not known her whereabouts all this time?

If not, she knows exactly why. Because she rarely sets foot outside the perimeter of the white picket fence-line—a barrier Charlie erected before she arrived. Unless it's under the cover of night to escape outside to pray and think about Tripp. Groceries are delivered to the farm, so she doesn't often need to go to the shops. *Everything is brought here.* The place names the family talk about: the school, the church, are unfamiliar, so she had no idea where she was. She still doesn't really know.

But perhaps Tripp was taken a long way from home and had been beside her all along. So near, so far. So near again.

Chapter Forty-Nine

Erin continually speaks of a miracle. She spent the first day simply staring at Tripp, looking shy and overwhelmed by the reconciliation. As soon as Fleur was introduced to him, they seemed to know and understand each other, like soul mates, the pair exchanging the first of a multitude of furtive glances—having an innate connection like his mother says she has with the girl.

Tripp soon begins his disclosures to his mother, Charlie and Grace about his missing years. At almost eighteen, he'd been living with Len Robinson since losing his mother as a young boy, working as a farmhand from a young age, staying on—feeling obliged to look after his mates.

Nothing seemed to ease his emptiness. Each day he searched his mind for clues to his real identity. Adrift at sea, waves pulling him to and fro, bearings lost. What he thought was his departure point had faded to a pale blur of background. His destination steadily faded too, and, after a while, he even forgot where he was originally heading. But he didn't forget to look for it. For her—his mother.

Tripp turned to the grog for a while to see if that would help; as with his mates, it didn't. He's decided not to talk about that.

But now Charlie has taken Tripp in, and he's letting him live in his house—with his mother in their own room—and Charlie is letting them eat with the family. He said he will pay Tripp a decent wage, and Tripp doesn't have a clue how all this could have happened.

When Izabella, Tripp and Fleur find themselves together in the lounge room on the evening of that first momentous day of reunion, Izzie's questions help Tripp reveal a little more.

'What are your memories from when you were with me, son?'

'I remember small things from home: you teaching me to read and write; the smell of wood burning; hot dinners; black cockatoos—they seemed more plentiful at our old place; both of us laughing as we romped about in the icy creek, remember? I remember your love. Your love.' Frowning, he looks down to his hands—the calloused patches on the palms, the fingerprints ingrained with dirty rivers going nowhere—then smiles up to his mother, his eyes twinkling now. 'Lots of happy times.'

'Ah, you remember! But, my poor boy, where've you been? What have you gone through? When you were taken from me, the pain broke my spirit. So much pain. You ... you were there in the water, then not there. Like some evil magic trick. You swam to the scarf because you knew it was ours. Your father gave it to me. I remember I told you to run, run, run! Back to your grandma. Away from that horrible man on the horse.'

'It's alright, Mummy. Really. I ran back to *nagymama*, but soon the man came.' Tripp looks away for a moment, lost in the horror, then back to Izabella. 'I remember what he said: "Hey, wog boy, where's yer mother?" and then he took me on his horse.' The words embarrass him in front of his mother and Fleur. Perhaps his mother has never heard the word wog—such a harsh term, like a disease. His recollections take him by surprise, and he realises it's the first time he has uttered such memories.

'I put the wet scarf under my cap. To hide it. Ha—he wasn't so smart. Thought he took everything from me, but not that, the piece of the puzzle that led me to you.'

'You remember *nagymama*! The Hungarian word for grandmother. Do you remember her?'

'A little. Where is she?'

Izabella averts her eyes from her son. 'With your grandfather, your *nagyapa*.'

'I don't remember him.'

'He was working away when you were little.'

'So that's why, Mummy.'

'*Anya*,' says Izabella.

'*Anya*,' says Tripp, grinning.

'How did they treat you, son, where you were living?'

Tripp's top lip starts to quiver, he eases it with his fingers. 'Alright, mother. My boss treated me okay,' Not willing to say otherwise yet. Not quite believing what he is calling her, that he can actually say the word *mother* to her in its literal meaning. Unsure of which language she'd prefer he use, he uses either, both—happy to be able to use any.

Tripp remembers being called a no-good refo wog, being slapped and punched—on the face, body, air punches when Robinson was too sozzled. For Tripp, any possibility of a pleasant exchange with that man was impossible. He knows there are many more confronting memories he has staunchly vaulted away for his own emotional protection, reasoning that time has a way of blocking things too painful to remember.

'He looks good, doesn't he, yes? Good, strong, handsome,' his mother seems unable to curb her impulse to compliment her son to Fleur.

Fleur returns her smile. 'Were you hurt, Tripp? We've heard stories about Robinson, about him having done some frightful things ...'

'No. I wasn't hurt.' What is hurt? Not having a home? Being tied up? Darkness? Hunger? Craving his mother—that was the worst hurt. He suffered all possible kinds of hurt. He doesn't tell them that he soon learnt that by playing the games obediently he could play it safe. He doesn't tell them the lies Robinson told him: that his mother never wanted him, that she couldn't cope, that it was for those reasons that she organised for Tripp to be taken from her. He doesn't tell them about his anger that raged like fire whenever he heard those lies. He wanted to kill Len Robinson. And at those times the last thing he wanted to do was to play it safe.

Like Tripp, most of the farmhands at the property felt like misfits, lost and abandoned, trying to make sense of past and present and their place in all of it. Cultures crushed, obliterated. Because a homogenised people are easier to control, Tripp supposes. Some of the workers were new to Australia and lived away from their families. Some years ago, the old man employed Aboriginal workers. They had been taken from their parents to live on a government-sanctioned church mission before working at the wheat farm. Some were told their parents were dead or simply didn't want them. One Aboriginal fellow told Tripp that it was curious spending so much time learning about a white man in a dress— Jesus Christ—teaching people to love one another, when they had lost everyone they had ever loved.

Tripp never stopped waiting for his mother to come to take him home, and Robinson became angry at the times he dared mention her name.

'At first it was hard, only being allowed to speak English, never our own languages. You can imagine what it was like for the Aboriginal kids—living on their own land and being controlled by a whitefella. I only realised I was Hungarian while once working with a fellow from Budapest on Robinson's property. He used the word *anya*.'

'You do remember some Hungarian words!' shouts Izzie, excited about things.

'Yes, I remember. I spent my time working on the farm. But I always read books, many books. The old boss fella gave them to me, to keep me quiet I think.' A twitch of smile, a deep breath. 'You know what? I want to learn more and be a teacher one day. I especially want to teach Hungarian to Aussies!'

His mother gives him a hug. 'And Greek, Tripp.'

'Why Greek?' asks Fleur.

'Because I am Greek, and so is Tripp! But Australian too,' says Izzie.

Fleur giggles at Izzie's words. 'I didn't know that.'

'I didn't know that either,' says Tripp.

'*Nani, nani*, my sweet baby *nani*,' Izzie sings to her son.

Despite himself, when he hears the familiar song sung with such heart by the mother he thought he'd never see again, he cries—big sobs.

She holds his hands, whispers. 'That, Tripp, is Greek. My mother was born in Crete. When she married my father, he took her to Hungary. He only allowed her to speak Hungarian, like my father did to me. But she wanted to teach me Greek, like I wanted for you.'

Beaming at Tripp, Fleur says, 'Ah, well then, you'll be busy Tripp. I like the idea of you being a teacher. And you know what? You seem clever enough. And if you are determined to do it, you will.'

Tripp wonders fleetingly if, how, Fleur could possibly admire his ambition. He gives her a shy, crinkly smile through the remaining tears, thinking to himself that this girl is a strange one, but a nice one, then changes the subject.

'So, you see, my life was busy, but I never, not for one day, didn't think of you, my *anya*, my mother.'

Izabella sheds tears now, too. Tripp studies her: hunched, tiny bird. With her paper-thin skin, he thinks she'd surely melt like soap in a hot shower.

Izzie speaks with him later, when she has recovered herself. Tripp tells her he thinks of his grandmother sometimes. Wonders how she is. Is she close by? Izzie has it in her mind that one day, when the time is right, she will find her mother again. She mumbles about Tripp's *nagyapa*—his grandfather, but isn't as keen to see him. She tells Tripp that she craves to tell her mother of her son's return, now she knows that Tripp's boss was an Australian, not a Hungarian friend of her father. Tripp is flummoxed about why the nationality of his boss is important to her. He might pursue that later.

Tripp hasn't known where he belongs for such a long time but being with his mother makes him realise he does have a home.

The following day, late afternoon. Tripp and Izabella sit together on her bed, in the room they share, Tripp unquestionably having moved in as soon as he arrived; Grace would have it no other way.

'I'll never forgive myself for losing you that day. I still don't know who took you.' Izzie places a small hand on her son's muscular leg.

'I went straight to Robinson's, I think. I don't remember being taken anywhere else. I was so young.'

'I fought so hard to keep you when you born, Tripp. You have to believe me.'

'What do you mean? Fought who?'

'I thought I'd done the right thing.' Izzie shakes her head despondently.

'What are you talking about?' Tripp sounds panicked.

'By keeping my baby. Keeping you with me. I wanted to love you, keep you safe. But Tripp, I must tell you, they wanted me to give you away.'

'Who wanted you to?'

'My father. Your *nagyapa*. You see, I was young, pregnant. *Apa*, my father thought I would bring shame to the family, so I was sent away to have you.'

'So, he didn't want me.' Tripp's voice is deep. Shakes his head, looks out the window.

'He didn't understand. If he knew you, he would love you.'

'Did you really want me, *Anya*?'

'Yes. Always forever! So much. I ran from hospital before you born, before they could take you from me. And you were quick to come into the world, my baby.'

'You must have been terrified.'

'Yes. But nothing would stop me. An angel, she help me to make you born. Then no-one was to take you away from me.'

Tripp is glad his mother believes in the divine. She would have had little left to hold onto. 'Oh, Mummy. And then later, someone did take me away from you. You can't blame yourself.'

'I died when you were taken from me. Fighting so hard for you. Always. I don't know who to blame anymore. You must tell me, Tripp, how that farm boss man really treated you. I've heard the Altons speak bad of him.'

'It was hard sometimes, to be honest. He always had a gun on him.

Sometimes he'd leave for weeks on end, which was good, but I stayed there with my mates, running the place. Robinson would threaten us before he left, ordering us not to leave or he'd call the police.' He doesn't tell her that he threatened their lives. 'We feared him. Robinson gave us some food, but it was never enough. So, we caught fish. But he didn't like that—thought he owned the river. We sheltered nearby the river—that was our home. Got some Government blankets to keep us warm at night.' His voice sounds panicky. 'I find this difficult to talk about ...'

'It's alright, my love.'

'I worry for my mates left behind on his land.'

'Perhaps one day we help them, Tripp. But for now, we have each other.'

'You know, *Anya*, when I was with the Aboriginal workers, they told me stories. About how the whitefellas took their land—they built fences and raised cattle which ate the grass. That grass was meant to be food for the kangaroos. Then the 'roos went away because they had no food. The whitefellas then built fences over the Aborigines' yam farms. Because they were starving, they took the whitefellas' cows. So the whites killed them with their muskets, their guns.

'I heard how the Aboriginal people reacted to their weapons: they dropped and then they got up and danced. They dropped because they knew the muskets were only good for one shot. They showed them, outsmarted them. Well, some of them did, the ones who didn't get killed. I sometimes wish I could have been there, hiding in the bushes, seeing those whites run and run! I'd be there cheering on the Aborigines. The mates I worked with are good people. Good skin, as they say. Peaceful people. But they weren't saved at the battle at Appin—white men on horses—Aboriginal men, women, children all gone.'

'They have been through so much. So, have you, Tripp and I don't know why. We came to Australia for safety. But there is suffering here, too.' Izabella cries a little, for the souls of those Aboriginal people, but not knowing what Appin was.

'What was my father like?'

Izabella's eyes avert from her son. Wipes them with her fists. 'You've seen men. Some good, some bad. Your father was good man when I met him.'

'And later?'

'And then he started drinking. He changed, for bad.'

'These are good people here in this house, aren't they?' says Tripp.

'Yes, lots of love here. But not our family. When I lost that scarf that day, when I lost you, I knew I'd lost everything. But it's done its job, that scarf—brought us together now. We are family, you and me.'

They hug so tight it is as if they can't tell one from the other.

Chapter Fifty

'What's that music?' asks Grace, as if Charlie would know. She sits up in bed, turning her ear towards the noise.

'Sounds like the gramophone. S'truth, it's a bit late for that. Must be nearly midnight!'

'Shush! Listen. Maria Callas. It's Bellini's "Casta diva"! It must be Erin. I didn't even know she had that record. I used to listen to it. Always sounds particularly plaintive to me. But that voice!' says Grace.

'I've a mind to march out there.'

'Leave it be. It's satisfying to the soul,' says Grace.

'What's gotten into you, wifey?'

'A voice so thrilling ne'er was heard in spring-time from the cuckoo-bird.'

'So, said …?'

'Wordsworth, "The Solitary Reaper". One of his finest,' says Grace.

'Whatever you reckon. From now on, I'll believe every word you tell me,' says Charlie. 'Can you believe what really happened today, Grace?' Charlie stares at the ceiling from their bed.

'No, not really. I'm still pinching myself about how the situation unfolded.'

Grace was initially worried that she should have somehow prepared Izabella for Tripp's arrival, thinking the shock may have been too much for her to bear. But she reasons that she didn't have time.

'They say truth is stranger than fiction, but I'm finding the whole thing hard to digest, too. Perhaps you can explain it better to me?'

says Charlie.

'I wish I were able to. I had absolutely no idea he would be there. I just knew about the connection to the scarf, Izzie, and a boy I suspected was her son. With the stories that have circulated about Robinson killing a boy, what else could I conclude?'

'Do you know how ridiculous that sounds? What, just by seeing the scarf you were able to put that together?' He looks as though he doesn't know whether to think she's stir-crazy, to be angry or simply intrigued.

'I know it sounds silly, which is exactly why I stopped telling people about my, my other side.'

'And you say you've always had this 'other side' as you call it?'

'Yes. I think my mother has it. And I have a feeling Teddy may have had it, too. Please don't be upset with me.'

'I'm not, silly sausage. I'm just, well, perplexed.'

'I know—I warned you before, you're married to a crazy person.'

'Remember after Teddy left us, how I said you could put your gift I think I called it, to good use? Well, to tell you the truth, I didn't believe in any of that stuff, thought you were grieving—that's it.'

'I can't blame you,' says Grace.

'Well, now I've seen you use your gift to do good. Grace, you've just reunited two people who love each other dearly, two people who were plucked from their home and taken to live with strangers, two people who thought they'd never meet again.'

'I hope we're not strangers to them now,' says Grace.

'No, I don't think so,' says Charlie.

'But I wonder if it's enough.'

'It's a beautiful thing, that's all I know.'

'But Charlie, Izzie was involved, too. It took a lot for her to tell us about her past. And Teddy was involved too; I have no doubt about it. I like to think he knew this would happen all along, which is why he hid the scarf. I don't mean he wanted to, to go. But he saw a wrong that had to be righted, and he did right it. Our darling little trouper.'

And Charlie looks as though he believes her words wholeheartedly, wondering why he should ever doubt her wisdom.

Tripp's homecoming, and that is how they view it, goes a long way towards bucking things up around the farm, on the surface anyway. The handing over of the sacrificial lambs to Len Robinson was somehow easier, lighter than Charlie expected, he told Grace. But it still hurt; he just had to make sure he didn't look the stock in the eye.

The issue of what to tell the family of Tripp's miraculous, or at least untimely return was handled as sensitively as possible by Charlie and Grace. They told everyone at the farm, including Marco and the boys, that Izabella had disclosed to them about her son named Tripp, and that she owned the scarf Teddy found on the Robinson property. So, Charlie and Grace had decided to ask Len if he knew anything about it. Which was the truth. What they didn't say was their fear that Tripp may have been killed. Of course, when Len had told them the scarf belonged to a fellow named Tripp who worked on his property, they'd naturally put two and two together and asked Robinson if they could bring Tripp to the farm to see if he and Izabella recognised one another.

How blessed is the family having Tripp to help Charlie around the farm? Grace somehow knows he will become his right-hand man. She sometimes wonders why Robinson inferred Tripp was lazy, because he seems so reliable and conscientious. Did that horrible man really believe the words he said? Or was Tripp lazy there, at his farm—so distraught with being there that he just plain gave up on work, on life, stopped trying? Or did Robinson not want him to leave? Was that why he spoke so unflatteringly about him? Did he let him go so as not to be questioned? And if he wanted Tripp to stay, why?

Charlie told the girls and his workers never to go near Robinson's property again, as he had treated Tripp appallingly. So far, no-one has broached the topic of why Tripp has not gone back, why the bastard hasn't dragged him back. Everyone is flying high on the reunion.

Grace told Tripp about losing Teddy, about the pain the family has gone through, about how finding Tripp alive has lifted them all in ways they've never experienced.

Chapter Fifty-One

From the moment Izzie arrived at the farm until now, Grace had felt ashamed because she couldn't bring herself to have a real talk with her. She knows why. It's because of the guilt Grace felt about using Izzie for help with the household without knowing her story. Why didn't they show enough interest for Izzie to feel safe enough to divulge her secrets? There was no real reciprocated trust. She must have constantly craved for her home and family, her culture. Grace always saw it in Izzie—the emptiness—and she didn't once pursue it. Were Charlie and Grace somehow complicit in keeping Izzie from all she ever loved? Perhaps not, because Grace also knew that for some reason that girl was hiding from her past.

'Sit with me, please,' says Grace as a cheerful, singing Izabella dries her wet hands on a dishcloth and pulls up a chair opposite her at the table in the kitchen.

'You have a lovely voice; you should sing more. Perhaps you will sing more now? Quite honestly, we never thought we'd see you happy like this, Izzie.'

'Of course,' a simple reply, her mood darkening a little, as if something as momentous as the return of her son happens every day. Grace can't help wonder what exactly Izzie means by her aloof reply.

'I hope you don't mind me asking, but this has troubled us greatly. Why on earth would you not have told us you had a son?'

'You don't understand. How could you? Please don't think me bad mother.' Tears start welling in Izzie's eyes.

'No, no, that's not what we think. We just want to know the truth.'

'Truth? I couldn't tell you.' She says it as if she doesn't know what truth is anymore.

'But why? That makes no sense. We could have helped. Surely there can't be anything worse than losing a son.' Grace sighs heavily, tears brimming in her own eyes. 'Dear God, I know how it feels. You shouldn't have suffered in silence. We had both lost sons, Izzie. We could have talked ...'

'Oh, I wanted to, Grace. If I could have cried and cried in front of you ...'

'But you didn't.' And I didn't, not once, ask you anything about your past, frets Grace.

'I did. Every night. Not in front of you.'

'What happened? How, why, when, did Tripp leave you?'

'So, so many questions I still have.' Izzie takes a breath, releasing it through pursed lips. 'Grace, my father is Hungarian. He wants me to marry Hungarian and have lots of children. But when I get pregnant with Tripp, and I not married, he was very, very angry. He told me he had friends who were going to take my baby from me at hospital. Do you know, Grace, I was in hospital with girls, many young girls, all having their babies taken from them? I could not let this happen, so I ran away.'

A chill runs up Grace's spine. Are there actually hospitals like this?

'So, you ran away from hospital?' She shakes her head to block out the visions of the poor girls.

'Yes. I not let them take my baby! I found my way home to live with my *anya*, my mother. Father was away.'

'But when did you lose Tripp?'

'One day, when Tripp nearly five years old, we were swimming. A man on horse came and took him away. I not know why or where he from. All this time, my boy was gone. Me wanting him, Tripp wanting his mother. What did he think of me?'

'Oh, Izzie, I'm so sorry. But why didn't you tell us? We could have helped you find him.'

'How could I? You tell me how much you want me here. I not know where Tripp is. I not know where I am. I walked for two days with no food or water to find him, for my baby. Days and nights! And for what? Bitten by snake. Who was the man to take him? From hospital? My father's friends? My own father? Perhaps, yes. Had I sign papers at hospital? I not know. I was, I am criminal. Criminal for stealing my own son!' Breathless now.

'No, Izzie. You're not a criminal. You were always meant to have Tripp. Look at you both together! You were never meant to be apart.'

'But how did you find him?'

'The scarf. Teddy found it where Tripp was working. When you said it was yours and you had a son, we had to find out if your son was there and had lost your scarf.'

'So, Teddy help.'

'Yes dear, Teddy help.'

'You don't know how it feels to want to escape, Grace. The worst was in Budapest—losing our home and people we loved. Losing our rights.'

'Losing control.'

'Yes, Grace.'

Do you feel we have taken control of you, Izzie? 'Loss of control is a terrible thing.' Grace can barely look at her.

'We escape and then we come here and I still wanted escape, feeling like bear on a tight chain.'

'What did you want to escape from?' *From us?*

'Control. Ha.' Her laugh is bitter. 'Sometimes inside here,' she points to her head, 'I cannot escape. My dreams—so dark.'

'Escape can take many forms, Izzie.'

'How you mean?'

'Sometimes I can use my thoughts to escape what goes on in the world.' *Or my thoughts use me ...* Grace has slipped into dangerous territory and doesn't want Izzie thinking she is strange. The woman needs stability. 'Anyhow. I guess at times life throws us challenges, and everyone faces things they want to escape from.'

'And some people we want to escape from too, Grace.' There is a far-away look in her eyes. Did Izzie fear someone from her past, as Grace feared Plasticine Man?

'Yes people, and sometimes places too, when those places become stained.'

'What is stain?'

'Ruined, broken.'

'So, you run from bad people and bad place. Everyone running! I hope Budapest is rid of stain now.'

'I am sure it will be as beautiful as ever, eventually.' Grace wonders if Izabella even knows that Hungary was invaded again in 1956.

'When did you want to escape, Grace?'

'Sometimes when I was young, I wanted very much to escape.' *And I did escape with the help of beyond. Do you ever want to escape from us, Izzie?* She wants to say it, but the lump in Grace's throat is preventing more of her words from coming out.

∽

Seventeen-year-old Fleur is on her bed again. Why can't she breathe out the pain? She can feel it right down the front of her; the hurt hits like a thud of grief when she breathes in, but the pain doesn't escape with her release of breath, which she feels logically it should. It's her but it's not her. How can that be? She's sure that if she could manage to cut out the front of her body from head to belly, the hurt would be gone, flown free in a whoosh—an escape of bloody flesh. But of course, she wouldn't have the nerve to do it.

Armed with her rudimentary tools of tweezers and nail scissors, Fleur moves stealthily into the bathroom and locks the door behind her. She tackles several more pores today, gouging out ever widening holes on her décolletage, breasts and stomach. With pedantic precision, she works with fine motor skills that would rival those of a surgeon. When the penance is done for now, calamine lotion and her mother's face powder help cover the evidence. Unsteadily, she edges back to her bed and collapses.

Surface wounds need the healing power of air; air turns toxic when it enters Fleur. Her surface wounds may eventually scar, but how can her heart possibly mend? She knows she's encumbered. Too fragile, too fast, too damaged, too … sleep.

Chapter Fifty-Two

One Thursday, Grace hears the old Chev truck chug up their driveway, wheezing to a halt outside the house. Peeking through from the lounge room, Grace notices a passenger up front with her husband. Charlie has returned home from the house of his old school friend Marmaduke (Dukie), who lives with his wife and son about ten miles away from the Alton farm. Having not seen his friend for several years, he'd gone there on Dukie's instigation to catch up on old times. Rather than being put out by not being invited, Grace was rather glad, as she'd always found Dukie and Carmen Harris tiresome, pompous. Charlie ushers a young man inside as Grace swiftly moves from sight.

'Grace, Grace, where are ya?' yells Charlie as the pair move through the kitchen to the hallway.

'What? What is going on?' Grace is flustered, worried, not used to being summoned by her husband with such verve. She races from the lounge-room, where she had been listening to her regular ABC radio broadcast of 'Blue Hills'—a daily indulgence she prefers to staring at the black and white television set Charlie has given pride and place. She's not happy about the interruption.

'What is it?' she snaps, knowing he has company but not caring. She catches sight of the young man.

'You remember Scott, don't you Grace,' Charlie states, leaving Grace no room for negation.

And now Grace is furious for not being warned of Dukie's son's arrival.

'Of course, I do. How are you?'

She attempts a smile, offering him a hand to shake as he comes in for an unexpected embrace. Grace remembers Scott from years ago—much shorter, in his mid-teens, rushing away after meeting her. Unfortunately, she remembers him as particularly spoilt.

Descendants of wealthy dairy farmers from the 1800s, Scott's family once owned substantial property in New South Wales. His parents decided to cut and run from the industry, preferring instead to buy out the family's art deco mansion in eastern Pig Peak, where they live out their days in luxury. Unless they feel the pull of a stiff sea breeze and ocean view, in which case they retire to their beach house.

'My, you've certainly grown into a handsome young man,' says Grace, truthfully—the dark red hair; piercing, dark emerald, almost black eyes—but kicking herself for bolstering what she's sure is the boy's already over-inflated ego. Unless he's changed.

'Thank you, Mrs Alton, but I think your flattery is slightly misplaced.'

'Oh, nonsense. He's handsome *and* clever. Grace, I'm here to tell you that this boy here is a miracle worker!' Charlie's eyes are gleaming with heated excitement.

'Well now, that's quite a title coming from Charlie,' says Grace, trying to lighten the mood, trying to avert her eyes from her sickening, grovelling other half.

'This is embarrassing. All I did was fix your car.'

'Baloney! It wasn't small change, Grace; it was *an engine fail.*'

As though Grace had addressed him. What's he trying to prove?

'My good old truck. I may not have made it home. Could've been stuck out in the middle of nowhere with no food, no water. Could even've skidded off the road, smack bang into a tree! This boy pulled the whole unit apart, then put it back together with all the new parts and all. Miracle worker—that's what he is I tell ya. He's a mechanic, he is. Done the whole apprenticeship. Works like a trooper—and so does the car now!'

'That's wonderful, dear. Thank you very much for helping us, Scott,' says Grace, wishing her husband would shut up; this fawning wasn't like him at all.

'And he wouldn't take a penny for all his troubles. A gem—that's what he is!'

Grace wonders if Charlie has been drinking, but as she glides past him on her way to the kitchen, shouting 'Who's for a cuppa?' she can't smell any grog on his breath. And that almost worries her more.

⁓

That certainly wasn't the last of it: Dukie decided to invite Charlie, Grace and both girls to dinner the following week.

The girls don't want to go. They haven't been out much since their brother's accident. But Grace imagines they won't regret coming when they see the house—magnificent, according to Charlie—when they see the handsome catch.

They take a slow drive along a long bitumen driveway lined with Illawarra flames and jacarandas, until the residence comes into view. A huge white stucco mansion beckons, looking as though it's just sailed in from somewhere grand; a house for suitably grand tenants, thinks Grace. Chimneys galore. Two levels, curved windows on both sides, and in its centre: two tiers of sweeping balconies. 'Ah' sighs Grace aloud, imagining what it would be like to have an upstairs bedroom with a verandah and view. She flashes back to the balcony scene in *Rebecca*. Shoos away the thought.

Grace reckons the rusty old truck looks so out of place she is on the verge of begging her husband to park out the back. Too late. One side of the glass entry door immediately opens and there stands Dukie smoking a cigar. The family clamber out and ascend the stairs to the verandah. Dukie greets them heartily and ushers them inside, competing with the melodic multilingual chatter of a lyrebird coming from nearby rainforest. The message of the lyrebird's call does not go unnoticed by Grace; she can't help but think that someone here is two-faced.

The four of them enter the large reception area and stand gobsmacked, staring up at the pale green patterns on the glass ceiling. Grace swallows her pride.

'Lalique—the ceiling—the house is Robin Boyd,' states Dukie, bored, as though he's had to explain these simple architectural facts to company a thousand times. Perhaps he has.

'Oh, it is truly spellbinding,' admits Grace, awestruck, angry at herself for being impressed.

When they look back down to earth, they notice the walls are dripping with paintings: watercolours, oils, bawdy sketches—Heysen, Streeton, Norman Lindsay—Gods of the Australian art world. Grace recognises the artists and their works; her Norman Park home held similar paintings; her mother's family having collected them.

Scott's mother Carmen—dressed to the hilt, her strawberry blonde hair coiffed and lacquered stiff—appears in the room, followed by her son. With casual flashes of smiles, they extend their hands in greeting. Erin and Fleur blush and batter the eyelashes of their come-hither eyes at the sight of Scott, the owner of his own pair of come-hither eyes.

'Grace!' Carmen's one extended hand is drooped like a begging dog's paw.

Grace suspects she is expected to kiss it. She backs up.

'How wonderful that you could make it,' Carmen says haughtily, retracting her paw. 'Did Dukie tell you what happened when Charlie arrived here last week? It was all rather deliciously funny, I must say. I thought he was one of the gardeners! I began to instruct him about pruning the rose bushes in the Monet—one of our many gardens—before Dukie stopped me. It was all a bit embarrassing at the time. I do hope he forgives me. It was just, just … his clothes, and the hat!' She cups her mouth, muffling the giggles which keep coming.

'Happy to meet you, Carmen,' says Grace. 'I was just admiring your paintings. Your Norman Lindsay is superb. My family in Brisbane has two of Norman's and one by his brother Lionel in the collection.' She can play bitch, too.

'Curious,' says Carmen, deadpan. She turns on her heels and walks away.

Dinner is served on gleaming silver platters and eaten from the best English china: a delicious spread of French onion soup, baked salmon with vegetables, and a peach Melba for dessert. Grace notices the girls trying to eat daintily so as not to stain the white linen serviettes. To impress? Scott guzzles with gusto.

After dinner, as they sit drinking coffee in the lounge room, the girls vie for Scott's attention, Erin fixing him with a flutter of eyelashes and her most coquettish glances.

'So, Scott, Dad tells me you're a top-notch mechanic,' says Fleur.

'Just something I do to keep my hands busy.'

Fleur blushes, and Grace imagines her daughter wishing she could help him keep his hands busy.

'Mum tells us we should be doing more things like fixing cars, but I'd rather be playing the piano,' says Erin.

What could Fleur say were her interests? Grace wonders. *I hate my sister. I hate my life. My mother blames me for taking Teddy to the river. I miss Teddy.* Grace nearly sobs as she watches Fleur flounder, opening and closing her mouth with nothing coming out.

'What a charming and impressive hobby. You must play something for us, Erin,' enthuses Scott.

'Mum and Dad,' says Scott loudly, interrupting the parents' conversation about farming enough to make Dukie stub out his half-smoked Scooters cigar.

'Erin plays piano! I was just saying that she should give us a little show,' continues Scott when he's sure he holds the room.

'Yes, please dear, we would adore that!' gushes Carmen.

Erin's eyes widen. 'What? Right now?'

'No time like the present, dear.'

Erin scans the room as though she's looking for a way out; the exit beckons. But she skulks over to the Steinway where she sits contemplating before playing a perfect rendition of Gershwin's 'Rhapsody in Blue'—all twenty minutes or so of it—aided by the perfect acoustics of the room.

'Do you remember sitting in the funicular together?' whispers Grace to Charlie. 'What you said about Gershwin? You were going to bring him to us that night.' She tries to remove herself to that other place, other time.

'How could I forget the girl in blue deserving of no less than a rhapsody?'

Applause breaks out around the room. Scott fixes Erin with eyes that light up that room, in a stare that Grace knows says: 'You're mine'.

As the family walks to the car, Grace hisses to Charlie: *'A plague on both your houses.'*

He shoots her a look of shock.

'Literally, Charlie—the mansion here, and the beach house.' Grace smirks.

Fleur won't let her sister sleep. Or is it just that she can't sleep herself? She's not quite sure.

'There's something a bit smarmy about him, don't you think?'

'Oh really? Is that why you were making eyes at him all night?' accuses Erin.

'I was NOT! I'm more into the less goody-goody type. Okay, I suppose you could call him good looking in a classic kind of way. A bit Gregory Peckish, I guess,' says Fleur.

'Hmm. *I'm* suddenly feeling particularly peckish for a classic kind of good-looking guy.'

'Oh, shut up. Me? Well, I'm more into the James Dean, Elvisy type. Rugged, outdoorsy, manly,' teases Fleur.

'So, you're saying he's not manly?' asks Erin.

To Fleur's delight, her sister has sweetly taken the bait. 'No, not at all, not really.'

'What, not manly, or you're not saying he's not?'

'Shut up and go to sleep.' Fleur turns her back on her sister and tries to sleep, unsuccessfully. Switches her position.

The good twin, the prettier twin. She'll get him—she probably already has.

Erin lies awake too. Fleur can see her teeth glowing in the dark; she's obviously smiling, aware of her sister's jealousy. Scott is exactly the type of boy her parents would want her to marry. But what about Cappi? wonders Fleur.

Chapter Fifty-Three

Len Robinson knew Tripp the minute his mate brought him to the farm. Plucked from his mother just as he'd organised—easy as picking apples. He has her eyes, her hair, even her smile when he managed to crack one. Everything about that lad is her, and it pisses Len right off; it's no wonder he can't stand him.

A funny thing: Len never really wanted him in the first place. The prize was imagining his mother pining for him, for all those years. Tripp has been nothing but a burden to Len, so he supposes he should be grateful the Altons took the boy from him. Funny too how in all these years Tripp never recognised his dear old dad. But that was a good thing really because Len didn't want Tripp asking questions about why his father never came back to him and his precious mother.

But it would've gotten all too boring. And difficult, what with the wife Dot back at the farm and all. And it was too hard to get grog out there in that never-never bullshit place where the bloody gypsies lived.

And Tripp and that scarf—talk about rubbing Len's nose in it. Funny thing is, Izzie had no idea Len had pocketed it from his little Italian ragazza—the wild dago he had before finding Izzie. A little memento of their 'time' together. And neither did Tripp obviously by the way he near worshipped the thing.

What the hell does Charlie Alton want with Len's son? Better not be something to do with that crazy wog Izzie. He will be keeping a close eye on Charlie. He's had the Alton farm on his radar for a long while now and Charlie doesn't have a bloody clue about it. So, Len resolves to keep an ear out at the pub now more than ever. His mates will keep things sweet. They'll keep him up to speed about exactly what kind of operation Charlie has going on there. Charlie had better keep looking over his shoulder. Len Robinson has friends in high places with a low tolerance for bribery.

'Where is the scarf, Mummy?' Tripp asks Izabella, scanning their room as though it will magically appear.

'With my clothes. Why?'

'Because I want you to get rid of it now.'

'Why, Tripp? We had some good times with that scarf.' Good and bad times.

'Because we don't need it anymore. And having it here is like having my father around.'

Izabella widens her eyes at her son. How much does he remember? 'And he must have become a bad man, or you would still be with him, we would be with him,' says Tripp.

Izzie wipes away a tear, goes to a drawer and pulls out the scarf. 'It's alright now, Tripp. We're alright together, aren't we. We're safe and happy together. Those times are gone. This thing here,' she holds up the material faded almost beyond recognition, dead long ago, 'this thing brought us together again, but it won't pull us apart. We'll burn it together.' Realising she hates it now.

And so, they make plans for the next day, when they'll hide it under the wood stack sitting neatly in the fireplace, ready and waiting for the next cold night when it will be extinguished forever.

One Monday, checking fences, Marco says to Charlie, 'I need to ask you a favour, mate. I would very much like to take myself and the boys to Italy for two weeks. It is my grandfather's ninetieth birthday. My children don't remember him, and I would very much like for them to see him before it's too late. I know you are short on hands at present, but the joining time for the sheep is over and things are fairly quiet here.'

'Of course, you can go. But you must promise to come back to us. I fear we wouldn't function without you lot.' Charlie is more than happy to grant his hardest worker this rare request, having not had a holiday since Charlie and Grace first arrived at the farm. And everyone at the farm reckons Marco, a widower, is a marvel, raising his kids with so little support.

'Ha, no worries there, Charlie. But if you want, I can find someone to take my place when I'm gone.'

'There'll be no need for that, Marco. I'll manage just fine. You go and have some precious, and much deserved, family time.'

The family prepares to leave the following Sunday, their bags having been packed for weeks.

Charlie buys a car, a sparkling green 1968 Dodge utility. Despite the car being brand new, Charlie decided he simply *had* to have Scott check it out. Of course, he did—Grace thinks he'd do almost anything to see anyone from that family. Scott returned it with a clean bill of health.

'I don't want you driving it,' Grace tells Charlie one morning at breakfast.

Izzie brings a fresh pot of tea to the table and refills both cups.

Charlie appears stumped. 'What? The new ute? Why would you say that?'

'I don't trust it. I have a bad feeling.'

'What? You have absolutely no reason to think the car isn't safe, Grace. Scott has just done a full inspection on it. Anyone would think you didn't trust Scott. And it's brand new, for goodness sake!' He leans back, crosses his arms.

She tries to keep cool yet give direct instruction. He needs to take note of her words. 'Just promise me you'll use Marco's car while he's away and get him to have a look at it when he gets back.'

'Alright, I'll have a word with him. But I must say I think you're being mighty paranoid.'

Grace could easily shatter the cups with the look she sends her husband.

'More tea?' asks Izzie, refilling the cups to almost overflowing, steadying them with a hand. Does she fear they'll explode?

Grace can't shake the dread. She knows Charlie was looking forward to dropping Marco and his family at the bus station in the new rig, but he will be doing so driving Marco's silver Holden panel van instead.

Izabella is alone. Earlier, Charlie drove the family to church and left them there for the annual picnic—under duress by the sound of the commotion they made before they left. Tripp even decided to go along to church to keep Fleur company. A parishioner has agreed to drive them back to the farm later in the day, Grace told Izzie, because Charlie would be dropping Marco and his family at the bus station in the afternoon and the station is in the opposite direction.

For the first time in years, Izzie has time to think, really think. Of her parents. She lets her thoughts drift to where the couple may be if they are still together. Far away probably, yes, but rivers join, and there's a chance her *anya* is out there waiting for her and Tripp. She knows her mother—even if she suspected she and Tripp were here—would never dare approach. Losing her daughter and grandchild would have aged her just like its aged Izzie. She thinks of her own greying hair, her wrinkled hands. Her mother would be getting old now. She may even be dead. She may even have died of a broken heart.

Izzie paces the kitchen floor, contemplating her options. Charlie will be back in a couple of hours, so if she is to get moving, she will have to do so now. She feels like Cinderella. But she won't be searching for her prince; she's after freedom.

Chapter Fifty-Four

Izzie layers herself: boots, a wide-brimmed straw hat and grey weatherproof jacket—gifts from Grace, items rarely worn, let alone tested for weather. She manages a smile in the mirror, approving of the disappearance of the white ghost. She has decided to start small, due to the time limit. Just to the river today. Another time, when she has much more time to spare, she'll try to discover what is left of her family. She can't worry about her father anymore; it is her mother she must find. One day.

Slowly opening the gate of the picket fence, Izzie takes her first tentative step—the first of thousands she will make this morning—scared at what she may find. Moves past the livestock shed, past the birthing dams, past Marco's place and the spare cottage that she and Tripp will move into soon. She dodges sheep, climbs over fences into the next paddocks because she finds the gates locked. She conquers the obstacles with an agility that surprises her. Gaining in confidence, her steps turn to strides.

Izzie feels it—something out here with teeth and claws that she must trap. She has her own weapon now: freedom, if only short-lived. She must keep an eye on the sun. Soon after midday, she'll return to the farm to be back in time for Charlie's arrival home.

She recalls the story of Cinderella—one she shared with Erin and Fleur many times when the girls were little—in her often-broken English, making them laugh. The girls were in awe when Izzie told them she, too, used to live near a beautiful real castle on the Buda in Hungary. They laughed at the similarities of the names—the rhyme:

Izabella Cinderella. But unlike the girl in that story, the Altons have always tried to make Izabella feel welcome. Perhaps Grace felt sorry for Izzie, as the reader feels sorry for little Cinders. But now, Izzie truly believes she could become a heroine. Although there'll be no coach to take her to the ball, no handsome prince to meet her there, she could do something worthwhile. Knows the catch: she must get back to the farm at a certain time, or things will go very wrong.

    The last paddock borders the Europa River. She climbs the fence and patters her sore feet across the bumpy stones towards the river. Izzie is awestruck by the strong current; she hasn't seen water flow like this for such a long time, and its clean rush and animation take her unawares, breathing new life into her. The need of freedom denied for way too long pulses in her temples like a welcome guest knocking at her door.

    She races along the river's edge, no longer so aware of the blisters which are forming on her feet today. When she tires, she crouches down and washes her hands in the invigorating water. She lets her hands and feet soak. Underwater, her palms look pink and mottled—larger and somehow stronger than they really are. Takes a long slurp of coldness, splashes her face, which provides pep—a boost of—

    She jolts at the sound of a gunshot, almost overbalancing in the stony shallows. A boost of bravery? The thought now complete. Terrifying memories of her last days in Budapest come flooding back. Perhaps the whole world is dangerous, she fears. When she again finds her feet, still in a crouch she retracts her head and limbs like a tortoise. Tries so hard not to move but she is shaking and could easily topple over again. Hears the loudening clump, clump of heavy boots coming towards her along the pebbly beach, disrupting the steady rush of water. There's nowhere to hide.

    'Who goes there? Show yerself,' a man commands.

    Izabella freezes. She wishes she were brave enough to get up and dance at him, like those Aboriginal people did all those years ago. But she can't, she lacks strength. She can feel him coming ever closer until shots of his hot breath hit her ear.

    'I said show yourself!' he yells, making her jump.

Slowly she unfolds her body and stands to face him. She looks up at the tall, hatted man, down to his grey bristles of beard, distended chest and stomach shadowing the ground in front of him as though announcing his tenebrosity. His vacant eyes remind her of two dull pits from poison fruit. He's carrying a rifle. She tries desperately to unravel her thoughts.

'Get your scrawny arse off my property *now*! I've had enough of you lot comin' here, on my land, my land. Now, git goin' before I call the cops.' He snarls, revealing a brown-stained flash of crooked teeth. He cocks his gun.

A burst of recognition, then nausea, as Izzie notices the man who is so angry and ugly is Joe. Does he not even know his own pretending wife? 'Jesus, Mary and Joseph.' Shaking her head, she can't stop herself from mumbling the words she only ever used with this man.

He fixes her with a stare. 'What the …? Izzie? What the blazes are you doin' here?' He returns the cocking handle to a safe position.

'I want to find my mother,' is all she can manage.

'Well, she sure as shit ain't here. Where did you come from? Are you alone?' His eyes shoot around like they're tracking flies.

'Yes. I'm alone.' She notices a small group of men working in distant fields, cutting wheat with sickles; she's seen them in books Fleur has read to her. It hits her with a thud: the evil neighbour employing men from Europe, treating them badly. *Where am I? No, not Robinson's? Please no.* He had Tripp … She trembles, one eye starting to twitch.

'Where did you come from?' he repeats, slowly, deliberately. Staring at her with apparently no recognition of times they'd had together.

'Over there.' She lets her arm make a wide arc in the general direction of the Alton's farm; it feels heavy and dead as though disconnected from her body.

'Over there, eh?' He mimics her arm movement, rubs his bristly chin. Knits his brows.

She notices a shadow directly under her hat, encircling her. Midday.

'I need to get going. I need to go home.'

'Izzie. Remember, I'm your husband. At least you could show me a little lovin' before you go back to your caravan or wherever bullshit place it is you live now, gypsy girl.'

She feels heat radiating from her body as she backs away. Can't think of what to say to this horrible creature.

'Look, darling, I'll make it easy for you. Just one kiss and you can go.' He moves to her, leans over and kisses her roughly—probing as though trying to claim her mouth, his stubble irritating her soft mouth and chin.

'Now I'll walk you home. See, I'm a man of my word.' The steel of his gun shines in the sunlight.

'I can walk myself home.'

'No chance. Come on. Let's go.' He grabs her by the arm. 'Lead on, McDuff!'

She has no idea what he has just said to her. There's no choice, she must go back to the farm—she knows of nowhere else nearby, but *she'll* lead *him*, so they will approach from the front of the property, along the roadside. Fleur once drew her a map to show her exactly where the farm was positioned, trying to reassure Izzie when she didn't know where she was, when she refused to go exploring with her. Izabella remembers the map's coordinates. So, she leads him, at right angles to the homestead, knowing they will hit more road than if they went back the way she came. And more chance of seeing Charlie. Biding time.

Just before they get to the roadside, he pulls her into the bushes, shoving her to the ground. Falling on top, he tugs at the zip of his trousers. It catches. Shocked, her immediate reaction is to fight back. But she soon realises the absurdity of her retaliation; he being about three times her weight now. Caught under his huge bulk she's barely able to draw breath. As he claws at her undergarments, she notices the rifle and its holster now on the ground. Fully clothed and grunting like a bush pig, she's aware he is losing control. Thinks how easy it could be for her to grab that gun, aim the barrel at his cruel face and shoot him, right at the moment of his climax. But she knows the gun is too large, too heavy, and so is he, so she doesn't—she just lies there, making sure she keeps drilling her dark eyes into his blank ones.

He catches her gaze and stops, simply stops. He rolls off her, jumping up and away, and he's shaking like a leaf. She's realising she has other weapons; she will get her time to dance soon.

The earth tilts on its axis. The illusion is of the fierce sun moving towards the western skies, as though it's had enough of the scene below. Ready to move on.

Chapter Fifty-Five

They are heading south beside the roadside, towards the Alton farm. The man has not released her arm, nor stopped digging his fingers into her soft flesh. The sting of her captor's ever-tightening pinch—piercing her skin with his broken, grubby fingernails—makes her want to scream, or cry, but she remains silent. She notices the menacing rifle slung back over his shoulder.

She hears the roar of a vehicle behind them. Both turn to see a silver panel van driven by a man slowly approaching them. Izabella knows the car Charlie is driving belongs to Marco.

The van stops, and for a couple of minutes the three of them stare blankly at one another. She watches as Charlie eyes the rifle, visible despite the man's lame efforts to hide it behind his shoulder as the car neared them. Not taking his eyes off the pair, or the gun, Charlie turns off the ignition and slowly gets out, standing at a distance of around ten feet to face them. Charlie would know to tread gently.

'So, neighbour, what brings you out on such a fine day?' asks the man.

Izzie is horrified. Neighbour. She knows the meaning of this word. Joe is the man who employed Tripp, who treated him so badly. Only he has a new name now. She shudders.

'I notice you're walking with our Izzie. Bringing her home, are you?'

'What d'ya mean, *our Izzie*? That's not a polite thing to say to a man about his wife.'

Izabella looks to the ground. With the man's words ringing in her head, she sees Charlie almost gag. She can imagine his thoughts: What the hell is he talking about? There is no way Izzie would have married a monster like Len Robinson. He doesn't pursue it.

'Come on, you two. I'll give you a lift,' says Charlie.

Izzie realises he is trying to make light of a situation which could easily fall apart.

'To where, my house or yours?' asks the man.

'Mine,' states Charlie firmly.

'That's good, because Dot hasn't vacuumed.' He smirks at his enemy, 'And I have some things I need to discuss with youse.'

The three of them get in the van: Izzie next to Charlie in the front, Robinson in the back. Izzie turns to glare at the bad man, noticing the steel gun prodding Charlie's back.

'Whose rig is this one?' asks Robinson.

'Belongs to Marco and the boys,' says Charlie.

'Not bad, but it's your little green bandit I like. I've seen you in it. Have had me eye on that beauty for a while now.'

Back at the Alton farm, they stand in the open garage where Charlie's green ute sits proudly. Robinson fixes his eyes on it, licks his chafed lips. 'Aren't you going to ask me in to the house?'

'No—I'd rather not,' says Charlie, obviously beyond playing games with this animal.

'Fine then. Let's do this here. I have a little matter to discuss with you. Two little matters, in fact. I'd love to know how you happen to have both my wife and son working for you.' Wide-eyed, Charlie flicks his head towards Izzie, who stares at him, deadpan, determined to give nothing away.

'Look Len, I swear to you, we had no idea you were married to Izabella. And I can tell you that Izzie had no idea you were living next door to us. She's hardly ever set foot outside this property!'

'Well then, ain't life strange? What a wonderful reunion we could all have!'

'What is it you want, Robinson?'

'Well, let's see, that depends on what she's worth to ya, to youse.' He looks Izzie in the eye, then stares back at Charlie hatefully, unflinching.

'I won't let you take her,' says Charlie.

'I don't think you have a say in the matter. We married, fair and square, didn't we Izzie?'

She refuses to look at him.

'What about that other woman at your place?' asks Charlie.

'Dot? Ha—she's the cleaning lady.'

Charlie raises his eyebrows, scratches one. Exhales.

'Like Izzie is to youse, I expect. Okay, here's my price. Everything has a price in this world, Charlie, about time you realised it.'

'Take that car!' Izabella yells passionately, pointing to the green vehicle. She does it for all the years he had hurt her son, for all the years Robinson kept Tripp from knowing that he was his son. But in fact, that's the one thing she's pleased about—she never wants Tripp knowing that this monster is his father.

Charlie's wide-eyed look of shock towards Izzie suddenly turns to something peaceful, with the faintest hint of a smile.

'She can still read my thoughts, bless her. She's right, I want your car—that one,' growls Robinson, pointing his finger in the same direction as Izzie's.

'And if I said *yes,* you'd never bother us again?' asks Charlie.

'That's correct,' says Robinson.

'I don't believe you,' says Charlie.

'I'll put it in writing if you want.'

Izzie knows Charlie believes in the power of the written word, knows this is the only way he will believe Len Robinson's words. Hurriedly, Charlie grabs some paper towels and a pen, and watches as Robinson transcribes his dictation, watches the misspelt words of the vow of restraint appear on the paper. Charlie pockets it deeply.

He rushes inside, then back out, having collected the keys to the green ute. Hands them over to his neighbour, the keys to the car Charlie was about to get checked by another mechanic following Grace's frantic plea—Izzie is sure of it.

As the portly man gets himself snugly into position and starts the engine after a few tries, he winds down the window.

'I'll look after her like a baby,' he says, as he flies out of there, kicking up a dust storm.

***

He takes the turn-off to the river, and drives that windy road, traversing it wildly like the maniac he is, over-steering in his excitement. Until the brakes fail during one of his crazy turns, and despite pressing the pedal to the floor he ploughs off the road and through a mass of wild lantana. In a shock of agitation and slurps, the dirty water rushes in through the open window, swirling around him, making the task of climbing through the only escape route impossible. He dies with his eyes and mouth wide open, caught dead in a place from where he once hoisted out so many living creatures to their deaths.

***

The Alton's heard that the congregation at Len Robinson's funeral consisted mainly of several police officers and other law enforcement personnel, paying their final respects to the man who got away with murder.

After the accident, Charlie's brand-new ute was so stuck in the river's muddy bottom, it couldn't be retrieved. When investigating the scene, he'd tried telling an officer that Robinson had effectively stolen the vehicle, but obviously charges couldn't be laid, and he didn't appear to believe Charlie anyway. It was just something he felt he needed to get off his chest.

On Thursday morning, two days after the funeral, Charlie and Tripp are at the Robinson farm. Appearing surreal, the cleared fields glow like velvet in cheery dormancy awaiting the next wheat planting, perhaps relieved their former cruel taskmaster will never be there again. Will there be another crop? Charlie has no idea, as the property will be going on the market very soon—Dot having returned to her sister in Sydney, taking the mangy mutts with her. Word has it she was pleased to get herself away from there. When alive, her husband often left her for weeks on end to go fishing all over the countryside, and when he was with her, he treated her like dirt, she finally admitted, so Charlie heard.

    Charlie and Tripp are at the property for one purpose only, to bring four workers—two Italian and two Romanian—to the Alton farm. There they will be paid and cared for; never again lied to, frightened or mistreated by their employer.

Chapter Fifty-Six

Dear Treasure, do you understand the good you have done? If not for you, Izzie and Tripp would not be together. If not for you, Robinson would still be practising cruelty and we would never have been able to rescue those workers. You were special, a chosen one.

The young may be new to this world, but I think they're also recent participants in a world where time and place don't exist. Some come here knowing more, remembering more than they should. Some see what has gone, some see what is yet to come in the context of our perception of time. I've always thought I may be one, and I think you may have been one too, my darling boy. I'm sure there must be conspirators here too, those who recognise hosts and work with them, for better or worse, relieved to give breath and voice to their knowledge.

Many people think the only action that happens is in life, but we found a way to work together, didn't we? And when I need your help again, you will be there for me, with me, guiding me. I have no doubt.

Did you ever intend on giving me that scarf, Teddy? Or did you know all along I would find it, that things would turn out this way? Izzie and I both had boys who brought colour to our lives, didn't we? Lasting, eternal colour. Unlike the colours in fabric, that will fade to grey, yours won't. They're bright and magical like you.

Ethereal—that's you, Teddy. Your mummy will ride the rainbow with you any time you like. Just ask.

Please ask …

May, 1968

Tonight, Grace encounters Teddy on her airborne journey. He looks happy, strong, unencumbered, brimming with love. And when he stretches out his hand towards his mother, and she takes hold of it, she's relieved to find it warm as they fly together through the rainbow's colours. He finally found that rainbow—the one she dreamed about, the one he painted. She is pushing back doubts, misgivings, to the point where she almost forgives herself. Her son is with her and he's okay.

She hears Charlie quietly close the bedroom door behind him so as not to disturb her, ready to begin his working day.

Grace is filled with a flutter of promise. A bird's tuneful song from outside floods the bedroom. From her bed she sees the welcome swallow perched on the window ledge, watching Grace through the glass. The two make eye contact. In words staunch and silent yet brimming with clarity, she wills the bird and its offspring long lives. Arising from the bed, she wrenches open the sash window, always a bit of a drama as it catches— the commotion causing the bird to alight. She watches, mesmerised, as it darts at speed like a tiny aeroplane high above the yard. It circumnavigates the old crying tree—indicating its significance to Grace—then returns to its nest on the rafters.

Grace hopes the crying tree need never weep again. She dares not give it more than a fleeting glance.

Acknowledgements

Thanks to author Cass Moriarty from the mentorship facilitated by Queensland Writers Centre Writer's Surgery. Your help and insight continue to resonate with me.

A huge shoutout to Alana Lambert from Book Burrow, who assisted with my second editions of both *Emigree* and *Niche*. Your professionalism and support have been immeasurable.

To Lauren Elise Daniels and Joshua Brockbank—both authors and editors—for inspiring me to give my early mishmash form. For your tough love, editor Peta Culverhouse, author Carleton Chinner, and my beta readers.

Thanks to all members of Writers Rendezvous—the warmest, most savvy writers' group in Dayboro. And to author Vicki Stevens, our group co-ordinator: you make writing fun! Thanks for your sage advice and friendship.

My heart swells in appreciation for the love, patience and input of my wonderful husband and children.

www.ingramcontent.com/pod-product-compliance
Ingram Content Group UK Ltd.
Pitfield, Milton Keynes, MK11 3LW, UK
UKHW020822140125
453709UK00011B/305